Nadia Marks

Between the Orange Groves

PAN BOOKS

First published 2019 by Pan Books
an imprint of Pan Macmillan
20 New Wharf Road, London N1 9RR
Associated companies throughout the world
www.panmacmillan.com

ISBN 978-1-5098-8972-3

1 3 5 7 9 8 6 4 2

A CIP catalogue record for this book is available from the British Library.

Typeset by Palimpsest Book Production Limited, Falkirk, Stirlingshire
Printed and bound by CPI Group (UK) Ltd, Croydon, CR0 4YY

Visit **www.panmacmillan.com** to read more about all our books
and to buy them. You will also find features, author interviews and
news of any author events, and you can sign up for e-newsletters
so that you're always first to hear about our new releases.

To my father,
Harilaos Kitromilides
(1916–2018)

Were there never rain
Could the springs so joyful be?
Were the sun not to shine again
Would God's nights ever an end see?
If love did not reign supreme
Would the world be enough for me?

—Orhan Seyfi Ari (1918–92)

Prologue

London, 2008

'There never was a more loving friendship than ours . . .' Lambros said, his eyes filling with the memory. '*Nowhere* on the island could you find such good friends as the two of us, despite our differences. Orhan and I would do anything for each other, we were family . . . we were like brothers. How could we let our friendship perish like that? It's unforgivable!'

Stella sat silently, listening to her father talk. She had heard these stories of love and friendship repeated many times over the years but she never tired of hearing them. She took pleasure in his tales from a far-off country, marvelling at the bond that had so closely tied those two boys and their families together. From a place and a past that was opening up to her through his words. Yet in contrast to the pleasure *she* received from her father's stories, the melancholy of recounting them invariably ended with the old man shedding tears of sadness.

Father and daughter were sitting in the garden among

the roses, basking in the sun on an unusually hot day in early June. Stella had come to visit him. This was her favourite month and even on days when the sun didn't grace them with an appearance, nature always did her best. This peaceful garden in north London was bright with flowers and sweet-smelling herbs, thanks to the hours Lambros spent tending them.

She came to visit her father often now that Athina, her mother, was gone, even though she knew he could cope perfectly well on his own. While her mother was alive her parents had always been busy, forever dashing off to something or other. It had been a constant source of frustration that they were less available for her than she would have liked them to be. She missed the old family house in the leafy London suburb favoured by many Cypriots and where her parents made their home when they first got married. She and her brother had been born there, her own children spent most of their pre-school days there with their *yiayia* when Stella was working. She missed her mother, she missed having little children, she missed the old days. Now that her father was alone she enjoyed recalling some of those times with him. Her visits gave them the chance to talk of the past, to remember. Lambros especially needed more than ever to recapture his youth, his friendships, a time of innocence and love, before he came to England, before he married and had a family . . . before he became someone else.

Stella had grown up with her father's stories from his youth but these days she was hearing them more often.

'We have to do something about it,' she told her brother one day while the two of them had lunch together. 'Honestly, Spiros, all he talks about when I see him now is Orhan. He remembers the old times, their youth, and what happened – and then he cries. What could have happened that was so bad to make an old man cry like that?' Stella looked at her brother.

'I know . . .' Spiros replied, 'I noticed it too and can't imagine. You've got to get him to talk about it; he'd tell you.' He gave Stella a little smile. 'You're good at that.'

'I've been thinking we should try and find him, bring the old men together.'

'You're right,' Spiros mused. 'Since Mum died he talks about Orhan and the past a lot. Do you think he's a bit depressed?'

'No, I don't think he's depressed, I just think he is very sad, and that's why I think we could try and find Orhan. You never know, he might still be alive.'

'He's the same age as Dad, isn't he?' said Spiros, reaching for his glass of wine. 'Eighty-something isn't so old, especially for these old Cypriot boys.'

The next time Stella went to visit her father he had just made himself a Turkish coffee and was about to carry it out to the garden. She let herself in and announced her arrival from the hall, hoping he could hear her – he was getting quite deaf these days, but since his hearing was apparently the only faculty that was failing him so far, no one was too worried. '*I hear what I need to hear*,' he would tell them.

'*Yiasou*, Papa!' she called out cheerfully. 'Where are you?' she asked, much louder than usual.

'In here . . . in the kitchen,' his reply came immediately. 'And no need to shout, the whole street knows you're here now,' he added with a chuckle.

The French windows leading into the garden were wide open, flooding the room with light, and Stella could see the newspaper spread out on the garden table outside where Lambros had been sitting.

'Come, I'll make you some coffee too,' he said, putting down his cup and picking up the *bricky* to make another. 'You like it *sketo* don't you?' he asked and pulled a face. 'How can you drink it without any sugar at all? Far too bitter for me . . . but then you ladies are always watching your figures . . .' he chatted on, glad to see her.

Once again Stella joined her dad in his fragrant summer garden with a plate of sesame biscuits she had bought from the Cypriot patisserie. Sitting down, she allowed him to transport her back in time to a world of people she could only imagine, yet which over the years had become as real as the world she lived in now.

Cyprus, 1946

The light summer breeze carried the call for evening prayer over the rooftops along the narrow streets of Nicosia to the two young men's ears. Lambros and Orhan had been taking a stroll inside the walled city after studying all day when the *muezzin*'s voice announced that the sun had started to set, so it was time for the faithful to remember Allah once more and make their way to the mosque for prayer.

'Is that the time already?' Orhan turned to his friend, incredulous at how late it was. 'I thought it was much earlier,' he added, as they turned left into a side street towards the mosque.

'It must be something to do with my stimulating conversation,' Lambros said jokingly, 'or maybe because it's high summer.' He looked up at the sky. 'I thought it was much earlier too.'

No matter where he was, or with whom, the Turkish boy, Orhan, always observed the prayer five times a day. More often than not, the two friends were taking their customary stroll together when evening prayer was called. The Greek boy, Lambros, was always glad to accompany his friend to the mosque and wait outside, guarding his shoes while the other prayed. Although one was Christian and the other Muslim, the two young men shared a deep friendship based on mutual respect and love for one another despite their different faiths.

'Don't you ever get mixed up with all of these shoes here?' Lambros pointed at the sea of footwear outside the mosque when Orhan re-emerged. 'I often wonder if anyone ever makes a mistake and walks off with someone else's . . .' He added, 'There are so many of them and they're all so alike.'

'*You*, my friend, might get mixed up but *I* do not,' Orhan retorted while doing up his laces. 'I'm well acquainted with my shoes – maybe you have too many to remember them all?'

'I think you know well enough that's not true . . .' Lambros replied, pretending to be offended, but aware that his friend's remark bore an element of truth. His family's apparent wealth bothered him only if it meant that it might set the two of them apart. Lambros's family was indeed quite well off; his father and uncle were the owners of the local bakery and general store which supplied the neighbourhood and beyond with bread and groceries, while Orhan's family lived less comfortably. But the disparity between the households hadn't always been there.

The two boys, born in the spring of 1928 in a remote village in the Troodos Mountains to the west of the island, had begun life quite differently. Orhan's father, Hassan Terzi, was a master tailor with a thriving business while

Lambros's father, Andreas Constandinou, owned a small and meagre general store in the village.

Hassan was the only decent tailor for miles, continuing in his father's and grandfather's footsteps. His reputation had travelled as far as Paphos, the third largest town on the island, supplying the entire male population of his own and most of the surrounding villages with his hand-made suits, shirts and overcoats. Andreas Constandinou, on the other hand, had to compete for his living with the municipal market and local farmers.

'The only way to make a proper living is to leave this village,' Andreas would often complain to his wife Maroula. 'If we want to prosper and provide for our children we need to go to Nicosia.' His grandfather owned a plot of land outside the city walls of the capital and Savvas, Andreas's older brother, who had been living and working away from the village for years and was now running a successful business in Nicosia, was always asking them to join him there.

'Savvas's business is thriving and I could be part of it,' Andreas would try to convince his wife. 'He has already started to build a house and we can all live together, we can give our children a better future there.' But Maroula was reluctant. She was happy in the village. She had no complaints or ambition for wealth. Her boy Lambros and her daughter Anastasia were growing up nicely out here in the country. The big city alarmed her. The children were still young, though it didn't stop her worrying about their future, especially the girl's. A daughter had to be provided with a dowry if they were to find her a good husband and Maroula was more than happy to help to supplement the family's income.

'God will provide, Andreas, there's no rush. We're managing, aren't we?' she would argue. 'We have enough to eat and I'm not frightened of work.' Maroula was a good seamstress and was able to take in sewing work which Hassan made sure came her way regularly.

'God bless him and all his family,' she would tell her husband when another garment came into the house for alterations. 'We couldn't wish for better friends, Andreas. If we lived in the city would we have such good neighbours?'

'There are good and bad people everywhere, Maroula,' was his reply.

'There is much danger in the city, Andreas. How could we marry our girl off to a good man when we don't know anyone there? *A patched-up shoe from your own village is better than a brand-new one from another.*' She would quote the old and much-used adage alluding to finding a good match from your familiars, close to home. 'I'm happy here with the people I know,' Maroula continued. 'Where would I find a friend as good as Hatiche in the city?'

The two families lived side by side. Lambros and Orhan were the oldest siblings in their families and they were inseparable, like their mothers.

1

Cyprus, 1920s

Kyria Maroula and Hatiche *Hanoum*, as the children politely addressed each other's mothers, were as generous in spirit as they were in spreading their love and laughter to their children and their families.

The Constandinou and Terzi houses were separated only by a row of orange, lemon and mandarin trees so close that often when Maroula threw open her kitchen window looking out on to the trees she had to battle with their foliage. When the blossom was in full bloom the heady aroma that flooded the room was almost over-whelming. Most mornings, after the two women finished their household chores, they would pause and take it in turns to make coffee for each other.

Whenever the weather was fine in spring and autumn, they would sit in each other's backyard enjoying the warm sunshine, while in winter they would sit beside a log fire as the rain, or sometimes snow, fell outside. Winters in the mountains were cold, often bitterly so, but they didn't last long, and when summer arrived, it was welcomed with jubilation. A mountain breeze kept the climate temperate and there was no shortage of trees in Maroula's and Hatiche's backyard to take refuge under if the temperature rose too high.

No fences or borders separated the two houses, and the hens roaming the yard as the two women sat drinking their coffee belonged to both households. When the children were small they would sit on a rug by their mothers' feet, and then toddle about chasing the chickens when they were a little older. First came the boys, Orhan and Lambros, then barely a year later came Leila.

'Oh, how I long for a daughter,' Maroula said with yearning as she cradled her friend's newborn baby girl.

'You'll have one soon, I know,' Hatiche replied. 'I saw it in the cup! The coffee grounds never lie. Believe me, it's your turn next.'

'*Inşallah*,' *God willing*, Maroula answered, using the customary Turkish expression which Greeks often used as well.

'Glad to hear you speak some Turkish, my friend,' Hatiche exclaimed in Greek. 'I've been thinking that it's about time to teach you some more. How many years now have I been speaking to you in Greek and all you say to me is *Inşallah* or *Maşallah*?'

As the majority of the Cypriot population was made up of Greeks, most Turks were obliged to have some knowledge of Greek and more often than not they were fluent. Hatiche was one of them, as were her parents and grandparents before her. Apart from the unavoidable mistakes many Turks made in not being able to distinguish gender, her vocabulary and pronunciation were excellent.

'I have tried,' Maroula protested, 'it's just that I'm no good at memorizing the words . . . Don't you remember when you were married, I tried to learn some phrases so that I could impress your grandmother at the ceremony? I was hopeless . . .' A sense of guilt and embarrassment made her stop; she knew her friend was probably right to be disappointed in her – most Greeks never made the effort to speak Turkish or indeed had a need to. 'Why don't you teach me how to say *Come for coffee*, then?' Maroula added to please her friend as she reached for a plate of sesame *goulourakia* she had baked the day before. These delicious biscuits, rich in butter flavoured with vanilla and covered in sesame seeds, were everyone's favourite and no one baked them better than Maroula.

'If you teach me the words, then when it's my turn to call you I'll say it in Turkish!'

'Well, let's start with *afiyet olsun*,' Hatiche replied with a smile, taking a biscuit from the dish Maroula held out to her.

'*Afiyet olsun* to you too,' Maroula repeated, recognizing the words for '*good appetite*'.

Maroula set her mind to learn the simple phrase

Hatiche taught her. She practised at home, repeating the words over and over, until one morning, throwing open the green shutters of her kitchen window, she proudly called out to her neighbour. The suppressed giggles and raucous laughter that came from across the garden were not at all the response Maroula had expected. She had hoped for praise not ridicule, but in her haste and excitement she had muddled her words and instead of asking if Hatiche had finished her chores and would like some coffee, she had said something along the lines of '*Have you finished your toilet ablutions?*' At which point Hatiche made her way round to Maroula's house to explain her mistake, amidst much laughter from both of them. Laughing was what the two of them did best; ever since they were little girls, their friendship had been based on good humour and fun. After that incident Hatiche gave up trying to teach her friend any more Turkish.

'Just stick to the few words you know,' she said and patted Maroula's hand. 'Since my Greek is so good we have no problem.'

'I told you,' Maroula said apologetically, 'I'm useless at this,' and their giggles were carried across the yard to the neighbouring houses.

Ever since childhood the two friends, both born in the spring of 1909, had always been inseparable, forever laughing and looking for fun together. When they were not at school they spent most of their time playing and inventing games. Their family homes were in the same street separated by three houses. Although they went to different schools, Maroula to the Greek elementary and Hatiche to the Turkish one, they had singled each other out to be best friends early on. The two schools were side by side so they walked there together each morning and after their homework they would meet in the street to play. On school days, their play was restricted to a few hours and they were not allowed to wander far. Some other kids on their street often joined in but when the time came to go inside to study neither of them minded; both girls were good pupils and took their homework seriously.

'I never had the opportunity to go to school,' Maroula's mother would say, unable to read or write herself but proud to see her daughter was keen on learning. 'But you have, and what's more you have brains. So, learn all you can *while* you can.'

School was free only until the age of twelve so most children, especially girls, would leave at that age, unless their parents could afford to send them to one of the towns or larger villages to learn a skill. For girls, it was usually sewing; for boys, a trade like carpentry or silversmithing, otherwise they would start to work in the fields with their fathers.

So during term time the girls were good, but come the summer they would run wild. For three whole months, they were free to roam the hills and valleys with nobody asking questions. There were many children in the neighbourhood: boys and girls, Christian and Muslim, or Mohammedans as the Greeks referred to them, and they would all gather under the big cedar tree at the end of Hatiche's and Maroula's road to plan their day. The hillsides with their lush vegetation were perfect for hide-and-seek and climbing trees. Away from the grown-ups' prying eyes, the boys' games would often turn mischievous; budding sexual curiosity would compel them to chase after the girls with one aim: to lift their skirts and look at their panties. The girls would protest amidst much yelling and screeching, but were also secretly thrilled with this wicked pursuit. At six and seven, they took each other at face value; they were all friends and they accepted their differences – Greeks or Turks, nothing mattered but fun. At around the age of nine, Maroula fell madly in love with Ali, a Turkish boy with huge brown eyes and golden skin who lived three streets away from her. He was a year older than her and if he chased her she willingly let herself be caught.

'When I grow up I will marry Ali,' she told Hatiche the first day he peeped up her skirt.

'Not sure your mama will agree,' Hatiche replied, having heard her parents more than once say that Greeks and Turks could never marry.

The two families were on good terms and their mothers

would often have coffee together to read the coffee grounds, but unlike their children, the friendship between the women only went so far. Hatiche's mama had a special gift for fortune telling and many of the Greek women in the street would join them to hear what she had to say.

'They are good people,' Maroula's mother would tell her when Maroula seemed to spend more time in her friend's house than theirs. 'But they are different from us, we are Christians and they are Mohammedans.' The last word rolled from her mouth with a certain disdain. 'They do not believe as we do in Jesus Christ. Maroula *mou*, *they* have their own religion which is not ours!'

She was always trying to convince her daughter of the difference between the two families, but apart from the religion that everyone always mentioned and the funny way Hatiche's mother spoke Greek, Maroula could never understand what set them apart. What she and most people saw were two girls who resembled each other, not only physically but temperamentally, too. When they were little they were both skinny and wiry, running around the countryside like two little mountain goats. Then when puberty set in they filled out in all the right places, which drove the local boys mad.

Plump and full-breasted, brown-eyed and pale-skinned, Hatiche and Maroula married for love, unlike the marriages arranged for most girls in the village. Maroula's childhood infatuation with Ali had long passed and her attentions turned to an older Greek boy who made it his aim to win her heart. Each of the girls fell in love with a young man from their village and both caused a scandal by choosing their match.

'She's stolen my heart, that little Hatiche,' Hassan, the son of the village tailor, would tell his friend every time he saw her collecting water from the spring in the village square. 'She's plump and ripe as a tasty peach and when she turns her eyes on me I lose my head.' Hatiche's eyes were all Hassan ever saw of her face, which was modestly covered with her scarf whenever she went out to get water, but for him it was enough to feel the thunderbolt of her gaze strike him.

'Her friend is a beauty too, and I aim to make her my wife one day,' Andreas, who worked in his father's grocery shop, told Hassan. Love's arrow had pierced his heart, too.

The girls were well aware of the attentions of the two boys, who miraculously always seemed to be in the square whenever they went to fetch water at the communal tap or when they sat outside each other's houses to do their embroidery. But meaningful looks were all that were exchanged between the four of them; no words were ever spoken.

The first time that Andreas summoned the courage to speak to Maroula was at the Easter Midnight Mass. He searched for her among the throng of people packed into the small church of Agia Ekaterini and seized the opportunity to stand near her without causing offence. He fought his way through the crowd and stood silently by her side, listening to the liturgy and breathing in her fragrance while waiting for an opportunity to speak to her. That moment came after the priest pronounced the *Kalos Logos*, the words proclaiming the good tidings of Christ's resurrection. *Christos Anesti*, he announced in a joyful melodious chant to the people, who responded in unison as each in turn lit a candle from his blessed flame.

The church was now lit only by candles, which bathed the congregation in a warm glow. As the room reverberated with the jubilant Easter singing of *Christos Anesti*, Andreas leaned a little closer to Maroula to light his candle from hers.

'*Christos Anesti*,' he whispered in her ear.

'*Alithos Anesti*,' she replied softly, confirming the resurrection in the customary response above the chanting of the service, and edged a little closer to him.

Although there was a small chapel in the centre of the village, most people chose the steep climb to the church of Agia Ekaterini, built on the summit of a nearby hill, in order to hear the long-awaited announcement of *Anastasis*, the glad tidings of life's victory over death. Those who arrived early were able to gather inside, but as the crowd increased many had spilled out into the churchyard and stood under the stars, their singing resounding across the hillsides.

Outside the church, in a far corner of the churchyard,

a huge pyre had been assembled, built during several days beforehand by the entire male population. It was to be set alight towards the end of the service in order to burn the effigy of Judas. This ritual could only take place after the priest had spoken the words of *Christos Anesti*, whereupon the fire would be lit. Soon the flames would rise into the night sky, followed by a series of explosions from the lighting of fireworks which would echo round the hills and mountains, signalling the start of two days of celebration.

After Andreas's success at approaching Maroula, Hassan was eager to do the same with Hatiche.

'I need to speak to her but I can never find her alone,' he said wistfully when his friend described how he had managed to be with his love without anyone noticing. 'The trouble is, I can't think of any time when she could be alone for me to approach her,' he complained. 'There's always someone around. Her father watches her like a hawk.'

'You could try speaking to her when she's with Maroula,' Andreas suggested. 'They're usually alone.'

Eventually Hassan found his opportunity one hot July day while Hatiche was outside her house buying some figs from an old man who passed by every week with produce from his trees. She was bending over to choose figs from the basket, examining each one before placing them on a tray as carefully as if they were eggs, when Hassan walked by and stopped, on the pretext that he too wanted to buy some fruit.

'I hope I am not intruding,' he said politely, gazing at the girl's face for the first time. In her haste and in the summer heat, when she heard the old man calling outside the kitchen window, Hatiche had run out of the house without covering her face. The sight of her naked features made Hassan's heart soar with desire and love for her. Unable to tear his eyes away from her, he tried to memorize every detail lest this was the last time he might see her uncovered.

'She has a beauty spot in the middle of her left cheek! You can't imagine how lovely she is,' Hassan told his friend, bursting with excitement later that day, 'and her lips are full and red like the ripe cherries on our tree. How can I find a way to make her fall in love with me?'

'Going by how I've seen the girls look at us, I think it might not be too difficult, my friend,' Andreas replied with a cheeky smile. 'I'm sure we can find a way.'

Andreas was not wrong; every time the girls went to the village square to fill their pots with water their hearts fluttered with anticipation at seeing the young men. Aphrodite's little love child had done his job well on them, too.

'Have you seen how he smiles?' Hatiche whispered into Maroula's ear once she realized she was in love with Hassan. 'He has the most perfect teeth! He's so handsome.'

'I have, and he is!' Maroula murmured. 'But have you noticed Andreas's eyes? I've never seen eyes that colour. Are they green, or are they brown? I just don't know . . . they're the colour of olive oil after a first pressing,' she went on in a whisper until she spotted her mother pushing open the back door into the yard. They were sitting with their needlework in the shade of a trellis covered with jasmine, daydreaming and talking about love and the boys when the appearance of Maroula's mother put an end to their secret conversation. Both girls agreed that each other's love was as handsome as could be but their own choice was the best. Besides, a Greek girl or boy would never have entertained romantic notions for a Turk or vice versa, no matter what Maroula had thought when she was nine.

'It's mainly our religion that sets us apart,' Maroula's mother had told her, not for the first time, when she announced at the age of seven that her new best friend was the Turkish girl Hatiche who lived three houses away from them. 'Their customs are different to ours,' she continued when Maroula asked her to explain the differences, but without much success.

'What customs?' Maroula asked.

'Their faith, what they believe in, who they pray to . . .' her mother tried again, aware of the quizzical look on her daughter's face. 'We go to church, we pray to our Agia Ekaterini and we cross ourselves, they don't.'

That much Maroula knew, yet it still didn't explain what divided them.

'They go to church, too,' the little girl replied. 'Hatiche told me they do.'

'No, they don't,' her mother answered, 'they go to the mosque . . . it's not a church.'

Hatiche had told Maroula that the place they went to pray was a church – *their* church – so why was her mother now telling her otherwise? She really didn't understand; as far as she was concerned they were neighbours who lived in the village like everyone else. In her friend's house she had even spotted an icon of the *Panayia*, the all-holy Virgin Mary, along with a blue evil-eye stone on top of a chest of drawers, just like the ones they kept at home beside her mother's shrine to the Virgin Mary. So, she wondered, what set them apart? Hatiche's mother, Ayşe *Hanoum*, seemed just like her own; like any Greek mother, apart from her asking them to take their shoes off when they entered the house.

At seven the two girls were inseparable best friends, recognizing no difference between them; not until later, when they were older, did Maroula become aware of a few disparities. For her part, she found most of them inconsequential, such as not eating pork, which she didn't like anyway. But some of their customs she found interesting and appealing, especially the beauty prepara-tions which Hatiche's mother concocted to use on herself and her daughters once they came of age. One of those was the use of *halaoua*. When her daughters reached puberty, Hatiche's mother decided that her girls must start depilating as she had at their age, and her mother and grandmother before her – she came from a long line of hirsute ladies.

'When you marry, your husband will expect you to be clean without too much hair,' she told her girls. This was around the time when Hatiche and Maroula fell in love with Hassan and Andreas. Although she had no inkling of this – the girls kept their secret well hidden – she realized the time had come to think about preparing her daughters for marriage.

The most effective and clean way to remove hair, Ayşe *Hanoum* explained, was with *halaoua*, a mixture of sugar and lemon juice which was heated over an open flame then left to cool off before it was kneaded into a gum-like paste. Once the correct consistency and texture was reached, she would apply it over the skin, pressing down with her palm onto the patch of unwanted hair before peeling it off with a swift action of the hand to leave the skin, as if by magic, smooth and hair free. There was only a little pain involved for just a moment or two, she reassured them, but the final result was so miraculous that it was worth the discomfort.

'So . . .' Hatiche whispered to Maroula conspiratorially, trying to explain about the ritual of *halaoua* one day, 'my mother thinks we have to start preparing for marriage! She says it's time to make our bodies look beautiful!'

'My mother hasn't mentioned anything like that to me . . .' Maroula replied, wondering if perhaps this was one of the cultural differences she had been warned about.

'I hope Hassan comes to ask for my hand soon, before they start arranging matches for me,' Hatiche said, with alarm in her voice this time.

'When is your mother going to do this hair removing for you?' Maroula asked, running her hand over her leg to feel the coarse hair that she had been cultivating on both legs and arms for at least two years now. What to do about it had been quite a worry for her: how would she ever take her clothes off in front of Andreas once they were married? All was fine when she was dressed, her long skirt and underskirt covered everything well enough, but she knew there would come a time when she would have to reveal all and she feared Andreas would run away in fright once she was naked. 'Do you think your mother would do this for me too?' Maroula asked hopefully.

'I don't see why not,' Hatiche replied, 'you're like a sister in our house.'

Maroula's mother knew all about *halaoua* but most Greek women didn't practise it; this was the Turkish women's custom. Then again, Maroula's mother thought it was immodest for women to be concerned with their appearance. Beauty, she believed, came with piety and not vanity; furthermore she didn't share her daughter's hair problem.

'If God didn't want us to have hairs on our body then he would have made us smooth-skinned,' she told Maroula when the girl first told her how Hatiche's mother could help her.

'I'd rather not be hairy like a man, whether God wants it or not,' was the young woman's reply, and the next time her friend's mother prepared the sugary mixture for herself and her daughters, Maroula took her turn to have the treatment applied to her upper lip. Her facial hair, she decided, was in more urgent need of attention.

'Next time we do the legs,' Ayşe *Hanoum* told her. Maroula soon learned to use *halaoua* on herself when her mother was out of the house, although she preferred to ask Hatiche's mother to do it for her. Maroula learned to follow several beauty rituals when visiting her friend. There were cream applications for the body and face, aromatic oils for the hair, black kohl for the eyes to make them look deep and mysterious, and mastic gum to chew in order to keep the breath fresh. Maroula's favourite was the application of henna. Often after *halaoua*, Ayşe *Hanoum* would apply henna using a transfer pattern on her daughter's palms, feet and nails. When the henna dried it would turn anything it touched a bright orange, leaving a pleasant aroma lingering in the room.

'What is the meaning of this?' her mother shouted when

Maroula turned up with henna on her hands one day. 'These are not our customs, my girl! What will your father say, what will people in the village say when they see this?' She turned her face to the little shrine of the *Panayia* and crossed herself. 'You've gone too far. What's next? Changing your faith?'

Maroula gasped. How could her mother suggest such a thing? What harm did any of this do to anyone? Her parents knew that she loved Hatiche like a sister, but that had nothing to do with wanting to abandon her own faith or her family. That would never happen. She was a devout Greek Orthodox, as Hatiche was a devout Muslim; Maroula went to church and believed in the power of prayer, while her friend observed her own religious rituals. There was never any conflict between them concerning their religion nor did they ever discuss it, whatever their parents might suspect. She had never doubted her faith, she always felt a particular connection with Agia Ekaterini, and every Sunday without fail when they went to the church with her mother she lit a candle in front of the saint's icon. How could her mother ever doubt her faith? When she was the one who always told Maroula that whether you were Christian or Muslim, what really mattered was to be a good person.

Nevertheless, it was one thing to believe something, and another to put it into practice.

'I'm worried for her, Kyriako,' she told her husband that

night. 'Hatiche is a good girl but our daughter is spending too much time with the Turkish family. She has a strong head, our Maroula. What if she comes home and tells us she wants to marry a Turk one day? Eh? What then?'

2

So it came about that when Andreas, a Greek boy, knocked at her parents' home to ask for Maroula's hand and confess that the two of them were in love, instead of kicking him out of the house for his audacity, and putting their daughter under lock and key for her immodest behaviour in claiming to be in love with a boy whom they had not vetted or chosen for her, Maroula's parents welcomed him with open arms.

As soon as Hassan heard the good news he proceeded to do the same and duly went to Hatiche's family to ask for her hand in marriage. There was much resistance from her father in questioning the credentials of the boy, which of course he knew were excellent – the small community was well acquainted with its inhabitants – but that was not the point. Any decent family had to be involved in the choosing of their children's match, whether Turk or Greek. That was one custom the two communities undoubtedly had in common. Making sure they knew and approved who their children – both boys and girls – were going to marry was very important for all families. Once a match was made it wasn't only down to the couple to make a life together because after marriage the two families would become one. Vetting and approving where a bride or groom came from was of utmost importance.

The girls were delirious at the fortuitous outcome, despite the wagging tongues of the villagers, whose vitriol was mainly directed at them for being female.

'You would never see a daughter of mine marrying for "*love*",' the women said as they gossiped by the well.

'I blame the parents for letting them roam about,' it was agreed.

'Girls need to be kept indoors in the name of decency,' said another.

'Love? What's love got to do with marriage . . .' they all tutted.

The two friends married their sweethearts a month apart, and each attended the other's wedding. Since a wedding was the main source of entertainment in those days for the entire village, celebrations would always last for three days and three nights, starting with the night before the ceremony.

Maroula and Andreas married in 1927, on a fragrant day in early May, after the snow had melted in the highest peaks and the streams and rivers were overflowing with ice-cold water, as sweet as nectar, that would keep everyone well supplied throughout the year. The village square was decorated in preparation for the evening feast.

Under the leafy branches of the old plane tree, trestle
tables and chairs had been set up in line to accommodate
the entire village, Greek and Turk alike, while the bride
was at home with her family getting ready for the church.
Andreas, too, was at his house, attended by his friends,
while the shaving ceremony was performed by his first
goumbaros, a custom always observed on the wedding day
to confirm the trust the groom holds for his best man. As
tradition has it, in Greek Orthodox weddings the groom
has several best men, but his first *goumbaros* is considered
the most honoured. He stands beside the groom during the
ceremony while the other best men stand in line next to
him. Throughout the wedding service the men remain by
the groom's side until at the end of the ceremony they
write their names in turn on a long piece of white ribbon,
to symbolize and confirm the *goumbaros'* lifelong loyalty
and allegiance to the groom. The same applies to the bride
as her own ribbon is passed down the line from her first
goumera, bridesmaid, then to the rest of the women.

Hassan knew that as a Muslim he could not be offered
the honour of being Andreas's first *goumbaros*; that position was given to Yiannos, Andreas's first cousin, but he
hoped that he might at least be one of the several men who
participated in the ritual. To their disappointment neither
Hatiche nor Hassan was granted permission by the priest
to participate.

'You are, and always will be, my best man,' Andreas

told Hassan, as they shared a glass of *zivania* a few days before the wedding. 'Our faith is the only thing that separates us, my friend. We each abide by the laws of our faith but it does not get in the way of our friendship! If my religion doesn't permit you to stand by my side in the church then, no matter, we will always stand by each other's side in life.'

The preparation for the religious service for both Greeks and Turks, which was always accompanied by music and songs, was almost as important as the marriage ritual itself, full of symbolism denoting fertility and prosperity for the couple.

At Maroula's house, all the female cousins and aunts had gathered to dress her. Hatiche and her mother were present, together with several other Turkish friends of the family. For some days before the wedding, Ayşe *Hanoum* had been applying all her treatments to beautify Maroula, as this was one occasion when her mother would have no objections. A bride must always be beautiful, smooth-skinned and fragrant for her wedding night.

When Maroula was finally ready, eyes kohled, cheeks and lips rouged, hair arranged to perfection, and helped into her wedding dress, the band started to play the traditional song that calls for all her relatives to give their blessing in turn by passing a red scarf around her waist to guarantee the new bride's fertility.

Although not a relative, Hatiche was determined to at

least participate in this ritual performed at home and not in the church, so she took her turn behind Soula, one of Maroula's cousins.

'*She* can't do this . . .' Soula whispered into Maroula's ear, pointing behind her at Hatiche, 'she's not Christian!' she gasped.

'She's not a cousin either . . .' Maroula snapped furiously in reply. 'She's much more than that, she's my best friend!'

The Turkish wedding rituals were similar to those for the Greek ceremony, based on the same intentions to evoke fertility and prosperity. On a hot day at the end of June, barely a month after the whole village had celebrated one matrimonial union, it was repeated all over again for Hatiche and Hassan. Like Hatiche, Maroula too was determined to participate in the preparations for her friend's marriage.

The night before Hatiche's wedding, all the women gathered together in her house for the henna ceremony, which Maroula – having never attended a bridal henna before – was anxious not to miss. Hatiche, clad in a purple and red dress and red veil, looked more like an exotic dancer than a bride-to-be, in contrast to the virginal white garments of a Greek bride.

The room was full of colour and movement as the women arrived, all dressed in reds and purples. At one point Hassan's mother, her head, shoulders and arms covered by a crimson and gold scarf, placed some henna in Hatiche's palm over a gold coin and covered it in gauze and a red glove; then she softly started to sing. One by one the women joined in the singing as they sat waiting for the henna to dry. Young and old, their voices blended together in a sad melody. Unable to understand the words, Maroula wondered why on such a jubilant occasion the songs didn't reflect the mood. Gradually the sounds became more joyful and she was told that the earlier songs displayed sadness for the departure of the bride from her parental home, but now it was time for them all to rejoice in her future nuptials.

At sunrise next day the preparations for the wedding party were already under way as once again the trestle tables and chairs made their appearance under the old plane tree in readiness for the wedding feast. Once again the entire village, Greek and Turk alike, came to celebrate the union of Hatiche and Hassan. Unlike the Greek ceremony, the Turkish wedding would not be blessed officially by the imam until the eating and drinking, dancing and singing were over. Only then would the holy man, in the presence of a few close relatives in the groom's parental home, perform the religious rites.

Once the festivities came to an end, as custom demanded, Hassan returned to his house and waited for Hatiche to be escorted to him. Maroula insisted on being one of her attendants, so together with several other female members of the family she accompanied Hatiche in their procession through the village, the bride dressed in white lace studded with colourful beads and sequins, her head and face covered by a red veil. Musicians playing drums and pipes led the bride with her attendants to her groom and her new family.

Both brides brought a good dowry from the parents. Maroula's father had already laid the foundations of a house for her with Andreas's help on the little plot of land which his own father-in-law had given to his daughter as part of her dowry. Now it was his turn to help the newly-weds in typical Cypriot tradition. Andreas and his father were struggling to keep their little grocery store going, so any help from Maroula's father was welcome. It was a modest little house made of used wood, stones and rough bricks. The bricks, a mixture of straw and mud, kept the house warm in winter and cool in the summer and in no time at all it was ready for the couple to move in; whereas Hatiche and Hassan had to continue living with his parents until her house was completed. She insisted that it had to be next to her friend's. The only request made by Maroula for her new home was for three bedrooms because, as she informed Andreas, she planned to have many children. 'They don't have to be big rooms,' she told her father and husband, 'but so long as they accommodate enough beds I am happy.'

'God willing, you will get your wish, my girl,' her father said and promised to build as many rooms as their materials allowed.

Maroula was granted her wish for three bedrooms but she didn't get her wish for the many children she had planned and hoped for; nonetheless she was more than grateful for the healthy son and daughter God did grant her and the house Andreas and her father had built for her. It was humble and compact but there was room enough for them all over the years. In the little garden that ran along the front of the house Maroula planted roses, and by the front step, a jasmine to climb around the door, which opened into an *iliakos* – a square entrance hall – leading to the rest of the house in typical Cypriot style. A huge fireplace in one corner, as in every room, kept them warm in winter.

After moving in, Maroula set about making the best of what she had, and her years of skilful embroidery and crochet work paid off in her decorative covers for the chairs, beds and tables, adding colour and warmth to the rooms. In the absence of the precious china or silverware displayed on shelves or in glass cabinets in more affluent homes, Maroula hung on the walls some of her patterned *paneria*, a kind of flat basket used to dry the handmade pasta that her mother prepared, which she had woven from reeds when she was a schoolgirl.

The toilet, as in all the village houses, was a hole in the ground at the end of the yard: no such luxury as the so-called 'European' flushing lavatories which, since the British colonization of Cyprus, were starting to make their appearance on the island. Maroula made it her first duty to wash down the floor of bare trodden earth daily with buckets of soapy water and try to keep it as clean as was humanly possible; she prayed for the day that civilization would arrive in their village.

'I've heard from Andreas's brother, that in Nicosia, when you go to the lavatory you sit on a kind of chair to do your business,' she told Hatiche almost in disbelief while they were planning their houses.

Just a few days after Maroula and Andreas had moved into their new home the village priest, Father Ioannis, came to visit. As the Greek Orthodox custom requires, a new home must be blessed and sanctified by a priest to ensure the well-being of its residents and banish evil from the house.

'Once the good father blesses the house it will be truly yours, Maroula *mou*,' her mother told her as they prepared for his arrival. She was busy undoing a string tied round a linen cloth in which she had carefully wrapped two icons as a gift for her daughter. 'God's blessing, and the people who live in it, is what makes a home,' she added, just as Father Ioannis entered the open front door holding a bowl of holy water, followed by a troop of fellow villagers who were seizing the opportunity to take a good look around the new house.

'Welcome, Father,' mother and daughter said in unison as they kissed the priest's hand in turn. Dipping a sprig of basil into the bowl, Father Ioannis made his way round the house, followed by the procession of villagers, entering each room to sprinkle holy water on anything and everything in his path and praying for the benediction of the home and its residents.

'The Holy Virgin and Agia Ekaterini will always look over you,' Maroula's mother told her after the priest and the rest of the village had finally left. She was lighting a candle in front of a little shrine she had just made in a corner of the *iliakos* where the two icons that she had unpacked earlier now hung, one of the *Panayia* and one of the patron saint. She had brought them both from her own home and was now passing them down to her daughter, as her own mother did for her when she first married. 'These are the essential things you need to make your home, Maroula *mou*,' she said again and crossed herself. 'Everything else comes with time. You'll soon have more possessions than you need and you won't know what to do with them all, especially after you've been blessed with a few children.' Maroula knew that her mother was right, as she so often was, and soon she would have her best friend living next door to complete the sum of all she had ever wanted.

Hatiche's house, due to her father-in-law's prosperity, was built of stone instead of mud bricks, and was altogether a more impressive affair when it was completed. Although it consisted of just one storey like Maroula's, the several steps that led to the front door gave it a grander appearance than her neighbour's. The same basic layout applied to the structure. The front door opened into a sunny entrance hall, the *iliakos*, with doors leading off to the rest of the house; however, the rooms here were bigger and included a large dining room separate from the kitchen, and a living room.

The two houses differed not only in size but also in appearance. Whereas Maroula and Andreas's furniture had been mainly handed down by both sets of parents, Hatiche and Hassan's house had an overall Turkish interior with newly constructed furniture in the Ottoman fashion. In the sitting room low divans, covered in opulent purple and red fabrics, lined all four walls to serve as comfortable seating areas, with low brass tables in front of them to accommodate the coffee hour, which was apparently any time of day if Hatiche had anything to do with it. Multicoloured stars and crescents were painted high on the walls near the ceiling, and above the divans a wooden shelf held ornamental china and gourds that Hassan had cleverly carved in ingenious intricate designs. When light fell on the gourds they shone and glittered as if they had been filled with precious jewels. As in the home of Maroula, whose mother had made a religious shrine with her old icons, in a corner of Hatiche's house there was now a little shrine with verses from the Quran and several wise sayings. Maroula knew the meaning of these proverbs, which had been translated for her by Hatiche's mother, Ayşe *Hanoum*, when as a little girl she had first seen them in the family house. These were now passed to Hatiche, just as her own mother had gifted her the icons.

'Let God keep away from us the man who has the face of a friend, and the heart of an enemy,' one saying read, and another: 'He who knows how to keep his tongue silent saves his head.' There were several more and Maroula thought them all wise. In a corner of the dining room, as in every home, Greek or Turkish, dangled a cluster of blue stones to fend off the evil eye.

In the backyard of Hatiche's house, Hassan had proudly built their very own *hamam*. Working with his father and learning the trade as a tailor was proving to be very profitable, so he was able to provide well for his family. The *hamam* was an enviable addition to their home: most people made do with the communal bathhouse in the grounds of the village mosque. Most Turks liked to make use of it at least once a week, and on days which were allocated for women only, most of the female population of the village would gather the children and visit the bathhouse for their weekly ablutions. Until the age of five, boys would accompany their mothers too; after that they were taken to the baths by their fathers.

Turk or Christian, everyone was allowed to use the

bathhouse and although many Greeks didn't deign to go, Maroula and her mother would often join Hatiche and her mother on ladies' days. But once Hassan finished building the *hamam* next door there was no more need for that; the two families had their own private bathhouse.

'You can never get as clean as you do after a steaming in a *hamam*,' Maroula's mother would try to explain to her friends who frowned upon the practice, considering communal bathing unsavoury. 'It's a hundred times better and more efficient to sit in the hot steam of a Turkish bath and have a good scrub than heating water and washing in a tin bath in the kitchen,' she'd tell those who criticized her. She knew well enough how most people bathed; only one or two families in the village were privileged enough to have a separate room for ablutions.

The pact made by the two friends from an early age, that when they married they would live side by side and continue to support each other, had eventually come to pass and nothing mattered apart from their families and their loving friendship. Giving birth to their two boys close together was also something that Maroula and Hatiche tried to orchestrate for themselves – and manage they did!

Maroula was the first to announce that she was pregnant, followed by Hatiche a month later. The saying that '*they knew each other from the cradle*' could not have been more apt for the two boys. Lambros was born in the first week of May 1928 and Orhan followed in early June; in fact, their mothers always loved to tell them how their first spoken words were each other's name.

When baby Leila was born about a year or so after the boys she was adored by everyone. Lambros and Orhan would toddle about while their mothers sat in the sunshine for their mid-morning coffee, shooing away the hens that circled around the baby's Moses basket. It was on one such morning that Hatiche told Maroula she was sure she must be with child as she had just seen it in her coffee grounds.

'Look!' she shouted. 'It's clear as the midday sun that you are pregnant, and what's more it's a girl!' Maroula leapt to her feet and hugged her friend. She needed no convincing; she knew that if Hatiche had said so it *was* so. Her friend had been well tutored by her own mother in the art of reading the cup, and what she predicted often came true.

'Our girls will grow up together like my Orhan and your Lambros,' Hatiche said, reaching for her friend's hand.

'God willing that it will all go well,' Maroula replied, making the sign of the cross for good measure, knowing too well how many pregnancies ended badly. Only a month ago their neighbour two houses down had died while giving birth to a girl, leaving the newborn and three boys motherless, and that wasn't an isolated case; many women still perished in childbirth. The village doctor was always kept busy, the nearest hospital was miles away near the coastal town of Paphos, and medical emergencies were often fatal. Death was unfortunately something both young and old were familiar with in the village.

'*Inşallah*,' Hatiche replied, and stood up to go and fetch some homemade lemonade and walnut *glygo* to celebrate her prediction. She knew that from all the fruits preserved in syrup, walnut was Maroula's favourite and she had a new batch made that year from her mother's tree. Sitting on her own while Hatiche was inside, baby Leila asleep in the basket and the two boys at her feet, Maroula felt almost certain that she could feel the new life growing inside her.

'*Maşallah*, my friend,' Hatiche said, returning with a tray carrying two portions of *glygo*, lemonade and sweet *bourekia* for the boys. 'You are strong and healthy, and you'll give birth to a beautiful girl as easily as you did with Lambros.'

As the two friends sat in the warm spring sunshine with their children around them, all was well with the world. Life so far had been good to them both. Maroula reached for her lemonade with a sigh of contentment and the boys tucked into their *bourekia*, covering their faces with the powdery icing sugar. As Hatiche bent to pick up her baby and place her on her breast their idyll was broken by an eerie sound that was all too familiar to them. The lamenting wail from a neighbour whose husband had died some weeks earlier was carried to their ears by the breeze, reminding them that sometimes one person could receive joy while another, pain.

'It's not been long since he left us.' Maroula looked at Hatiche. 'She still needs to express her grief.'

'It takes everyone in different ways,' Hatiche observed. 'Sometimes even after you think the pain has passed it rises unexpectedly and you just can't hold it in.'

'I know . . .' Maroula added with a sigh, 'I remember when my *bappou* died, my *yiayia* would suddenly start her lament in the middle of the night months after he had gone.'

The lament for a loved one when the grief took hold was an intrinsic part of grieving in the village. Hearing their neighbour voice her pain in the rhythmic sound of her wailing did not alarm them, but reminded them that they must pay her a visit. It was a collective duty to help a fellow villager through their grief.

3

Maroula's pregnancy was as difficult as it had been easy when she carried Lambros. The complications were manifold. First she bled throughout most of her early stages, making her fear that she would lose the baby. After that stopped, Dr Elias explained that she must pay attention to her diet because she had too much 'sugar' in her blood. She didn't understand this. How did *sugar* get into her blood? she repeated.

'It's only for a short while,' the doctor tried to explain. 'Once you have given birth you will return to normal and you can eat all the *glygo* and *baklava* you want. But for now, you must be good if you want yourself and your baby to be healthy.'

'I don't understand, Hatiche,' Maroula complained to her friend, who was always at hand to help. 'With Lambros, I ran about and did everything and more, but now I must be careful what I do *and* I have to give up eating!'

'Every pregnancy is different. Do as the doctor says, eat the right foods and you'll be fine,' Hatiche told her friend. But Maroula wouldn't listen and she was told she must spend the last few weeks of her gestation in bed. Hatiche, as always, was there to help.

'Stop apologizing,' she told Maroula. 'I have to cook for all of my lot, what difference does it make if I cook for yours too? Besides, wouldn't you do the same for me if I needed it?'

Anastasia was born after three whole days of agonizing labour. Maroula's screams could be heard all over the neighbourhood and there were moments when even Hatiche, with her optimistic nature, wondered if she would survive the birth. For three days and nights she stayed by her friend's side assisting the midwife while Andreas and little Lambros moved next door with Hassan.

When at last she entered the world, Anastasia looked as defiant and alert as she would grow up to be, which was quite the opposite of Leila.

'Well, look at this little one!' the midwife had said after washing and wrapping the newborn in her swaddling clothes. 'I'm sure she's been here before . . .' she added, handing the baby to Hatiche as Maroula had fallen into an exhausted sleep. 'I've never seen one *just* born with eyes as bright and open as this one's.'

Thus the first few hours of Anastasia's life were spent cradled lovingly in Hatiche *Hanoum*'s arms, which her mother always believed was the reason why the girl felt a closer affinity with the Turkish woman than with herself.

'She'd rather spend time with you and Leila,' Maroula would say to Hatiche when Anastasia was big enough to wander off on her own across the yard to the house next door. 'According to both of my children, you are a better cook than me,' Maroula would tell Hatiche, pretending to feel hurt, 'but then again I remember saying something similar to my mother when I was that age.'

'Don't you know that food tastes better in someone else's house?' Hatiche would remind her. 'I always preferred your mother's cooking to mine at home, too.'

'Why don't I cook *dolmades* for us all today,' Maroula suggested one day, aware that of late Hatiche had been responsible for most of the cooking for both families. 'Andreas has brought home some succulent vine leaves,' she continued. 'I'll show you the way my mother taught me to make them.'

The truth was that Andreas hadn't been bringing home much of anything lately, and since the death of his old father the previous year he had been left alone to run the grocery shop, making business harder than ever. One of the farmers from the nearby town had taken to driving his horse and cart to the village every other day with fresh produce as well as poultry from his farm, and once a week he arrived with newly slaughtered meat. The competition hit the small store badly.

'I don't know what we are going to do, wife,' Andreas

often complained to Maroula. 'The shop is being hit hard, I hardly make a profit these days. Now the old man is gone maybe we should listen to Savvas and try our luck in the city.'

'The city! The city! You're always going on about the *city* . . .' Maroula replied, alarm rising in her voice. 'If things are hard here, how much harder would they be there?'

'Savvas has a plan.' Andreas gave a sigh. 'He knows people in the city, we should listen to him.'

Hatiche and Hassan were aware that their friends were struggling to make ends meet so they discreetly tried to share whatever they could with them. Aside from Hassan passing on sewing work to Maroula, taking meals together was another way in which they could help and it was an event that they all enjoyed.

'So how about it, shall we start?' Maroula asked Hatiche eagerly as she fetched the bag of freshly cut vine leaves. 'There's enough here for all of us,' she continued and went to fetch her biggest pot.

Their boys had already started school by then, and as their mothers had done before them, they walked to and from their different classrooms together. Anastasia and Leila, still pre-school, were out in the yard playing in the sunshine while the women sat at the kitchen table stuffing vine leaves. A huge bowl full of minced lamb and rice spiced with salt, pepper, oregano from the hills and cinnamon sat on the table while a plate held the blanched leaves.

'The leaves have to be softened in hot water first,' Maroula said, picking one up and spreading it on the palm of her left hand, ready for stuffing.

'And you think *this* is news to me?' Hatiche teased Maroula. 'I think your mother's recipe is the same as mine!'

'Yes, well, that might be the case,' Maroula smiled, 'but does she cook it with *kolokasi* in tomatoes and lemon juice and does she also stuff onions to go in the dish?'

'Well, if you stop talking and start cooking, I'll be able to tell you,' the other woman replied and their laughter spilled out into the yard where their little girls were playing. Their mothers' laughter always made them feel safe; they didn't need to see them, so long as they could hear their voices, they knew that all was well.

When she was very small, Anastasia liked playing with Leila and dolls, but soon enough she discarded these girlish pursuits to join Lambros and Orhan in their rough-and-tumble scrambles around the countryside, leaving Leila behind to trail after them wailing that she was being left out.

'She's as tough as any boy,' Orhan would tell his friend when he complained that he didn't want his sister around.

'She should be playing with the girls, not running after us,' Lambros objected. But Orhan was very fond of Anastasia, in fact he preferred her to his own sister who was always whining about something. By the time they reached puberty, Orhan's feelings for Anastasia had tipped into longing, but he would never ever admit it or speak about it to anyone, especially to Lambros. It was his own lonely secret that he carried around with him.

He never tired of looking at the girl, not just because he loved her: Anastasia was growing up to be a beauty and no one could help but look at her. At twelve she looked sixteen, her figure already that of a young woman's, her skin white and smooth as satin. Her huge eyes the colour of deep amber dominated her face, framed by long black lashes that curled upwards towards her eyebrows, which looked as if they had been painted in a straight line across her high forehead. Her perfect Greek nose gave strength to her delicate oval face, while her lips curved faintly upwards at the corners, making her look as if she were perpetually smiling.

Comparing his own physical appearance to the object of his love made Orhan's heart sink with dejection. She was a beauty and he was mediocre. Examining himself in the mirror, he wished he had grown to be taller, stronger and generally more of a match for the girl. He had a kind face, warm brown eyes and a wide smile but he would have preferred Lambros's broad shoulders and strong muscled arms. However, his wit, kindness and brains made up for any physical shortcoming and Anastasia loved that in him. He always treated her with consideration and respect and listened to what she had to say even though she was a girl, which was more than most people in her life. For her part, she treated him with sisterly familiarity and affection which kept Orhan in a state of concealed hopefulness.

With time and age the boys' rough games were deemed inappropriate, and Anastasia, who had always loved running wild around the countryside with them, was encouraged by her mother to consider more feminine pursuits.

'You are getting older now, my girl,' Maroula would say, remembering how she had been at her daughter's age, 'and there are things you need to learn. It won't be very long before the *proxenia* start to arrive. There are many young men in the village who'd want you as their bride,' she continued, forgetting how she had broken all the rules and had made her own choice of a husband when she was a girl. The main way a marriage proposal was ever made in those days was through *proxenia*, either through a match-maker or by the family of the young man. Rarely did a decent and pious girl ever choose her own mate and if so it was always frowned upon.

Leila was willing enough to give up childhood games and become a 'young woman' but Anastasia was reluctant;

she missed the freedom of childhood, although spending time with her beloved Hatiche *Hanoum*, who took it upon herself to teach her how to cook some of her favourite dishes, was a bonus. On discovering that she had a willing pupil, Hatiche decided to seize the opportunity to teach her some Turkish too.

'Unlike your mother you're doing well, Anastasia *mou*,' she joked, pleased that finally a Greek was picking up Turkish as well as she and her family had learned Greek.

Spending time with Hatiche was always a treat for Anastasia, but if an opportunity arose to do something with the boys she was ready and Orhan was more than willing to include her. One treat they all enjoyed was attending any performance of the shadow theatre on its tours of the villages in the summer months. Its arrival was eagerly anticipated by the entire village, Greeks and Turks alike; they couldn't wait to be entertained by the puppeteer, who would set up his screen, a large white sheet, in the main square to entertain them with the tales of the popular fictional character called Karagiozis, his son Kolidiris, and all his friends and foes. The chairs would be supplied for the spectators by the village *kafenion* and set in rows under the night sky. Standing behind the screen, illuminated by a lantern, the puppeteer would masterfully make his paper puppets caper on their sticks, representing a host of characters speaking in different voices and acting out comic stories, as his audience, young and old, erupted into raucous laughter.

They would sit for an hour or two and be transported by these shadowy figures into an exaggerated world of farce that spoke of family squabbles, misunderstandings and wrongdoings. They laughed to their hearts' content at the expense of the protagonist, Karagiozis, a simple-minded peasant who was always getting himself into scrapes.

These moonlit summer nights in the mild, scented mountain air, sitting next to Anastasia, feeling the warmth from her body, her laughter mingle with his, made the young Orhan's heart explode with happiness. Anastasia too was flooded with tenderness and affection for the boy beside her who always made her feel cherished and loved.

Orhan and Lambros were excellent students, and as they were now in their last year of compulsory schooling, their parents were urged to encourage their sons to continue their education further.

'You'll do him a great disservice if you don't allow him to carry on learning,' Lambros's teacher had said to Andreas and Maroula one winter's day when he asked to see them. 'I understand it is difficult for you financially, as with most people, but your son is my most promising student. He has always been the best in the school.'

Bursting with pride, Andreas and Maroula couldn't believe their ears; nobody in their family had ever been praised so highly before. 'I can't promise anything,' the teacher went on, '*but* I would like to try to arrange a scholarship for him to continue his secondary education at a high school. It might take some time but it's fine to wait, even if it takes another year.'

Both Lambros and Orhan were keen on their education and they had been hoping they would be allowed to continue with school and eventually be trained as teachers. But they also knew it would be a costly affair; schooling from then on would not be free. Whereas Hatiche and Hassan had the means to pay for their son to continue learning, Andreas and Maroula knew that the fees would be an unmanageable burden for them. Besides, there was no high school, Greek or Turkish, in their village and both boys would have to travel to Paphos or to one of the bigger villages near the coast and stay in lodgings that would only add to the cost.

That night, after speaking to the teacher, Andreas and Maroula sat in the kitchen on their own by the roaring fire and tried to go over what they had been told.

'One thing is for sure,' Andreas said, 'we can't stand in the boy's way. Let's see if this scholarship comes about and as the teacher said, there's no rush, so the boy can come and help me in the shop while we wait. God only knows how I need the help now the old man's gone.' He let out a long sigh and stretched his legs under the table. 'If I had been given the same opportunity I wouldn't be struggling now to scratch a living . . .' He folded his arms behind his head and exhaled again. 'Look at my brother Savvas.'

'What about your brother Savvas?' Maroula replied. 'Savvas didn't go to school for any longer than you did, so it's not just down to education, is it?' she reminded her husband, but her voice didn't carry much conviction; she knew well enough that schooling led to opportunities and that was something none of them had ever enjoyed. 'Anyway,' she continued, 'Savvas was lucky.'

Maroula was right. Andreas's brother, five years his senior, *was* lucky. He too had only completed the elementary school, like most children in the village; nevertheless he seemed to be doing well. He was always urging them to join him in the island's capital, Nicosia, but Maroula's reluctance to leave her home and her friends, especially Hatiche, would always put an end to any such discussions. Then again, even if over the years Andreas had thought it a good idea to relocate to the city, he too was reluctant to leave the village and abandon his old and ailing father. After his mother had gone he felt duty-bound to stay with the old man, but now that he had gone too he had started to think all the more often about it.

'That shop is like a noose around my neck,' he said under his breath, as if he was talking to himself. Then, looking at Maroula, he added, 'If the good teacher manages to get that scholarship for our boy then we have no option but to go. God will provide and Savvas will also help us.'

'Maybe you're right.' Maroula let out a long sad sigh and got up to make some mountain tea for both of them. 'Maybe Savvas is right, things have worked out for him, but then again that was a long time ago and *he* had no option but to leave.'

4

Savvas was trouble. Andreas adored his charming brother, he could do no wrong in the younger boy's eyes, but to everyone else, especially his father, he was nothing but trouble. There had been four boys in all: Elias, Stavros, Savvas and Andreas. Their mother had kept trying for a girl and praying every night in front of the icon of the *Panayia*, but it never happened; instead she lost two of the boys she already had. Her first two sons perished in childhood, one dying of pneumonia, the other from a snake bite. 'Why is God punishing me?' she wailed in despair after each child's untimely death and vowed to Agia Ekaterini, the patron saint of their village, that she would do whatever she asked, if only she kept her remaining boys safe. She doted on her two sons, especially Savvas.

Every morning without fail, at sunrise – just as the saint had instructed her one night in a dream – she would walk up to the church on top of the hill, through rain, snow or storm, to light a candle in front of the saint's icon and pray for the safety of her two sons. On religious holidays she would visit twice daily, and she did this until her dying day.

'You spoil that boy,' the father would tell his wife on hearing about his elder son's latest exploits. 'He thinks he can do whatever he likes regardless of the consequences.' His father was right – what Savvas liked to do, *regardless of the consequences*, was fall in lust and seduce every girl in the village, making each of them think she was the only one for him. Tall and slender, with mischievous hazel eyes and a head of black curls, he was easily the best-looking boy of his age, and it wasn't hard for most girls to respond to his advances. Puberty and sexual awakenings hit Savvas early, at an age when most boys were still running around the countryside climbing trees and making up childhood games. *His* idea of fun was to chase whichever girl had captured his attention at that moment and then move on to the next one.

'You are not being honourable,' his father would try to reason with him when he was a little older. 'We are a decent family. Choose one girl of your liking and we will go to her family and arrange a match.'

But Savvas was an incorrigible flirt; he couldn't contain his seductive urges and had a string of girls of marriageable age dreaming in their beds at night that they would be his bride.

'I have a bad feeling about your precious boy,' his father would tell his wife anxiously. 'One of these days a father or a brother will show your son what he thinks of him.'

'They egg him on, those females,' she would jump to his

defence. 'Don't you see how they provoke him? What's the boy to do? He's a hot-blooded male.'

'You won't be saying that if he gets one of them in trouble and one day ends up lying in a pool of his own hot blood,' he'd hit back, despairing of his son's misdeeds.

Angeliki was easily the prettiest girl among all of Savvas's conquests but she was also headstrong and difficult; the only girl in her family, adored by her brothers, she was used to having her own way. She had also decided that she wouldn't give in to Savvas's sexual advances, even if she wanted to, until she had him all to herself. *She* would be nobody's fool. He was going to marry her or else . . . but Savvas was as stubborn as she was and no one was going to tell *him* what to do. He was certain he would eventually have Angeliki and as many other girls as he wanted to.

He heard the flick of the knife opening before he saw the blade flash in the moonlight. He had taken a shortcut through an apple orchard and was merrily making his way home after a secret meeting with a new girl. The knife missed his heart by inches. Angeliki's three brothers had followed the couple to their lovers' hideout and ambushed him on his way home. Nobody was going to make a fool of their sister and dishonour their family name. He hadn't stood a chance – he managed to drag himself to the front door of his house, where he collapsed bleeding into his mother's arms. No one needed to tell Savvas's father what had happened, he knew in an instant.

'You see, woman,' he shouted at his wife, 'you see? I told you this was going to end badly! You can't treat people's daughters like this and get away with it. It was only a matter of time.'

'Stop your shouting,' she wailed, 'our boy is dying! *Do* something.'

But Savvas was lucky. He didn't die. For three weeks he lay in bed while his mother and the doctor saw to his recovery, and then one night under the protective veil of darkness he left the village. He left like a thief, on horseback, with his cousin and uncle, his mother's brother, who took him to their village on the coast, where he stayed, not daring to return home again. He kept in touch with his family through letters to Andreas, who was the only member of the family who could read, while his mother cried and sobbed at what she called the *loss of another son*. His father was relieved to see him go.

'He has disgraced our family,' he would tell his wife whenever he saw her weeping. 'Stop your crying, woman, you should thank God and all the saints that they didn't finish him off and pray that the village won't blame *us* for *that* boy's wrongdoings.'

'He didn't commit a crime,' his wife would wail. '*He* didn't kill anyone, but *they* tried to kill him . . . and for what?'

'Admit it, woman, it was coming to him, that's all I'll say and you know it's the truth. I'm just grateful that we have one son with morals. Our Andreas is a good boy.'

In the years that followed, a question would often flash through the father's mind – could it be that the decline of their grocer's shop had something to do with Savvas's legacy? Perhaps, he thought, the village didn't forgive and forget so easily.

However, as Maroula told Andreas when he was trying to convince her that they should follow his brother to the city, Savvas *was* lucky and luck seemed to follow him wherever he went. Some months after his departure, he had found a job with a man called Christos, to whom his uncle introduced him. Christos owned a bakery just outside the city of Paphos, a good forty miles away from their village. With the job, Savvas also found board and lodging with Mr Christos, who, as luck would have it, not only had a beautiful wife but also three still more beautiful daughters.

'Now, my boy,' his uncle told him on their last night together before he left them to move in with his employer, 'I know this family. You will be surrounded by what has previously nearly been your downfall and my advice to you is you *must* resist.'

Savvas was sitting at the kitchen table with his uncle and cousin and their glasses of wine while his aunt and his two female cousins bustled about producing little dishes of mezze for them. This ritual usually took place when the men decided to have a night of drinking and discussion, which of course had to be accompanied by food. They were steadily downing one bottle of village red wine after another and even when the food finally stopped and the women went to bed, they would continue talking and drinking into the late hours of the night.

'I know you're a hot-blooded male, my boy, you are my nephew after all,' his uncle said, flashing a knowing grin, 'and passion runs in all the men in our family.' He reached for the bottle to refill their glasses for a toast. 'But you have to govern your desires, or you could be in danger again. This is a good job for you, do the right thing and you'll be fine.' And at that they all raised their glasses to Savvas's future.

'I'll do my best, Uncle,' he replied and meant it.

Despite his good intentions, Savvas, faced with four women and a maid all under one roof, found it almost more than he could manage to avoid temptation. However, in moments of weakness his uncle's words would visit him and he would refrain from acting on his impulses.

'*They are a good family and they treat me well,*' he wrote to his brother Andreas a few weeks after he arrived in Paphos. '*I like Mr Christos. He's a good man, but the best thing about living with this family is the women! You should see them, brother, they are magnificent creatures and so well bred, too.*

There are three pretty sisters and the maid isn't bad either, and . . .' Savvas continued enthusing, *'there is the mother, too. You should see her . . . but yes, I know, I know, don't get upset . . . I know I must behave myself or I'll come unstuck again.'*

But, as much as he wanted to, it wasn't easy to break the habits of a lifetime. Savvas therefore came to a serious decision. For the first time in his life he decided that he would choose one girl as the focus for his romantic attentions and put the others out of mind, even if they were not out of sight. He took his time in making his choice between the sisters and finally he settled on eighteen-year-old Penelope, the middle one. She, he concluded, was the fairest of all three and with the nicest disposition. She was slender and tall, with hair as black as a raven's, while her skin was as white as the dough he kneaded for bread every day. Her eyes, the colour of mountain honey, were framed by thick, black, arched eyebrows and her easy smile held sensual promise. He was subtle with his attentions, making them known to her whenever possible but taking care that no one else was aware. The girl didn't take long to succumb to his charms; she thought he was the most handsome young man she ever saw. Rarely, if ever, did any of the girls come in close contact with such a fine-looking young man.

The baker's house was a two-storey imposing building made of limestone. On the ground floor a veranda ran along its entire facade and wrapped itself around both sides of the house. All doors, reaching from floor to ceiling in every room, opened onto the terrace, while on the upper floor the four bedrooms led out onto balconies over-hanging the garden with a view of the sea. The garden itself, like the veranda, occupied only the front and two sides of the house as the back was reserved for the bakery. This included a big oven house, a storeroom, a work room, plus Savvas's sleeping quarters. Savvas had never seen such luxury. He had grown up in a house made of mud bricks, with a hole in the ground in the backyard as a latrine, and a tin bath in the kitchen for bathing once a week.

This was the house of a man with money and status, and one day, he vowed, he would have all this and more for himself.

Although he was expected to spend his free time in his room, Savvas did take his meals with the family and from time to time, with the approval of their father, the girls would insist that he spent some evenings with them. Mr Christos was a kindly man and he gradually started to regard the hard-working boy as part of the family. Those evenings spent in the house, sometimes playing cards or simply sitting and talking, gave Savvas the opportunity to secretly convey his affections to Penelope – a furtive glance here, an accidental touch on the arm or leg under the card table there, were enough for the girl's heart to be set alight.

It wasn't long before she started to initiate contact with him.

'If you really love me you should speak to my father,' Penelope cooed in his ear one hot summer's night after secretly stealing into Savvas's room.

'If your father would have me as a son-in-law, I'll ask him tomorrow,' he replied, pulling her close and kissing her full on the mouth.

What more could he want, he asked himself? He would have a pretty wife, a big dowry and a job for life!

'If my daughter agrees and wants you too, I would be a happy man to welcome you into our family, my boy,' Christos told Savvas when the young man asked to see him in private the next day after work. The baker had always been regretful that his wife had failed to produce a son for him – if he had had a boy he would have been able to teach him his trade and pass on the business, in which he knew his daughters had no interest. His biggest concern of late was what he would do if Savvas ever left him. The boy was proving to be an asset: he was a natural baker and had a good head for business. Christos's bakery had enjoyed the monopoly in Paphos for many years and his wish had been to expand to another city; perhaps now with Savvas on board this could be a possibility. The boy was turning out to be the son he had always wished for.

*

The news of the engagement was received with great jubilation by all the family and friends and the wedding plans were already on their way for a spring wedding. May as always was considered the best month for a marriage, when the earth was exploding with the scents and colours of wild flowers, and the heady aroma of roses followed you from every garden.

It was about six weeks before the big day and the preparations were well on their way when Penelope's mother, Martha, unexpectedly walked into the bakery looking for her husband. Savvas had been up since dawn firing up the clay furnace with wood and had been hard at work for hours making the loaves which now lay on the wooden slab in rows ready for baking. He had just finished placing a batch of loaves in the oven when his fiancée's mother came in.

'*Kalimera*, Savvas,' she greeted him cheerfully. 'Have you seen Christos?' she asked, glancing around the empty room. 'I can't find him anywhere, I thought he might be going into town.'

'He's gone already . . .' Savvas replied, perplexed as to why his future mother-in-law didn't know this since he was sure he had seen Christos wave goodbye to his wife that very morning as he got into his carriage.

'Really?' she said absently, moving closer to him. 'I must have been in the kitchen and missed him,' she lied. 'I wanted to ask him to pick up some things from the market for me,' she continued, reaching out to touch the young man's bare forearm. Her hand on his naked flesh lingered there a little too long for comfort and sent familiar shock waves through his body; she was standing so close that he could feel the heat emanating from her, and the smell of rose water which she used on her skin and hair clouded his senses.

'Are you going into town sometime soon, Savvas?' she asked softly as he tried to move a little further away from her. 'If so, can I come with you?'

She edged closer, her breast almost touching his arm now.

'I'll . . . I'll . . . let you know,' he stammered and his throat felt as dry as a sand thistle.

'Good!' she replied and then, turning her back, she walked out of the oven room, tantalizingly swaying her ample behind, leaving him standing drenched in sweat. His employer's wife had been an object of desire ever since he arrived in that house, but he had tried to turn a blind eye to her charms, until now.

In the days that followed, Savvas couldn't get the woman out of his mind. She stirred up feelings he'd been trying hard to suppress and which were now rising to the surface to taunt him again. He had done well over the last year or so, he had managed to fight back his old weaknesses and bury his bad habits. He had made up his mind he was going to marry Penelope and nothing was going to stop him . . . but the fire that his future wife's mother had ignited in his loins was proving hard to ignore. He tried to avoid being alone with her but she, on the other hand, always seemed to pursue him. When she stood close to him the sap would rise, and in spite of himself, so did his lust towards her.

Whenever she happened to be alone in the house she would make an excuse to visit him while he worked. It was on one such day that she followed him into the store-room where he had gone to pick up a sack of flour; she slipped quietly into the twilight of the room and closed the door behind her. He had tried so hard to resist her but, despite himself, that day he could not.

A solitary porthole high up on the wall near the ceiling let in a beam of light that barely illuminated them, and in the musty darkness of the room he could see her eyes glistening as she moved closer and reached for his hand. In a swift movement of his arm, he pulled her tight against him searching for her lips, his hands moving over her monumental buttocks, which he had been fantasizing about cupping ever since he set eyes on them. No words were exchanged; she moaned with pleasure as he kissed her neck and ran his hands over her body. Then as quietly as she had glided in she pulled away from him, turned around and walked out, leaving him rooted to the spot and wanting more.

Despite her age, Savvas found Martha sumptuous; she

was as ripe as the plums from the orchards in the mountains whose juice ran down your face when you bit into them. The old saying he'd heard so often in the village coffee shop when he was a boy suddenly came to his lips – '*It's the older hen that has the juice*' – and for the first time it made sense to him. He had no idea what they were referring to then, but now he understood; how right those men had been, he nodded in agreement to himself, and wondered if Martha was possibly more exciting and sensual than her youthful daughter. He had not desired an older woman before, his experience had always been with girls of his own age who had to be coaxed into his lovemaking. So how could he resist a woman like Martha who was now not only provoking him, but evidently eager to taste the illicit fruits of desire.

Savvas had never been one to restrain his lust even if of late he had tried his hardest. This, however, was too much to forgo. Besides, Martha knew well enough that he was to marry her daughter and she was apparently not concerned, so why should he be? This was a gift from heaven, he kept telling himself, he was being rewarded for being so good for so long. It was an offering from Aphrodite, the goddess of love herself, who just like Martha was a daughter of Paphos.

And so once again Savvas yielded to his natural inclinations and decided to sample the delights that Aphrodite had sent his way in the form of his mother-in-law, who was apparently proving to be a true descendant of the goddess of love. *'What harm could it do?'* he asked himself. *'To resist would cause more pain than to accept.'* So eventually Savvas reached the conclusion that it bore no harm to bed the mother of his future wife and, moreover, that it was his duty to spread his love and carnal pleasure to a woman who was so obviously in need of it.

During the following weeks that led up to the wedding, whenever they had the opportunity, Savvas and Martha swam in a sea of sexual bliss.

Sometimes, if they were sure they were alone with no one around, they would sneak into his room, and there in the dark, on his bed, they'd make hurried love without even bothering to undress. It was always rushed, fervent and sinful, and feverishly exciting. Never had Savvas been so aroused or relished a more willing and complaisant sexual partner. The girls in the village had been economical with their favours and even the ones who yielded to his passionate pleas and allowed him to go further always proved to be awkward and inadequate in comparison to Martha. She, as it turned out, was what he had been looking for all along during those years of chasing girls.

The flurry of work for the wedding preparations seemed to offer ample opportunities for Martha to be alone in the house. Christos was always out and about; now the maid and the girls were also busy running errands most days. Trips to the dressmaker for fittings, or visits to the *zaharoplastio* – the finest confectionery in town – for the sugared almonds and the *loukoumia* which Penelope was so particular about, without which no elegant wedding could be complete.

'I will make the *loukoumia*,' Christos had announced to his daughter, believing that as the top baker in Paphos it was for him to make these traditional sweet pastries stuffed with pistachios and almonds for his daughter's wedding.

'You are a master baker, Papa, everyone knows that,' Penelope had said, trying to appease her father. 'No one bakes bread as delicious as yours. But you are not a *zaharoplastio* and I think the job for my *loukoumia* should go to the best.' The father of course relented – how could he refuse her – and the girls continued to dash around town making their orders and purchases, leaving the coast clear for Martha to visit Savvas at her ease.

Although Savvas was now spending all his spare time with the family, he was still sleeping in his room next to the bakery, which he would soon be giving up in order to move into the house with his bride.

'What are we going to do when we no longer have this room?' he heard himself murmur wistfully into Martha's ear one day as she lay beneath him on his bed, her skirt raised, her legs wrapped around him. He waited for her reply but none came; assuming she hadn't heard, he repeated the question. Still she didn't speak, and when after a long pause she finally replied, to his dismay her answer was not at all what he had anticipated.

'*We* will do absolutely nothing!' she said sharply, not looking at him while she sat at the edge of the bed adjusting her clothes. Her voice had a steely edge to it and her reply came as an unwelcome surprise as well as carrying a sting to his heart. The words he had expected to hear from her were something along the lines of '*nothing can stop us*' or '*nothing* can come between us'. '*Do nothing*' had never crossed his mind.

The realization that he was falling in love with Martha dismayed and confused Savvas; when it came to matters of the heart, or rather of the flesh, he had always been in control. He had embarked on this erotic journey with his mother-in-law the way he had always done – knowing exactly where he was going with it, and for no other reason but purely for his sensual gratification and excitement. However, he had never entertained the possibility that for the first time in his life he might lose control. *That* was something he didn't know how to handle.

The wedding day was fast approaching and he was at a loss about what to do. He had wanted to speak to Martha, confess his love, but after her brisk reply he hardly dared; yet he had to let her know how he felt. He could wait no longer, time was running out; he had to do it now. Perhaps, he convinced himself, if she knew how he felt she would change her mind.

It wasn't that he didn't love Penelope, he told her, when he finally summoned up the nerve to speak to her. On the contrary, he was very fond of the girl; she was a delightful young woman with beauty and charm, which evidently she had inherited from her mother, and would make some man happy, but he was *not* that man.

'What I feel for Penelope doesn't compare to what I feel for you,' he told her. 'I love you with all my heart; you are the woman for me.'

He reached for her hand and clasped it in both of his. 'Say yes, and I'll put off the wedding,' he continued passionately. 'You can leave Christos and marry me!' Martha stood motionless and speechless, staring at him as he searched her eyes for clues. He held his breath and waited for her reaction.

'Have you lost your mind?' she finally hissed at him, articulating every word, and pulled her hand away from his grip. 'You will do no such thing!' she hissed again, her eyes flashing. 'You will marry my daughter and you will stop this crazy talk at once!'

'But . . . what . . . what . . . about *us*?' Savvas mumbled, looking pitiful and confused. 'Surely you love *me*, not Christos. We love each other, don't we?'

Martha took a step back and glared at Savvas.

'Christos is a good man, and I have no intention of

leaving him for you or for any other man, and as for *love*, whoever said anything about that and what does it have to do with this? You listen to me, my boy, we've had our fun, be grateful for that and stop all this nonsense, do you hear me?' And with that, Martha turned round and walked out of the room, leaving him, as she always seemed to do, trembling in his shoes.

From that day on she stayed well away from Savvas and kept him at a distance, as if nothing had happened between them. The wedding preparations continued as before and nothing was ever said again about the affair.

For the first time in his life Savvas was experiencing rejection. No woman had ever treated him this way. How could he have let himself be swept away like that, he scolded himself. What a fool he had been – of course he must marry Penelope, who was as fresh as a rosebud and who adored him. Martha was right, he had surely lost his mind to even contemplate wanting to take a woman so much older than himself as his wife. Yet he had to admit that even well past her first bloom of youth, his mother-in-law had got under his skin and her indifference distressed him.

After the wedding, as it had been planned, Savvas moved into the house with Penelope and the rest of the family, which was what he had been looking forward to long before his affair with Martha but which was now turning out to be a liability.

Try as he would, there were times when his anger towards her, still mixed with desire, made living under the same roof intolerable, and for the first time since he had left his village and family he wished himself back at home living the simple life of the mountains.

'Wouldn't it be good if we had our own house, just the two of us?' he would say to Penelope sometimes when the burden of having to see Martha day in and day out became too oppressive for him. Soon any longing and passion he might have felt for her turned to fury alone.

'Why would we do that?' she replied, surprised that Savvas would even think of such a thing. 'Our house is large enough for all of us.'

'But when we start having children, then what?' he would insist.

'There is plenty of room for us all,' she would tell him and kiss the top of his head.

Luckily for Savvas his misery was short-lived. The solution to his predicament came when his father-in-law suggested that it was time to think seriously about expanding their business in another town, and wanted Savvas to be in charge.

'I think you know that for a while now I have been thinking of taking the bakery to Nicosia,' Christos told him one night after they had finished their supper. 'I have an old friend there, Petros is his name; we go back a long way and he's come into some money problems.' He picked up his glass of wine and drained it. 'He owns a grocery shop and he wants to sell it and I am thinking of buying it off him.' He reached across for the bottle of wine and continued talking. 'My plan is that while Petros continues to run the shop you will set up a bakery and when that's up and running you can take over the shop, too.' Christos looked at Savvas and filled up their glasses again. 'The capital, my boy, is where you could make a fortune. So, what do you say?'

Savvas didn't have to think for long before giving his reply with genuine enthusiasm.

'I say *yes*, Father!' he said eagerly and raised his glass. 'I'll do whatever you want me to and will help you as much as I can.'

'That's my boy!' Christos picked up his glass too. 'I was worried that you might not want to leave Paphos, but believe me, my son, as much as I don't want to see you and my Penelope go, Nicosia is the city of opportunities.' Smiling broadly, Christos stretched across and noisily clinked glasses with his son-in-law.

'*Stin ygia mas,*' they both echoed as they drank to the future and to each other's health.

Unbeknown to Savvas, Martha had played a hand in convincing her husband of the idea. She too could see how hard it was for the two of them to continue living together under the same roof. Now, they would both regain their peace of mind and she was glad to have him out of the way. Savvas was delighted with the prospect of leaving the paternal home with his bride for Nicosia, which could hardly be further away. Marrying Penelope was the wisest decision he ever made, he told himself – or perhaps, he mused, it was the wisest thing that *Martha* had decided for him. He had often heard people say that he was lucky; now he began to believe it.

His father-in-law's offer was a great gift and he vowed to work hard and make a success of the business, not only to repay Christos's kindness but also as an act of atonement for the way he and Martha had behaved. He threw himself into work and started to make plans for their departure, deciding that once he set up the bakery in Nicosia he would send for his brother Andreas to come and help him.

'*This is a great opportunity for us both to make some money at last,*' he wrote to Andreas with excitement, telling him of his future plans. '*You, my brother, know all about being a grocer, you've been managing our father's shop since you were in short trousers. You know exactly what to do, while I know all about baking bread.*' Savvas needed his little brother with him, he'd been away from the family for too long. '*There is no great urgency,*' his letter continued, '*the old man who runs the shop is still managing it, but when the time comes you and I will make a great team and have a family business of our own.*'

Savvas's enthusiasm was infectious and Andreas was

delighted to hear that things were finally looking up for his brother. However, what Savvas didn't know when he first wrote home to announce his future plans, was that Andreas was not the kind of man willing to make the decision without the consent of his beloved wife and Maroula was in no hurry to leave their village. But Savvas wasn't going to give up easily. He was certain that he could have no better partner than his younger brother and so he made up his mind to wait.

'*It will be good for all of you,*' he pursued every so often in his letters, '*the children will benefit too, it's time to make the move, my brother. The bakery is running well now and making good profits, soon it will be time to think of the grocery shop, too, and I need you for that to keep it in the family. I've already started building our house, which will be big enough for all of us. As you know, Penelope and I haven't been blessed with children, so your Lambros and Anastasia will bring joy to our lives, too.*' Savvas's letters were now being sent all the more frequently and each time another arrived the temptation and call from the city was becoming greater for Andreas.

5

Both Andreas and Maroula were conscientious parents and wanted the best for their children, and now after the conversation with Lambros's teacher, the issue of education was playing heavily on their minds.

'If he is as clever as the teacher says then we must do something about it,' Andreas told his wife. 'We can't ignore it, intelligence is a gift from God.'

So that very evening when the couple sat at the kitchen table discussing their son's future and the likely award of his scholarship, they at last made the decision to accept Savvas's offer for them to join him in Nicosia and help to expand his business.

'One thing is certain,' Andreas repeated, sipping the cup of hot tea his wife had placed in front of him, 'we can't stand in our boy's way. Savvas is doing well and maybe together we can do better.'

'We could use some of your brother's good luck,' Maroula said and reached for her husband's hand. 'If you think this is the best plan for us, Andreas, I have no objections now to leaving for the city; we must do what's best for our children.'

'You never know, wife,' he replied, 'maybe Hassan and Hatiche will follow us. Orhan needs to carry on with his studies too.'

'*Inşallah*,' Maroula replied, and looked over her shoulder at the icon of Agia Ekaterini, hoping that the saint had heard her plea. 'I couldn't be happier if that was to happen,' she sighed, and promised that she would speak to her friend the very next day about their plan. Yes, you never know, she thought – given enough time, their friends might decide to make the move too. But if her family had to leave without the Terzis, it would be the first time they had been separated. She didn't want to think about that.

The snow had been falling all night. Unlike Lambros and Anastasia, who were already up and calling each other excitedly, Maroula could hardly drag herself out of bed, unwilling as she was to leave its cosy warmth. Her thoughts had kept her awake most of the night and the eerie silence which comes with falling snow had prepared her for the sight she was faced with when she finally pushed off the heavy eiderdown and swung her legs to the floor, searching for her slippers. The room was as cold as she had expected; shivering, she reached for her dressing gown on the chair next to the bed. Wrapping the warm fabric around her she let out a long sigh and made her way to the kitchen. Andreas had already been up for hours and was now feeding the stove with more wood while Anastasia was cutting thick slices of bread for toast.

'We'd better set off for school early,' the girl said to her brother, who was still standing at the window.

Although snow was not an uncommon sight in their mountain village during winter, it was usually more of a flurry; the previous night's snowfall was surprisingly substantial, bringing joy to the young and irritation to their elders who knew how much tougher their work would be in the bad weather. Lambros stood looking in wonderment at the village and forest ahead of him. Every rooftop and every treetop was covered in a clean crisp blanket of snow as if the whole village had just been white-washed. He couldn't wait to run out with Orhan and fill his lungs with fresh clean alpine air.

'LAMBROS!' Anastasia's irritated voice snapped him out of his reverie. 'Stop dreaming and come and help, it will take us longer this morning to get to school.'

With a heavy heart, Maroula walked into the kitchen and sat herself down at the table, watching as everyone busied themselves with their morning chores.

'*Kalimera*, Maroula *mou*, how are you?' Andreas greeted his wife. 'Have you seen outside?' He pointed to the window with his chin. 'The chickens haven't budged from their coop.'

'What's wrong, Mama?' Anastasia asked, surprised to

see her mother so out of sorts. 'Father said you weren't feeling so well.'

'I'm fine, Anastasia *mou*, just a little cold, it's this weather,' she replied, unwilling to explain what was bothering her just yet. 'You'd better call round for Orhan and Leila on your way,' she said to change the subject. She and Andreas needed to have a long discussion with their children and this morning was not the time.

'Don't we always?' the girl replied, surprised at her mother's suggestion. 'When do I ever walk to school without Leila?' she added with a quizzical look.

'I know, but with this snow . . .' she didn't finish her sentence. She got up slowly and reached for the *bricky* hanging on a hook above the sink. She had a heavy heart but she also had a heavy head this morning, and she knew that a large cup of coffee would at least deal with the latter and help her to think.

She stood at the window watching the four children disappear noisily down the road, throwing snowballs at each other, and her eyes filled with sorrow. She must go next door soon and talk to Hatiche. She gave yet another long sigh: how would they all manage to live without each other?

She pushed open the back door and stepped outside with a broom to clear a path. The snow, dazzlingly white in the sunlight, squeaked beneath her feet like the cornflour she used to make *mahalepi*, which in turn always reminded her of snow. She breathed in the crisp fresh air; the pure blue sky and the sun beating down on her back would normally have lifted her spirits, but today nothing seemed to work. It took her a surprisingly long time to clear the path, delaying the moment of having to speak to her friend.

Hatiche sat in silence for a long while after Maroula stopped talking. She was afraid that if she spoke too soon she would not be able to control the flow of tears she was holding back and she knew that would only add to the distress of them both. What good would tears bring, she told herself. Maroula wasn't leaving her in order to punish her; this was equally painful for her, she was leaving for the good of her family, and Hatiche would do the same in her place. But Hassan's business was thriving and if Orhan wanted to continue with his studies, Paphos was a good deal closer than Nicosia.

When Hatiche at last managed to speak, her words brought no surprises to Maroula; in fact, she later thought, she should have expected them.

'I knew it, my friend,' Hatiche said, her voice barely a whisper, 'I read it in the cup. I have known for a while now but I didn't dare breathe a word about it in case it was true.' She reached for her friend's hands and held them tight. 'For the first time since I've been reading the coffee grounds, I hoped the cup was lying.'

*

The news of their impending move affected everyone in different ways. It would be a life-changing event for all four members of the Constandinou family; none of them had ever ventured far away, and apart from their lack of money, Andreas knew that his family was content with life as it was.

'Even if you don't get the scholarship your teacher hopes for, we have a duty to help you to continue with your studies,' Andreas told his son after their evening meal a few nights after he and Maroula had made their decision. It was a bitterly cold night and they were huddled around the crackling fire in the kitchen, discussing future plans. Anastasia had just finished helping her mother to clear the dishes from the dinner table and was now at last about to join her father and brother by the fire; Maroula was handing out cups of sweet black Russian tea for further warmth.

'I can earn more in Nicosia for your school fees, and your uncle Savvas has pledged to help us,' Andreas continued and reached for his tea. 'The family house is almost built, and it will be big enough for us all to live there. We wait and see about the scholarship; in the meantime you help me in the shop.' He took a sip and looked over the rim of his cup, anticipating the boy's response. Maroula darted worried looks at her husband; they had never discussed leaving the village before and her anxiety was mounting at how her son would react.

'What do you think?' Andreas said again, hardly giving Lambros a chance to reply. 'This will be a good move for you, my boy,' he continued. 'Your future isn't here, your future is in the city. I stayed in this village and look where it got me. So, what do you think?' He looked eagerly at his son.

Lambros took a sip of his tea, looked at his father and was about to speak when Anastasia interrupted him.

'Does anyone care what *I* think?' she blurted out, her voice raised, her cheeks flushed. 'Doesn't *my* opinion count to you?' She looked from one parent to the other. 'No one asked *me* if *I* wanted to go to Nicosia' – her eyes flashed with anger now as she spoke – 'and what about *my* school, do neither of you care about that at all?'

'You will finish your schooling in the city,' Andreas replied, open-mouthed at the girl's unexpected outburst, having never imagined that Anastasia would have an opinion on the matter. 'Besides, you have only one more year of school to go and you don't even have to go if you don't want to.'

'Of course I want to finish school!' she burst out again. 'But that's not the point – the point is that neither of you thought about *me*, or asked what I think. You never do!' She darted a look at her mother.

'I didn't think you cared one way or another about school,' Andreas said, bewildered. 'Haven't you been saying that you want to learn to sew with your mother?'

'That might be so, but the fact is you only ever care about what Lambros thinks.'

'Of course we care about you, my girl . . .' Maroula said gently, trying to appease her daughter, and moved closer to take her hand.

'It's because Lambros is a boy,' came Andreas's feeble excuse, confused about his daughter's outburst. 'We have to think about *his* future. As a girl your future will soon be with your husband.'

'Who said I want to get married?' Anastasia gasped. 'I'm too young, I'm not even thirteen yet! And who told you I want to go to Nicosia?'

'Your father is not talking about getting married now, Anastasia *mou* . . . but it won't be too long before you do; things are different for girls, you know that.'

'It shouldn't make any difference that he is a boy and I'm a girl, Mother. You should still care about what I think. I've never been to Nicosia. How do I know if I want to live there?'

'None of us has ever been to Nicosia, Anastasia *mou*,' her mother replied. 'It will be an adventure. Just think how much warmer it will be there than up here.'

'Do you think I care about that!' the girl snapped angrily at her mother and snatched her hand away from hers. 'I can't believe you're all willing to just get up and leave. What about our house *here*? What about our friends?' Her voice, though still raised, was now wavering, her eyes filling with tears.

'She is right, Father,' Lambros said finally, having sat silently listening to his family talking across each other. 'I am really grateful that you are willing to give up our home for me, but if Anastasia doesn't want to leave she has a right to choose. I could always go alone and stay with Uncle Savvas.'

'Oh no! No!' Maroula spoke out this time. 'We will *not* be separated, we shall stay together.' The thought of losing her beloved friend and her home was bad enough, but the idea of splitting up her family was even worse. Nicosia was as foreign and unknown to them as the moon. The distance of seventy miles or so that separated their village from the capital and the treacherous mountain roads between them made it a daunting journey to undertake, and unless it was essential few people braved it. Andreas knew it was an uphill prospect to uproot his family, but he had also hoped that the big city's potential would be an attractive proposition to his children.

'It could be exciting, Anastasia *mou*,' Maroula began again, trying to defend their decision.

'What about Hatiche *Hanoum*?' the girl burst out once more, giving her mother a hard look and ignoring her comment, 'and Leila and Hassan *Bey* and Orhan?' She glanced around the room, first at her parents and then at Lambros. 'How can we leave them all behind? Don't any of you care?'

'They will come and visit us, and stay as long as they

like,' Maroula replied, 'and you can spend all your summer holidays up here with them. I've already spoken to Hatiche, and we have agreed.'

The next day after school Anastasia went straight to Hatiche's house. She threw her arms around the woman and started to cry.

'I don't want to leave you,' she said through her tears. 'It's not fair that we should all be separated because of Lambros.'

'Now, now, *askim mou*,' Hatiche said, stroking the girl's hair and using the Turkish word for love, that Anastasia had learned so well from her. 'Your mother and father are only doing what they think is best for *both* of you and all the family, not just for Lambros. Besides, you're not leaving yet. By the time you have to go you'll be used to the idea.'

'I'll never get used to it, and I'll never see any of you again if we leave.'

'Do you think I would let that happen?' the older woman replied. 'Do you think I'd let your mother go without ever seeing her again? So, come and sit down and tell me the reason why you are so upset.'

'It's not that I don't love Lambros, and Orhan . . . I do, you know I do, but what about me and Leila? It's always about them, about the boys!'

'Do you want to go to high school too, Anastasia *mou*?

Is that what this is about? What's upsetting you?' Hatiche asked, looking the girl in the eyes. Anastasia averted her gaze, avoiding the older woman's scrutiny.

'No, it's not that,' she finally said and wiped her tears with the back of her hand. 'I can read all the books I want, I don't need to go to school for that.'

'What is it, then?'

'I know you've always said education is freedom and that you and Mother didn't have enough, but a skill is freedom too, isn't it? I want to learn to be a seamstress like you and Mama, so that I can earn a living and be independent.'

'But you can do that in the city,' Hatiche interrupted. 'You can learn from your mother or do an apprenticeship somewhere.'

'But I wanted to learn from Hassan *Bey*, he's the master tailor, I wanted to work in his shop.'

'You can do that when you come to stay with us in the summer. I can teach you and Leila more, and then when you are older and know the trade, Leila can come to Nicosia and the two of you can open a dressmaker's shop. Now doesn't that sound like a good enough reason to go to Nicosia?' Smiling, Hatiche gave Anastasia a kiss on the cheek, got up and made her way to the kitchen. 'Now stop crying and let's have some of the *baklava* I made this morning,' she called from the other room.

*

By the time Anastasia arrived home she had cheered up and the future looked brighter.

'That smells good, Mama,' she said chirpily, walking into the kitchen where her mother was stirring a pot of steaming hot *trahana* soup made from cracked wheat and yogurt with chunks of halloumi cheese floating in it, perfect comfort food to warm them up on such a cold day.

'You sound cheerful, Anastasia *mou*,' Maroula replied, relieved to see her daughter in better spirits. She had felt guilty all night long, thinking about their conversation. The girl was right, none of them had really thought about her; their focus was always on the boy.

'Maybe Nicosia isn't such a bad place to live in, after all,' the girl said and started to pour herself a glass of water from the earthenware jug standing in the middle of the table. 'I went to see Hatiche *Hanoum* after school.'

'Ah! Of course! That would explain it,' Maroula said and let out a long sad sigh. She would miss her friend more than she could ever explain to anyone or even want to at this point. But she knew that once the decision was made and their plans had been set in motion they must start to prepare for the move. There would be no looking back.

'I heard the news . . .' Orhan said to Lambros on their way home from school the next day. 'My mother told me.'

'I'm sorry . . . I wanted to tell you myself,' Lambros

replied, stealing a sideways glance at his friend. The joy he felt at the prospect of going to high school was mingled with a sense of guilt, knowing that the reason for this upheaval for everyone, for leaving the family home and his best friend, was himself.

'Even if I don't get the scholarship, my uncle has offered us a place to live and my dad a job,' he tried to explain further.

The snow was now rapidly melting and the sun beamed down on them as they trudged through mud and slush. 'It all happened so fast,' he said again apologetically.

'I'm not really surprised,' Orhan replied. 'Isn't that what we both wanted? To go to high school?'

'I know, but we wanted to go somewhere together . . .' Lambros's voice trailed off.

'Yes, we did,' Orhan said and turned around to look at his friend with a beaming smile. 'The way I see it, there's only one thing for it. If they were going to send me away to school in Paphos, then they can send me away to school in Nicosia with you!'

'The boy is right,' Hassan said to Hatiche that same night after Orhan came to them with his suggestion. 'We were seriously considering sending him to Paphos, so why not Nicosia?'

'Yes, yes!' Hatiche interrupted in agreement. 'He'll be safer with our friends.'

'I just pray to Allah that Andreas will accept some money for the boy's lodging,' Hassan added, concerned that his friend might refuse out of pride.

'I'll talk to Maroula,' Hatiche said, knowing that between them the two women would never allow such matters as foolish pride to interfere with a good plan.

And so it was agreed that if, as hoped, Lambros was awarded a scholarship and the Constandinou family were prepared for Nicosia, Orhan would leave with them to attend the Turkish high school.

The boy was family, there was no question that they would refuse. He would live with them and they would look after him as one of their own, as the two families always did for each other.

6

The bus stopped in the village just twice a week. Visits to nearby villages were usually made by foot, donkey or mule, but for longer journeys a bus would arrive every Tuesday to deliver and collect mail and carry the few passengers who wanted to travel further around the island. Paphos and Limassol were the most common destinations while hardly anyone ever ventured as far as Nicosia.

The arrival of the bus was always an occasion of interest and excitement. Bambos, the driver, was well known and liked in the village. He worked for the main office in Limassol, which contracted drivers to pick up passengers from remote mountain locations; since he often had few or no passengers, he was given the job of postman too, as an added incentive to make the hazardous journeys.

Bambos's Bedford bus, which he leased from the company and was painted in a riotous assortment of colours, was his pride and joy. Half-metal, half-timber, the bus was painted a brilliant shiny red on both sides of the chassis, while the upper part, including the window frames and bonnet, was an equally glossy bright green edged with yellow stripes. The bumpers, front and back, were white, with gold, red and green stripes round the edges framing the number plates. The luggage, on the occasions when the bus had more than a handful of passengers, would either be hoisted onto the roof rack to be tied down with tough blue fishing ropes, or if anything was deemed too precious by its owners, it would be carried into the bus. Luggage consisted of numerous wooden or cardboard boxes, often filled with livestock, wicker baskets filled with an assortment of foodstuffs, and earthenware pitchers filled with olives or olive oil.

On fine days, when rain, wind and mud hadn't yet splashed the vehicle, it would arrive looking almost as bright and festive as when Bambos had set off. After parking in the village square he would make his way to the *kafenion* with his postbag and sit at a table for a well-earned coffee and some walnut, cherry, or bitter-lemon *glygo* in syrup, whichever was in season, while he waited to pick up any return mail and, with luck, any passengers. All the while that the bus was parked in the square it became the object of intense curiosity, mainly among the children, who would spend the entire time while Bambos was having his break examining the vehicle. No matter how many times they had seen it, they never tired of climbing all over it and pretending to drive it.

'Just make sure none of you rascals do any damage or,

God forbid, release the hand brake, or there'll be hell to pay,' Bambos would shout good-naturedly at the children who were, of course, in no doubt that his threats were sincere.

When the day finally arrived for Bambos to take the Constandinou family and Orhan to Nicosia, the whole village had gathered in the square to see them off. Over the years people came and went, especially young men, looking for work in the bigger villages and towns, but no entire family had ever left in this way before.

'*Dear brother, I am so happy that you have finally decided to take the plunge and leave the village,*' Savvas had written to Andreas when he heard the news. '*Penelope has prepared your part of the house and we are looking forward to being a family again at last. It's been lonely with just the two of us in this great big place. Orhan is welcome too, Hatiche* Hanoum *and Hassan* Bey *have been like family to you.*'

Preparations for the move had been taking place for weeks before their departure and it was agreed that Xenia, one of Maroula's cousins, and her family, who had been living with her husband's parents, would take over the house.

'Bless you, Maroula *mou*, and your Andreas too,' the cousin said with tears of gratitude. 'I shall take care of your home as you have always done and whenever you come back to visit us you will live here with us.' Maroula was not only pleased to be able to do a good deed for her relative but also content in the knowledge that she was leaving her house in good hands.

'I want to stay with Hatiche *Hanoum* when I come back to visit, not with Auntie,' Anastasia had told her mother as they packed their belongings to be sent ahead with Bambos one day in early June.

'I don't suppose Hatiche would let you stay anywhere else even if you wanted to,' Maroula replied with a smile.

'How will it be when we get to Nicosia, Mama?' Anastasia said again, her curiosity now aroused by the prospect of their move. 'People say it will be very hot!'

Reports of heatwaves and droughts down on the plains were always rumoured and as high summer was fast approaching they found it hard to imagine. The Troodos range was their terrain, their world. Heavily forested, heather-scented, with cool streams and water-falls, these mountains covered a great deal of the western part of the island. Cold and crisp in the winters, hot but fresh in the summers, that was the only climate they had ever known.

To the north of the island across from Troodos, another mountain chain in the form of a narrow limestone ridge ran along the entire length of the coastline, acting as a barrier to the sea and creating a vast hot, dry flatland between the two ranges, and that was where the city of Nicosia lay.

*

By early July they were on their way. The journey was long, tiring and dusty; for Maroula it was also heart-breaking, although she tried her best not to show it. The others were delighted for their own different personal reasons. Lambros and Orhan were happy not to be separated as they had feared they would be, and to realize their dream of attending high school at last. Orhan had an extra reason for joy in the knowledge that he would not only not lose his best friend but he would also be living under the same roof as the girl who had stolen his heart. Andreas was looking forward to and ready for the challenge of working with his brother, and Anastasia was now eagerly anticipating a new life in the big city. Maroula, it seemed, was the only one looking back. She sat on the bus quietly reflecting on what she had left behind: a life she was content with, a house she cherished, family and loved ones, and for the first time ever she would be separated from her beloved Hatiche. At least, she thought, her parents were long dead and buried or that would have been one too many separations to endure. She sighed deeply and swallowed her tears. She had lived a happy life so far, she told herself; she had no complaints. Now it was her children's turn. Their future was what mattered and she must start to look ahead.

As the bus trundled slowly down to the foothills of the mountains and started to leave behind the familiar slopes, the landscapes they encountered were a revelation. Apart from Andreas, who had travelled elsewhere on occasion, no one else had ventured further than the neighbouring villages. Gradually, as they made their descent, they watched as the familiar fresh green lushness of the mountains was replaced by shrubs, cactus plants and dusty carob trees. Once they approached the flatlands the green vanished entirely, giving way to a parched yellow and dusty grey plain. They watched with keen interest as herds of goats and sheep grazed under the unforgiving sun on what appeared to be nothing but thistles and tumbleweed, with only an occasional lonely olive or fig tree providing shade for the poor shepherd.

The day before their departure Maroula had visited Hatiche for a last morning coffee together. They sat as always in the backyard under the mandarin tree and pledged never to lose touch with each other. Hatiche was the more pragmatic of the two.

'How can we ever let go of one another, my friend?' she said. 'Can sisters ever forget each other? Because that is what you and I are.'

'I know I would never find a friend like you again,' Maroula replied, her eyes tearing up.

'Besides, you will have my boy. Do you think I would allow too much time to go by before I come to visit you?'

But despite their million promises to visit each other, Maroula had a premonition, a foreboding, warning her that somehow their easy companionship would never be the same again.

They arrived in Nicosia just before sunset. The sky, the faintest of blues, was tinged with blushing pink and alive with the darting flight of swallows in a last attempt to feed before nightfall on a wealth of insects.

Normally the bus stopped at the terminus in the main square, within the Venetian walls encircling the old city, but since there were no other passengers and Bambos was almost family, he took it upon himself to make a slight detour and deliver them to their front door.

The house that Savvas had built, on a plot of land that had been passed down to him and Andreas by their maternal grandfather, was an almost exact replica of that of his father-in-law in Paphos, just as he had promised for himself one day. Standing in front of the house, only a few metres outside the city wall and facing the dry moat, they were all mesmerized as they glanced over the ancient fort onto the city beyond, imagining what wonders it contained within. Just inside the wall, which surrounded the city like a serpent, and no more than a stone's throw away from the house stood a mosque, its minaret soaring above any other building in the vicinity, while in the distance the Byzantine domes and bell-towers of Greek Orthodox churches were visible.

The sound of the bus and Bambos's loud beeping

announcing their arrival propelled Savvas and Penelope out into the yard to welcome everybody amid much jubilation and embracing.

'*Kalosorisate, kopiaste,*' *welcome, come in*, they repeated excitedly, helping the newcomers off the bus and into the dusty road.

Andreas's brother and his wife couldn't have been more welcoming and their new home surpassed all expectations. The house, made out of local limestone, was solid and spacious; on entering through the front door they stepped into an *iliakos* almost the size of the entire house they had lived in before. Anastasia was thrilled with the bedroom her aunt had given her, which was double the size of her old room and furnished with a rosewood chest of drawers, a single four-poster bed festooned with lace, ribbons and a mosquito net, and a wardrobe with a full-length mirror on the door. She was made to feel like a princess; Penelope was compensating for the absence of a daughter she had always longed for. The two boys had to share a room but it was spacious enough for their two beds, a large wardrobe and two small desks complete with an electric lamp for their evening studies. Everyone was more than happy. Above all, the most impressive item in their new home, they unanimously agreed, was the installation by Savvas of one of the European lavatories they had heard so much about, complete with a flushing device which they all had to learn how to use properly. There was also a tiled room in which Savvas had placed a small wooden bathtub under a metal pipe acting as a kind of shower, so that when the boiler was fed with wood it would heat enough water for bathing – though arrangements had to made in advance as there was only ever enough water for one person to wash at a time. Once again, it was unanimously agreed that the shower device was nowhere near as good or effective as Hassan's Turkish bath.

They had now all been living together for over six months and their cohabitation had proved to be more successful than Maroula had imagined, even if at times she was aware of Penelope's reservations about the Turkish boy. If any negative comments were ever made about Orhan they fell on deaf ears. Maroula was determined that he would be part of the family, no matter what. Both boys had now enrolled into their high schools, Anastasia had started as an apprentice with *Kyria* Thecla, a seamstress in the old town, while Andreas was getting used to running the other part of the business, the grocery shop with its now ailing proprietor, Petros.

At first Maroula had a few reservations as to how they would manage with two women running a house – she was used to being in charge of her domestic domain and worried that Penelope might not take too kindly to her interference – but on the contrary her sister-in-law, after a few initial hitches of getting used to another mistress in the home, welcomed her participation with pleasure. Penelope was proving to be a good friend, even if she couldn't replace her dear Hatiche.

'I had never imagined that I would not be able to bear a child,' Penelope confided in Maroula as they sat drinking coffee between their household chores one day. 'Each month I would wait and each month I'd be heartbroken. I visited every doctor in Nicosia, I've had every examination under the sun and I have even been to the fortune teller to find out if it might happen someday . . .' her voice trailed off. 'Having a full house now with all of you here, especially the young ones, has brought me so much joy. Bless you and bless your children, although,' she hesitated, 'they are hardly children anymore.'

'That's true, Penelope *mou*, they're growing up; a year or two more and we'll be looking for a husband for my Anastasia. She's nearly fourteen now. And the boys, they are turning out to be fine young men, but then again they'll always be our *children*,' the other woman replied with a smile. 'My old mother used to treat me like a child even after I got married.'

'My sisters and my mother hardly ever visit me,' Penelope murmured, sadness resonating in her voice. 'I'm used to a big family, Maroula *mou*, and I miss it. My mother has never visited, not *once*, she says it's too far to travel for her health . . .' Her voice trailed off again. 'Savvas sends me to visit her once in a while but it's not the same.

Having you all here makes me feel like we're a real family at last, and I thank you for it.' She reached across to squeeze her sister-in-law's hand.

'You have no reason to thank me, Penelope *mou*, *we* should thank *you* for sharing your home with us.'

'It shows how lonely they must have both been these past years, especially Penelope,' Maroula told Andreas. 'She is one of three sisters, it must have hit her hard leaving them all behind and starting over again on her own. I can't understand why her mother never visits her, it's not normal. Poor Penelope.'

'Yes, but see how nicely my brother has provided for her?' he replied. 'She wants for nothing.' His expression darkened. 'I, on the other hand, Maroula *mou*, have never managed to provide well for you in all the years we've been married.'

'Having money doesn't bring happiness, Andreas, a good family does that,' replied Maroula. 'Penelope was rich before she married your brother, but being childless and alone can bring sadness no matter how wealthy a person is.'

7

The fire started from a single candle. Electricity had been introduced to the village only recently and the supply was unpredictable. The power would frequently cut off, unexpectedly plunging everyone into darkness, so candles and oil lamps were still essential and no one was in a hurry to get rid of them. On one such night when Hassan was working late, the bare electric light bulb hanging from the ceiling in his workshop faded and he was suddenly enveloped in darkness. He was used to these power cuts so he was well prepared. Fumbling in the dark, he lit the candle which he kept ready for such occasions, then turned round to light the oil lamp – when a remnant of fabric was accidentally caught by the naked flame.

Piled high with bolts of textiles, yarns, samples and offcuts, the workshop was a fire trap. In no time at all the building was set ablaze. He tried to save what he could, beating back the flames with a rug and battling with the raging fire while his strength lasted; but he couldn't help inhaling the thick smoke which rapidly filled his lungs. By the time the alarm was raised the flames were lighting up the night sky. Hassan was found unconscious outside the building and could not be revived.

The news hit the family in Nicosia like an avalanche. Their return journey was immediate to avoid delaying the funeral for more than a day, since for both Christians and Muslims, the dead must be buried straight away.

They arrived in a village plunged into mourning for the untimely death of one of their own. They found Hatiche and Leila at home, surrounded by black-clothed friends and neighbours who were caring for them. Dying had always been a communal affair in their close-knit community, for Turk and Greek alike, and demanded that everyone lend their support and help of every kind to the bereaved family.

Hatiche was inconsolable. How would she live without her Hassan, what would happen to her and Leila without him? Orhan was as heartbroken as his mother and sister and insisted that he must give up his studies and come back to the village at once to try to rebuild the family business. The months spent helping his father while they were waiting for Lambros's scholarship to be approved had given him some knowledge of tailoring, although when Hassan suggested that Orhan should take on the business after his studies he had vowed to himself that it would never happen. He was not going to follow in his father's and grandfather's footsteps; he was not a born tailor, he was going to be a teacher. But now things were different, his mother and sister needed him and he must do the right thing to support them.

Hatiche was thrown into further turmoil. She did not want her son to give up his education but how could she afford to continue paying his fees, let alone give Andreas and Maroula money for his lodgings?

'No matter how bad things are, I would *never* ask you to give up your dream,' she nonetheless told her son a few days after the burial, trying to show a brave face. 'Allah is great and He will provide for us, my son.'

The solution to their problem came a few days later when Andreas and Maroula sat Hatiche down and in no uncertain terms told her that from now on Orhan's education would be their responsibility. Lambros's scholarship would see him through his education, and the grocery shop and Savvas's bakery were now providing them with a good income; for the first time in his life Andreas was earning enough money for them all and Orhan was almost a second son to them.

'If it was the other way round, wouldn't Hassan have done the same for me?' Maroula told her friend and took her in her arms.

'You have both helped us so many times when we were in need,' added Andreas when Hatiche tried to protest. 'Now it's our turn.'

It was nearly the end of the school year and summer was already upon them, so it was decided that although

Andreas had to return to Nicosia, the rest of them would remain with Hatiche and Leila to help one another through their grief. It had been previously planned that the three children and Maroula were going to spend the summer in the village, but none of them could have ever anticipated the circumstances of their return.

They had been looking forward to spending two or three months with family and friends in the cool of the mountains, especially Maroula and the boys, but Anastasia, surprisingly, had been in no great hurry to leave the city. She was enjoying her apprenticeship with *Kyria* Thecla and more specifically she was enjoying the attentions of her bosses' two handsome young sons, who had an eye for a pretty girl. The rest of the family was finding the heat of Nicosia oppressive and longed for the fresh air of their village but Anastasia, despite her concern before arriving in the city, found that she actually liked the heat, without knowing exactly why it suited her. Somehow it felt not unlike the flurry of sensuality she experienced when the eyes of *Kyria* Thecla's sons were upon her.

'Why don't you open all the windows at night?' she told her mother when she complained that it was too hot. '*Kyria* Thecla's house is cool and breezy because she keeps the windows and doors open for a nice draught and we look into her garden when we work. This house is like a furnace! Uncle Savvas's oven at the back isn't helping either.'

Four other girls were working out their apprenticeship with Anastasia, all between the ages of fourteen and seventeen. Two of the older girls came from villages across the island and were staying with relatives while the other two were local, living at home. Anastasia struck up a close friendship with one girl who came from a remote village in the north of the island and who was now living with her aunt and uncle not far from *Kyria* Thecla's house; her name was Victoria.

'My mother told me that I was named after the queen of England,' the girl explained to Anastasia, who had never heard of the name before, nor did she know anything about England or her queen. 'But you can call me Rioula if you like. I prefer it, that's what my *yiayia* calls me.'

'You can tell your friend Victoria that she might have been named after an old English queen but you are named after a Russian princess!' Orhan retorted when Anastasia told him and Lambros about her new friend and her grand name. High school had already made its mark on the boys' education, the colonization of the island by the British being given much emphasis in their school curriculum. The British occupation after centuries of Ottoman rule had been initially well received by the Cypriots, even prompting many to name their baby girls after the victorious queen, but sixty years on the empire was losing its lustre, and islanders were now beginning to view the colonials through less favourable eyes. While the girls were ignorant of developments in the political domain, the two boys were beginning to pick up a wider awareness of their place in the world, sensing the rumblings of anti-colonial, anti-British feelings from certain Greek Cypriots that were creating some tensions between the two communities. Orhan and Lambros stayed neutral – politics was not for them.

Whether Anastasia wanted to spend the summer in the village or not, the death of Hassan *Bey* changed everything and there was no question of her not joining the rest of the family in supporting their beloved friends.

The summer of their return was useful to them all and the time they spent together sharing the rituals of grief helped them on their way to recovery.

For Orhan, that summer also proved to be the most significant of his life so far. The unexpected death of his father hit him with force, and the realization that he was now the man of the family and would have to take care of his mother and sister was weighing heavily on his young shoulders. He had always been a pious boy and from a very young age he had attended the mosque daily, first with his father and then alone. Now he came to realize that for himself, solace could be found only through prayer and reflection.

Although the three friends had lived under the same roof for the best part of a year, Nicosia had held many distractions for the youngsters. Orhan and Lambros had their studies and Anastasia was busy with her apprenticeship and helping her mother and aunt around the house. Returning to the village of his birth under the sadness of his loss, Orhan was flooded with childhood nostalgia which emphasized the importance of his relationship with his friends. He loved Lambros like a brother, as he always had; but now he had to also recognize and acknowledge that his feelings for Anastasia, which had been contained for so long, were far from brotherly. Suddenly he found himself torn between two conflicting emotions: faith and love.

8

That summer spent at their childhood village was like no other. The death of Hassan *Bey* brought the two families together once again and prompted Anastasia to be still more affectionate towards Orhan, who, during his solitary reveries, imagined that the girl was perhaps a little in love with him, too. But what to do about it? She was a Christian, he was a Muslim: a union between them could never take place unless one of them changed their faith, thus committing a great sin. He knew that for him it was out of the question and he was more than certain that Anastasia was a devout Orthodox, like all her family. How could he ever speak of such love to her? Or even worse, to Lambros? He was certain that his friend would be angry with him; he would consider Orhan's declaration as an act of disrespect and betrayal. This, he told himself repeatedly, was a love that could not be declared; besides, he had no idea if Anastasia felt the same way that he did. But his feelings were so strong that when his imagination carried him away and fantasy took hold he looked for glimmers of hope in everything she said or did. *Does she know how she makes my heart ache?* he would think to himself whenever she was near him and paid him attention, making his heart soar with happiness and misery all at once.

For her part, the girl loved her childhood friend as much as she had ever loved anyone who was not her mother, father, or brother.

Hatiche was grateful to have Maroula with her again, the friend who was always ready to hold her, comfort her and listen to her laments. More than two months had passed since they had buried Hassan and although the pain of his death was as raw as the day when they had found him unconscious outside his workshop, they were all trying to come to terms with the loss. Andreas had gone back to Nicosia and soon the others would have to follow in time for the start of the school term.

'God bless you and your family, my friend. Knowing that my boy will be taken care of lifts a huge burden from my soul,' said Hatiche, wiping away her tears.

'Wouldn't Hassan *Bey* have done the same for Lambros if it was the other way round?' Maroula repeated and reached for her friend's hand. The two women were sitting under an orange tree in the backyard with their coffee while the hens pecked at their feet, almost like old times. Maroula had been staying with her cousin in the old house while Lambros and Anastasia were next door with Hatiche.

'Why won't you come with us?' Maroula asked her friend again. She had spent the last half hour trying to convince Hatiche that a trip to the city could be just what she needed. 'I don't want to leave you alone,' she went on.

'I won't be alone, I have Leila. She's a good girl, and she helps me with the sewing. How else are we going to make a living now?'

'Never forget that you always have us, Hatiche *mou*,' Maroula replied.

'I have never doubted it, my friend, your friendship is what gives me peace of mind. And there is also Ahmet, Hassan's brother in England, who has promised to help us.'

This time, saying goodbye before their return journey to Nicosia was harder than ever and once again the villagers gathered in the square to see the Constandinou family off. Bambos waited patiently as they said their tearful good-byes before boarding his bus. They sat in silence, sad and pensive during their long trip, deprived of the excitement and anticipation which they had felt the summer before on the way to their new life. Maroula couldn't help thinking that she should have stayed longer with her friend but Hatiche wouldn't hear of it, insisting that the family needed her in Nicosia more than she and Leila did.

'Who would take care of them if you don't go back with them?' Hatiche told her when she agonized about staying longer. 'Your sister-in-law is not used to looking after so many people. They all need you there, my friend. Leila and I will be fine, we have the whole village to take care of us.'

Gradually life in Nicosia resumed its normal pace, for the three young people at least, although Orhan felt that nothing would ever be the same again without his father. Leaving his mother and sister alone in the village to fend for themselves weighed heavily in his mind and heart. He vowed that he would study hard and make good so he could provide well for them in the future. Living with the people he loved almost as much as his own parents eased his pain a little and his proximity to Anastasia inspired feelings which helped to soothe his soul. He threw himself into his studies with more passion than ever. While his ambition to become a teacher was still strong, now his spiritual and religious education seemed to hold extra significance.

'I still want to go to the teachers' training college with you,' he told Lambros during one of their early evening strolls inside the city walls after their day at school, 'but I also want to carry on with my religious studies.'

The death of his father had left a void in the young man's life and he struggled with his grief. The Constandinou family was providing him with the love and security they were giving their own two children and Andreas did his best to be something of a father figure to him. However, when it came to matters of faith there was little he could do to advise or help him. For that, Orhan turned to his local imam. Allah and the Quran were now giving him the solace and comfort he needed.

The apparent reversal of fortunes between the two families, which sometimes troubled and embarrassed Lambros, didn't bother Orhan at all. What mattered to him now was the affection he received from his adopted family, being close to Anastasia, and the new spiritual path he was following.

Anastasia was thriving at *Kyria* Thecla's workshop. She was developing into a talented seamstress and was beginning to dream of the future.

'*It won't be too long now before I finish my apprenticeship,*' she wrote to Leila, '*then you will come to Nicosia and we will open our very own dressmaking shop just like your mama said we would.*'

'First of all, my girl, we have to arrange a marriage for you before you start thinking about opening a shop,' Andreas and Maroula said, alarmed at their daughter's apparent ambition.

'You will do no such thing!' Anastasia gasped. '*You* will *not* be marrying me off!'

'In any case,' Andreas continued, well acquainted with his daughter's rebellious spirit by now and ignoring her outburst, 'what kind of an unmarried girl from a good family sets up a shop on her own?'

'*Kyria* Thecla has one, and she is a respectable lady from a good family—' Anastasia started to protest.

'*Kyria* Thecla is a married woman and no doubt her husband had a hand in setting up her business,' Andreas interrupted. 'It's one thing to be willing to work like your mother did when we were struggling, and another to have grand schemes at your age!'

'Hatiche *Hanoum* thinks it's a good idea,' Anastasia protested again.

'I'm certain that Hatiche thinks it will be a good idea once you and Leila are married and settled, not while you are both looking for husbands!'

'She's too headstrong, this girl of ours,' Maroula told Andreas after Anastasia flounced off in a fury at her parents' inability to understand that they were living in the twentieth century now and women could be independent.

'Who is going to want to marry her if she acts like a man?' added Andreas. 'The sooner we find her a match, the better.'

But of course, Anastasia was her parents' daughter and they had both apparently forgotten that no one had found a match for *them*. They had found each other and had married for love at a time and place when such things were unthinkable.

After their little dispute Anastasia made a mental note not to discuss what was on her mind with her parents in future. She was going to do what she wanted when she wanted and she was determined that she would find a way to follow her ambitions. Besides, she was certain that Hatiche *Hanoum* was on her side and so was Orhan, who was the only member of the household who took her seriously and listened to what she had to say. Since moving to Nicosia, he had taken his mother's place as her confidant and mentor and she regarded him as her best friend.

'They just don't understand,' she told him one day when she tried to explain that she wished to work more than she wished to be married. 'How can I accept a marriage proposal from someone I don't even know, who doesn't respect what I want out of life and who has only asked for my hand on the basis of my looks and my dowry?'

'If I was your husband I would be *more* than respectful that you want to work,' Orhan replied, emboldened by the heat of the moment and the intimacy of their conversation. Then he instantly regretted it. 'What . . . what . . . I mean,' he stammered, 'is a wife of mine would be free to pursue her interests, I wouldn't stand in her way.'

'I'm sure of it!' Anastasia replied ardently. 'And what's more, she'd be a lucky woman who takes you for her husband, because you're intelligent and sensitive and you never dismiss what I have to say because I'm a girl,' she continued, pink with emotion. 'I've seen the types my parents have found as a suitable match for me, and *thoughtful* or *sensitive* is not how I'd describe any of them. You, Orhan *mou*, are an exception.'

Anastasia's little speech swept over him like a tidal wave of happiness. He sat quietly listening to her speak, soaking up her every word. What did she mean, he wondered, as his mind raced to interpret her comments. Did she, perhaps, love him as he loved her but he'd been too blind to see?

'So, yes!' Anastasia carried on. 'The girl who marries you will be a lucky woman – but as we know,' she quickly added, 'that's not going to me . . . is it? But maybe if I'm lucky I'll find someone like you one day.'

'Ermm, well, as they say . . .' Orhan stammered again. 'As they say,' he continued, summoning up courage. 'Sometimes if there is a will there is a way,' he finally blurted out as the blood rushed to his cheeks.

'I don't think there could *ever* be a way when it comes to a match between a Turk and a Greek, Orhan *mou*, *you* know that!' Anastasia said gently, reaching for his hands. 'You are my best friend, my mentor, my adviser, we are family! To my mind we're even closer than if we were married. In fact, we're like an old married couple already,' she added cheerfully as a smile started to spread across her face. 'In any case I think there's more to life than marriage, don't you?' she concluded and started to laugh, putting an end to their conversation.

*

Orhan basked in the memory of Anastasia's words for weeks after their conversation. Although their meaning was ambiguous they allowed him a glimpse of the possibility that she loved him, even if marriage was an impossible dream.

Now he had hope as well as love, and faith in his heart, making his days brighter and his nights easier, which was enough to sustain him for the time being, at least. Besides, as school was coming to an end the work he had to do for both his academic and his religious studies was consuming most of his time and energy, and any spare time that he and Lambros had was now filled with helping out at the bakery.

First deliveries were usually made early in the morning by Andreas in a horse and cart before opening the shop. However, more recently, demand was growing and some families inside the city walls were ordering more than one freshly baked loaf per day.

'Let us help with deliveries, Father,' Lambros offered when he realized that his father and uncle were struggling with the orders. 'Orhan and I like to take a break from studying and it will give us something to do.'

So most afternoons the boys would set off, carrying a basket each full of bread and sesame *goulourakia* or whatever other pastries people had ordered, timing their deliveries to be finished before the call for evening prayer. If the call came when they were far from home, Lambros would wait for his friend outside one of the mosques in the old city. If they had already returned home, Orhan was able to observe prayers at the local mosque, which was a hop and a skip across the dusty road in front of their house. He would run across the street, down the slope into the dry moat, climb the wooden ladder that people had made to climb the wall and then jump down onto the back of the minaret, thus gaining entrance to the mosque without having to follow the long way round through the streets and the city gate. Bayraktar Mosque was Orhan's favourite, because it was not only close to home but also one of the oldest and in his opinion the most holy of Nicosia's mosques. Built against the Constanza Bastion of the wall, it was surrounded by a fragrant garden where worshippers gathered to use the pool and basin for their ablutions before prayer. Above all, perhaps the most important reason why he preferred this mosque was that the wise old imam who led the congregation there was his mentor and spiritual adviser.

'He is a righteous and honourable boy, if a little too pious,' Penelope had commented to Maroula about Orhan, soon after they all moved in.

'Well, he was brought up by Hatiche *Hanoum* and Hassan *Bey*,' she replied. 'You couldn't meet a more honourable family, so what do you expect?'

When Savvas first told Penelope that Orhan would be coming with his brother's family to live with them, she was not in favour.

'The boy is a Turk . . . a Mohammedan!' she protested.
'What business does he have living with us?'

'He is family!' Savvas replied sharply, making it clear
that she was not permitted to raise any more objections. It
didn't take long for Orhan to win her over with his character and charm and, regardless of their differences, she
soon accepted him, although never quite as a fully fledged
member of the family. As a Christian she struggled with it
but knew well enough to keep her opinions to herself.

9

London, 2008

'The older I get, the more I regret what happened . . .' Lambros said with a mournful sigh. 'And the older I get, the more I regret that we allowed our differences and the turn of events to come between us.' The old man shifted in his chair and turned round to look at his daughter: 'Tell me, my girl, tell me, what will become of the world if we all carry on like this?'

'I know, Papa,' Stella replied, cupping both of her hands over her father's on the garden table. 'We believe we're tolerant but, in the end, we prove that we're nothing of the kind!'

'Human beings, eh? We think we're so superior, we think we know everything and more, but in the end we fall back into our stupid pride and prejudices.' Lambros reached for his coffee and took a sip.

'I have a feeling that our stupid pride and intolerances have a lot to answer for in many of life's calamities, Papa.'

'Why did we allow it all to go so wrong?' he asked again

and looked at his daughter, searching her eyes as if to find the answers there. 'We had such respect for each other, such love, such trust, so much life together. You know, Stella *mou*, I remember once . . .' Lambros's eyes took on a faraway expression as his mind reverted to the past.

'I remember one time when Orhan had to disappear for a week. I didn't quite understand why. It was part of his religious studies, which required him to spend time alone for a week's retreat from the world, in order to pray and meditate. He wasn't allowed to see or speak to anyone.'

Lambros reached for his coffee again as he continued with his story. Stella believed she had heard it before – she had heard most of her father's yarns many times over – but to her surprise this wasn't familiar.

'For almost a week he had to be by himself,' the old man continued, a smile starting to spread across his face. 'So he took himself off to a kind of shepherd's hut about a mile away from our house. And of course I was the only one who knew where it was; he told me, not only because he trusted me but also because he needed my help.' He chuckled at the memory. 'He needed food, you see, he couldn't stay without it for all that time. And who else would do that for him but me! Provisions wouldn't last long in the middle of a field, so every evening I would sneak out of the house with a bag of bread, water, some olives, a tomato, and maybe an onion, and leave it at a place we agreed, for him to collect after I left. When the week was over he came back to the house looking lean and serene – he'd told everyone that he was studying with his imam, so no one asked any questions. They knew how important his faith was for him.'

Lambros pushed back his chair, stood up, stretched his arms and started to walk to the end of the garden, where an olive tree he had planted many years ago had now grown almost as tall as the plum tree that stood next to it.

'And you know, Stella *mou*,' he called across the grass to his daughter, 'that's just one of so many stories. Did I ever tell you the one about the bicycle thieves?'

'I think so, Papa,' Stella called back, knowing she was destined to hear it again even though she'd heard it a dozen times before. 'But tell me anyway,' she added, humouring him. 'I've forgotten most of it.'

'I remember it as if it was last night,' he began as he returned to the table with a yellow rose he had cut for her. 'It was during our last year at the teachers' training college in Nicosia.' He handed her the stem and sat down. 'It was only about a week before graduation and we joined a group of students who were spending a week in the holiday campus in the mountains, visiting a few of the village schools. Orhan and I were staying on the campus with some of our fellow students, and one day a relative of his who lived in a neighbouring village invited us both to an engagement party.' Lambros's face lit up at the memory. 'Happy to be going to a celebration but having no other means of transport, we decided to hire a couple of bicycles for the journey. The relatives were hospitable and kind and we had a great time. We ate, we drank and danced till late in the evening before we got on our bikes for our return journey.'

Stella poured a couple of glasses of water from the jug on the table and pushed one in front of her father. 'The night was warm, the stars were bright, the world was ours and we sang at the top of our lungs as we rode through the moonlit forest.' Lambros lifted the glass to his lips, amusement etched on his face as he continued with his story. 'Suddenly over our singing we heard loud shouting and leaves rustling in the dark. Four or five masked men rushed out from the trees and stood across the road to block our way, some of them brandishing what looked like shotguns and demanding our bicycles!'

The old man leaned on his elbows and glanced at Stella to make sure he had her attention. 'We braked to a sudden halt and both came crashing off our bikes on top of each other! We were terrified; these bandits looked mean and obviously meant no good. We picked ourselves up and waited for our fate. They ordered us to hand over our bicycles and our money and then they vanished back into the forest with the loot, leaving us stranded in the night far from the village, to make our way back on foot. Well, what could we have done? We had no option but to do as they said and were relieved at least that they'd let us go without beating us up into the bargain. We started to trudge down the road in the dark, bruised from the tumble and thoroughly miserable. The bikes you see were rented and would have to be returned and paid for the next day, but they had taken all our money!'

'What did you do, Papa?' Stella prompted, enjoying her father's pleasure in retelling his story. He'd been so sad lately when he remembered the past, she was glad to see him cheerful.

'We'd been walking for about half an hour,' Lambros continued animatedly. 'We were still in shock after our ordeal, when suddenly we saw something glittering in the moonlight. As we got closer we realized it was our two bicycles lying in the middle of the road, one on top of the other. We stood gazing in amazement, trying to work out what this meant, when out of the forest we were pounced on again by the same bandits! This time though, Stella *mou*, this time something made us react differently and in a brave moment Orhan lurched forward and pulled off one of the bandit's masks – only to discover that this was no thief but one of our fellow students! They all were, all five of them! They wanted to get their own back on us for going off to a party without inviting them along and this was to punish us for having fun while they stayed behind!' Lambros's smile broke into laughter. 'Their disguise and their toy shotguns were convincing enough in the dark and had us both well and truly scared. What rascals, eh?'

'That's one of my favourite stories, Papa, and you tell it so well,' Stella said with a grin and meant it. She gave her father a kiss on the cheek. 'You should write them all down, they'd make good reading. I've always said that your grandson gets his talent for storytelling from you!'

Stella was convinced that her son, who was Lambros's namesake, was more like his grandfather than anyone else in the family, not only because of their shared name. 'Did you know that Lambros wants to study journalism?' she added.

'He mentioned it, but I thought he was more interested in teaching,' her father replied, hopeful that his grandson would follow in his footsteps.

'*Teaching, my boy, is a job you can do wherever you are, and always guaranteed to earn you a living,*' he would advise the young Lambros at every opportunity.

'He's still thinking about it,' Stella replied, 'but he loves to write and he's very good at it. His teachers are advising him to go for an English degree and then maybe do a course in journalism.'

'He can always go into teaching later,' Lambros said, refusing to give up his hopes for the boy. 'He's still so young and I'm sure whatever he does he'll be a success; he's got brains!'

'I told you,' Stella smiled, 'he takes after his *bappou.*'

'And what about our girl?' Lambros asked after his granddaughter this time. 'What does our Erini want to do?'

'She wants to be a fashion designer,' Stella told him. 'She's been accepted at the London College of Fashion. It's a big deal, Papa,' she added, beaming with pride. Stella was proud of both of her children and took credit for always encouraging them to make the most of their talents, while trying to distinguish between pushing and motivating. She was especially glad that she had encouraged them to become bilingual, although it was their grandfather who took on the hard work of teaching them to read and write in Greek, as he had done for her and her brother while they grew up in London. For young Lambros and Erini the experience was less easy; whereas Stella and her brother had had two Greek parents who spoke the language at home, Stella's children had an English father with no knowledge of Greek, making the task much harder. Passing on her mother tongue required effort and patience from Stella and fortunately when hers ran out, *bappou* Lambros had plenty of both. *'I just want you to be able to talk to your grandparents and know what people are saying when we visit Cyprus or Greece,'* she would tell one or other of her children when they were younger, exasperated when they rebelled at the extra work they had to put in after school.

Now as young adults they were both more than grateful for the second language their mother and grandfather had passed on to them.

'So, Erini wants to be a fashion designer, eh?' Lambros asked again.

'Yes, Papa, she's very talented, you should see her work. She makes the most wonderful clothes. In fact, look! She made this blouse I'm wearing now.' She stood up to show it off to her dad. 'I don't know where she comes up with the ideas, certainly not from me!' Stella beamed again.

'If Lambros takes after me then Erini must take after my sister,' the old man said and his expression clouded over. 'Anastasia was a very talented seamstress, you know . . .'

10

Cyprus, 1950

To describe Anastasia as a free spirit would have been an understatement. Where that unconventional disposition of hers came from neither she nor anyone else knew, considering the way she was brought up.

She was living on a far-flung island in one of the easternmost corners of the western world, touching the fringes of the Middle East, yet Anastasia behaved as if she was familiar with life in Paris, Vienna or Milan. Did the Italian and French fashion magazines she devoured at *Kyria* Thecla's workshop or the cinemas she frequented with her friends on Sunday afternoons have anything to do with it? Perhaps that was part of the explanation. Yet it was still far from clear how a girl who had spent her formative years in a remote village high in the mountains of Cyprus, where girls were expected to conform to strict local traditions, could find such confidence to voice her own opinions, not only to her family but to anyone who would listen. Perhaps, if the midwife who delivered her was to be believed, Anastasia had visited this world before – otherwise how else could her understanding of things beyond her experience be explained? With time her poor mother decided that the midwife's surprised observation must be the only reason for her daughter's irrepressible independence; she could see no other explanation.

'We need to marry her off as soon as possible,' was Andreas's only solution to his daughter's rebellious nature. 'Once she's married with a couple of babies she'll be like everyone else.'

'She doesn't want marriage, Andreas,' Maroula reminded her husband in despair. 'We can't force her, and she won't listen to me.'

'*You* never listened to your mother, either, when she wanted to find you a husband, if you remember.' Andreas insisted, 'We must keep on trying.'

'I didn't want to be married off because I wanted to marry you, not because I was against marriage, in fact I couldn't wait to be married, unlike our daughter,' Maroula countered. 'She insists that she doesn't see the point of marriage unless she falls in love.'

'Just like her mother!' Andreas teased.

'Yes, Andreas *mou*, but by the time I was her age I'd found you,' Maroula replied, 'and we were already engaged . . . but our daughter, on the other hand, doesn't seem to be interested in *anyone*!'

'It's simple,' Andreas replied confidently. 'We'll find

someone she can fall in love with. Savvas and I know plenty of well-to-do young men that she might approve of.'

Anastasia was a notable beauty in the city, and despite her mother's concerns that she would soon be left on the shelf if she didn't accept a marriage proposal, at twenty she was still young enough and with a substantial dowry to be considered an excellent catch. It was not as if no one was interested in her; on the contrary the *proxenia*, the marriage proposals, arrived with alarming frequency via a matchmaker or directly from men who happened to see her and liked what they saw.

'I don't know who this man is, why would I want to marry him?' was the girl's invariable reaction when Maroula informed her about a new proposal. 'When I agree to marry, it will be to a man I know and love, not to some stranger!'

'You will get to know him, then love will follow,' her mother would try to reason. 'That's how *proxenia* works.' But Anastasia would not be convinced.

'I'm not ready for marriage. When I am, I'll know, and then I'll let you know,' she would tell them, hoping they might relax their relentless campaign.

Maroula was at a loss; her daughter had a mind of her own and of late had given her even more reason to worry, due to her startling modern ways.

'What man is going to find her attractive, looking like a boy?' she asked her husband when Anastasia came home one day having had her long dark curls cut *à la garçonne* into the fashionable bob worn by the models in the French magazines. 'As if wearing trousers in public isn't enough, now she has no hair either,' her mother despaired. 'Do you think she has a secret love and won't tell us?' Maroula asked her husband, not knowing how else to explain her daughter's behaviour. 'Do you think she's unhappy?'

'How should I know? She's your daughter. You're a woman, *you* find out,' Andreas replied.

Maroula's fears were unfounded. Anastasia was more than happy with her life; she had her family and friends, she had her brother and Orhan who were always ready to take her out to the fashionable cafes and movie theatres any time she wanted. She found much to enjoy in her work which kept her stimulated and interested. For now she desired nothing else; life was fun enough without being bound by ties and duties to a husband.

Most young girls of marriageable age stayed at home with their mothers waiting for *proxenia* and learning the virtues of housekeeping and modesty. Anastasia, on the other hand, wanted none of this. She had decided that after completing her dressmaking training she would apply for work with *Kyria* Thecla, who was expanding her business and had offered a position to her star pupil along with young Victoria. The stylish new look from Europe was taking the capital by storm and all the prosperous ladies were eager for the latest exciting designs. Anastasia had a feel for the drape and fall of fabrics, and a knack for adapting the basic cut from existing Vogue patterns for each customer, making every outfit unique.

She insisted on walking daily to the workshop without a chaperone. Her route took Anastasia via Nicosia's commercial quarter, past the municipal market and bazaar and through the back streets that crisscrossed the old town, past diverse shops and stalls whose Greek, Turkish and Armenian vendors had become well acquainted with the cheerful young beauty who never failed to greet them when she passed.

'*Kalimera*, Anastasia! God be with you,' they called as she breezed past them like a breath of sweet air and a good omen to the start of their day. Working made her feel free and independent and her heart swelled with new possibilities ahead.

'There is no need for you to work,' her parents protested when she first decided that earning a living was her plan.

'Your father and uncle earn enough between them to support all of us,' her mother tried to convince her.

'Yes, but you won't always be there to support *me*, will you?' she replied, having already made up her mind.

'Your husband will be there to take care of you,' her father said. At which point Anastasia stalked out of the room in a rage, refusing to engage in further discussion with them.

*

'I have no option *but* to work,' Victoria told Anastasia when the latter complained of her parents' inability to understand why she wanted to earn a living and their obsession with finding a husband for her. 'If I had a chance not to work I'd be more than happy, but my family depends on what I can bring home . . . And as for marriage?' The girl gave a hollow laugh. 'Without a dowry *that* would be a fine thing!'

'If a boy falls in love with you the dowry won't matter,' Anastasia replied, knowing that her friend was sweet on one of *Kyria* Thecla's sons and forever encouraging her to give the boy a sign. What Victoria lacked in a dowry and breeding she made up for with her good looks, even if she herself was unaware of them. Dark and sultry, with intense fiery black eyes and full lips, she exuded a raw sexuality that no male could ignore.

'Dino can have the pick of any girl from a good family,' was her response, 'so why would he want *me*, or *Kyria* Thecla have me as a daughter-in-law? What can I bring to the bargain?'

'He likes you! I've seen the way he looks at you!' Anastasia replied. 'And in any case,' she protested, 'love is not a transaction!'

'Believe what you will,' the other girl replied, and looked down at her sewing. 'Anyhow,' she sighed, 'I think Dino looks at all the girls that way.'

'He certainly doesn't look at me that way,' Anastasia

insisted. 'It's you he favours, my friend, I know it, and if you gave him some encouragement instead of scowling at him every time you saw him you might be surprised!'

'The trouble is, Anastasia *mou*,' Victoria said, looking up from the collar she was stitching, 'you and I are different. For a start, boys always look at you adoringly, *and* like Dino you also have the pick of the best if you ever want to get married. *You*, my friend, have the support of your family, their money, their connections.' She paused to take a deep breath before continuing. 'I, on the other hand, have to fend for myself, because nobody is going to look after *me*.'

Victoria's words lingered disturbingly in Anastasia's mind. Her friend's brief outburst, she decided, wasn't vengeful or mean: it was simply realistic. Victoria was speaking the truth. Not only did her words highlight Anastasia's privileged position, making her sound like a spoilt child, they also had a surprising impact in revealing to her how she had been behaving towards her parents. She acknowledged that, unlike Victoria, she was fortunate to have parents who supported and protected her and that perhaps it wouldn't hurt her to become a little more thoughtful and tolerant towards them. After all, she reflected, they only wanted what was best for *her*.

Panos was a fine young man from a family as affluent as the Constandinous, and was acquainted with Lambros and Orhan from around the neighbourhood. He was aware of

Anastasia, having noticed her a number of times, chatting with the boys in cafes or at the movie theatre, or walking alone to work. He found her intriguing; she was distinctive, like no other girl in Nicosia.

His mother, *Kyria* Froso, was a regular customer at the bakery and shop and the *proxenia* came directly from her in the way of an afternoon visit to Maroula and Penelope. The two women didn't often meet their prosperous customers in a social context, so when *Kyria* Froso's maid called round one morning with a message that her lady wished to pay them a visit that afternoon the two sisters-in-law were impressed and curious to know the reason for the call.

It was pleasantly warm for early summer so they decided to receive their guest in the front garden, which was still in bloom and shaded by a small orchard of citrus trees and one tall, majestic palm laden with yet unripe dates, providing plenty of cover. Maroula and Penelope fussed about with preparations for their visitor, laying the table with their best linen and china and deciding to serve lemon tea, a more elegant variation on their usual Turkish coffee. *Kyria* Froso was one of their most valued customers and frequented the Nicosian social circles with whom they wanted to make a good impression, because no matter how long they lived there they would always be considered provincial.

'What prompted this all of a sudden?' Maroula asked Penelope, moving the table under the date palm, her curiosity getting the better of her. 'Do you think she has something to say to us?'

'Well, she does have a son,' Penelope replied, giving her sister-in-law a knowing smile and a nod.

'Could it be that she wants our Anastasia for him?' Maroula said with hope in her heart.

'And why not? Where are they going to find a better bride than our girl?'

'And do you honestly think there is any chance that *our girl* is going to accept?' she replied with a sinking heart. 'That, Penelope *mou*, would be nothing less than a miracle!'

While Anastasia was hardly eager to meet Panos, given her recent resolution after her chat with Victoria to behave more reasonably towards her parents, she agreed.

'They are a good family and there's no harm done by meeting with them,' Maroula had said to her when she realized that for once Anastasia was not going to storm off in a rage at the suggestion. She knew by now that the whole practice of *proxenia* infuriated her daughter, who told her often enough how she perceived it to be primitive and demeaning.

'If he likes me so much, why didn't he come himself instead of sending his mama?' was her only response to her parents when they broke the news of *Kyria* Froso's visit.

'His mother said he had asked her to come and speak to us out of respect,' Maroula explained.

'Respect is important,' Andreas added. 'It shows he's a good boy, and in any case, this is how we do things here, my girl, get used to it,' he said, starting to lose his patience with his daughter and her defiant ways.

'I'm just doing this to appease everyone,' Anastasia told Orhan, explaining why she had agreed to the meeting. 'I've refused so many times, I thought I'd comply just this once to keep them happy. But honestly, Orhan *mou*, as you know, I have no interest in getting married to anyone.'

Orhan had met this Panos. He and Lambros had seen him in town and had often exchanged a few words when they came across each other. He had to admit that he was a personable young man, while wishing with all his might that he wasn't. His heart ached with the prospect that his beloved might find this match to her liking.

'I know they only want what's best for me,' Anastasia continued, oblivious to Orhan's silence and sudden queasy expression, 'but I promise you, I'm not interested, especially in some stranger. Besides,' she continued with a mischievous glint in her eyes and suppressing a giggle, 'who needs a husband when I've got you?' She moved closer and nudged him with her elbow. 'Haven't I always said we're like an old married couple?' Her giggle turned into infectious laughter.

*

Panos thought he recognized a little of himself in Anastasia. He had recently returned from Athens, where he had been studying architecture, and saw himself as something of an artist, a nonconformist, unlike most young men in his circle.

He was twenty-seven years old and as an only child he was now being urged by his parents, especially his mother, to think about marriage.

'You're not getting any younger,' *Kyria* Froso told him repeatedly. 'You need to find a suitable wife and start thinking about setting up your practice. You didn't spend all those years and all our money on your studies to sit around doing nothing.'

He had been aware of Anastasia for a while and although his mother introduced him to plenty of girls of marriageable age from prosperous families, his thoughts kept wandering back to the girl who looked as if she had stepped off the pages of a fashion magazine.

'I've met her brother,' Panos told his mother when he tried to explain his interest in Anastasia. 'He's a nice boy, studying to be a teacher, and they live quite close.'

'I know exactly who they are,' *Kyria* Froso replied. 'She's the grocer's daughter!'

'And is that a problem?' Panos replied, well aware that his mother was a snob.

'Not quite our class of people, but they have money. The family own the bakery and the grocery shop.'

'Oh, Mother!' the young man replied, exasperated. 'Why does everything have to come down to money?'

'It helps,' she said, and quickly added, 'So would you like me to go and pay them a visit?'

Anastasia's first impression of Panos was one of pleasant surprise. Here was a young man who she thought was indeed likeable and who appeared to shun convention, despite conforming to the extent of sending his mother to ask about her – although after spending some time talking to him she was willing to overlook that. The fact that Panos was older than she was and had lived for several years in Athens met with her decided approval and she considered it an asset in his favour. She was at last meeting someone who was well read, had travelled abroad, and had experienced a life she had only ever imagined from reading magazines and watching films.

He was fine-looking too: tall, slender, bespectacled, with a good head of brown hair and a preference for casual yet well-cut clothes which gave him an avant-garde air. At first glance she established that his sartorial taste was to her liking; then, after talking to him for a while, she decided that she liked him enough to agree to see him again and get to know him better. In fact, she thought with amusement, something about Panos reminded her of Orhan, but with better taste in clothes.

'I liked him!' Anastasia announced after the young man

left. 'I think we could become good friends.' She looked at her brother and Orhan to gauge their reaction.

'What do you mean, you could become *good friends*?' her mother shrieked.

'The boy didn't come here to ask you to be his new pal, Anastasia!' her father added sternly. 'He came here with a serious proposal of marriage!'

'And you all know how I feel about *that*,' Anastasia replied defiantly, stealing a look at Orhan, who had sat silent throughout the entire visit. 'I liked him, isn't that enough?' She looked around the room at them all. 'I only just met him!'

Panos, on the other hand, was sure Anastasia was the right girl for him. He liked her unconventional spirit. He could see from just the two hours they had spent together at her parents' house that she was an intriguing and exceptional person, unlike the young women his mother had been trying to foist on him, with their dowries and social status and bland and tedious ways. Here was a girl, he thought, who had not only beauty but also individuality and a personality that sparkled. Other girls he had been presented with since his return from Athens had been far too submissive and eager to please. Anastasia reminded him of young women he had met in Athens; she, he thought, had a slight air of defiance, aloofness and self-assurance which he found challenging, making him all the more determined to wait and win her over.

'So, what did you agree?' his mother asked eagerly the minute Panos walked through the door of their house when he returned from the meeting with the Constandinou family. Panos had insisted he must go alone for that initial introduction meeting for the marriage proposal, not with his parents as tradition requested. Sending his mother to make the first approach had been conventional enough and against his modern beliefs. 'So . . . tell me!' *Kyria* Froso insisted impatiently. 'Did you give the word?' The word being the promise that a marriage proposal had been agreed.

'No, Mother,' Panos replied, 'I'll leave that to you in due course, but we will meet next Sunday with Lambros and Orhan and the four of us will go for a drive.'

'What exactly does *that* mean?' his mother persisted. 'What do you mean, go for a drive? What did the parents say?'

'What it means, Mother, is that Anastasia has a mind of her own,' Panos said, exasperated, 'and we shall get to know each other better, unlike most girls around here . . .'

Meetings in cafes with friends as chaperones, with Lambros and sometimes Orhan too, walks and excursions in the countryside, and meals with both their families, soon led the way towards the blossoming of a friendship between Anastasia and Panos.

The young man was the proud owner of a green Ford Anglia automobile which he shared with his father, a rare sight in Nicosia at a time when it was still common to see a horse and cart on the roads. Piling into Panos's small car for trips to the neighbouring countryside, and sometimes even as far as the foothills of the Troodos Mountains, caused great excitement for them all. Anastasia was enjoying this new friendship, and she soon decided that if she was going to marry anyone, Panos wouldn't be a bad choice. She was getting her wish; she was going to live her life with a man she had come to know and like. A man who, like Orhan, was fast becoming a good friend. Panos didn't make her heart race in the way she had heard Victoria describe when Dino was near, or as she had gathered from movies and romantic novels, but then again, she didn't greatly value that. Love wasn't lust as far as she was concerned – not that she knew much about lust and its mysterious ways; that would come later, she thought. *Love*, Anastasia insisted, was a meeting of minds: having fun with someone who respected you and made you laugh. Panos had it all. She *loved* his company, she *loved* his character and *loved* being with him – therefore she *loved him*.

'I told you it was only a matter of time,' Penelope told her sister-in-law. 'The girl has a mind of her own and she was going to do it her way.'

'I'm glad you thought so, because I was prepared for her

to end up as an old maid with that mind of hers,' Maroula sighed.

Everyone in the family, with the exception of poor Orhan of course, was delighted with Anastasia's choice. Even though he understood in his head that he and Anastasia could never be a couple, his heart still clung to a wild fantasy that somehow they could continue living their life together as the '*old married couple*', to borrow her words. *But*, he was obliged to concede to himself, if Anastasia was actually going to marry someone, it might as well be Panos.

'I want your opinion,' she had said to him before she made her final decision. 'Your opinion always counts, and I want you to tell me in all honesty what you think of Panos.'

'He is a Greek, he's a Christian and he is a good man,' was Orhan's reply, which he gave to her in all honesty, even though the lump which rose in his throat made it hard for him to speak the words. 'I think you are making the right choice,' he finally added, and hoped she would never ask his opinion on the matter again.

The one other person with whom Anastasia discussed her decision to accept Panos's marriage proposal was Victoria, who herself had taken the plunge and had given Dino a sign of how she felt. They were now secretly seeing each other.

'Apart from Orhan, I have never liked a man as much as Panos. Well . . . perhaps one or two others,' she told Victoria, laughing, 'but not as much!'

'That is a very good sign and I'm so happy for you, Anastasia *mou*,' Victoria replied. 'I was really worried that you were set against marriage.'

'Only because I didn't want to marry someone I didn't know.'

'I didn't know Dino, but I knew he was for me the minute I saw him!' The girl's eyes sparkled with the memory.

'You were lucky,' Anastasia said. 'It doesn't happen to everyone.'

'It was like, you know what they say, it was like a thunderbolt! I felt the blood rush to my head.'

'Well, I can't say that's what happened to me when I first saw Panos,' Anastasia giggled. 'The blood didn't rush to my head . . . but I did like his suit,' she said again and erupted into laughter. 'But seriously,' she reflected, 'he is a good man and he always makes me laugh.'

'Laughter is good,' Victoria said and picked up some mother-of-pearl buttons for a blouse she was working on. 'Dino makes me laugh too, as well as tremble.'

'To be honest,' Anastasia replied, looking up from her work, 'no one has ever made me tremble. Orhan is the only boy I have ever really cared for . . . I sometimes think I could easily marry him if he wasn't a Turk, we are so well suited, I feel so good when I am with him, but neither he nor Panos has ever made me *tremble . . .*'

'Well, they do say that sometimes you can fall in love after marriage,' Victoria said with a mischievous glint in her eyes. 'Apparently that feeling can come after the wedding! Obviously you are not going to marry Orhan, no matter how well he makes you feel, but you never know, Panos might make you tremble yet!'

The family were all agreed that Anastasia and Panos would make a good match, including Lambros, who approved of his sister's choice for a brother-in-law. Even Panos's parents approved, despite *Kyria* Froso's desire that her one and only son should have chosen a bride from the more aristocratic circles in Nicosia.

Once everything was agreed between the two families, the engagement ceremony was arranged swiftly. Amid much anticipation and jubilation, Hatiche *Hanoum* arrived with Leila a few days before the ceremony, which was held on a Sunday afternoon in late February, just a couple of weeks after Anastasia's twenty-first birthday. Their local priest was summoned for the religious ritual, which was to take place at the Constandinous' house, for the blessing of the couple and the exchange of rings, which would each be placed on the third finger of the other's left hand. The so-called *aravones*, simple bands of gold symbolizing the couple's pledge to each other, would remain there until the wedding ceremony, when the rings would be moved to the third finger of the right hand, thus sealing their union forever. A small group of friends and relatives were gathered for the occasion together with Victoria, who was chosen as the maid of honour and who would then become Anastasia's first *goumera* at the wedding ceremony, while Lambros was chosen by Panos to be his first *goumbaros*. Orhan did his best to hide his sorrow; having his mother and sister there gave him some comfort and he started to consider that once his studies were complete, he should perhaps return to the village. He had hoped to find work in Nicosia but the idea of seeing his love with another man was too painful to contemplate.

Anastasia was in favour of a long engagement and wanted the wedding to take place in the summer of the following year, but her mother and aunt vehemently disagreed.

'Why would you want to wait so long?' Maroula and Penelope asked with surprise. 'What benefit can a long engagement have?'

It was typical of the girl, they both thought, to continue to be difficult. But Anastasia had her reasons.

'I just want to enjoy myself, before I start to have babies,' she replied, knowing well enough that women were usually with child within a few months of their wedding. 'Also,' she added, 'we're still getting to know each other.'

'How much more do you need to know each other?' her aunt demanded.

'You've known Panos for three months – isn't that long enough?' said her mother.

'We shall get to know each other even better now we are engaged,' she continued, facing her mother and aunt and ignoring their questions. Anastasia knew that in the eyes of the world a betrothal meant that a couple were permitted to spend time together without a chaperone. Her wish to postpone the wedding for a while was in order to give her and Panos the opportunity to spend some time alone and be able to sample the fruits of sensuality, of which, despite all her modern ways and ideas, she had no experience. A betrothal was like a trial marriage, but full intercourse should take place only after marriage, thus postponing motherhood for a little longer.

Panos's family house was as substantial as the Constandinous', if not more so, and since Anastasia's house was far too busy to give them any privacy, they started to spend time together there on a regular basis. Although *Kyria* Froso found it painful to hand her precious boy over to another, she knew the only normal and decent thing to do after the engagement was to allow the couple time alone.

Panos was gentle, considerate and loving and found Anastasia irresistible, yet took his time in the way of his lovemaking. Anastasia was open, curious and eager to learn and absorb everything that her fiancé had to give her. Physical contact was pleasurable to her, but even more than that she loved everything else that Panos could offer, aside from his kisses and caresses. The wall-to-wall library of books in his study held works that the young woman had never imagined existed. Poetry, history, geography, novels. Panos would spend hours leafing through art books with her, introducing her to the paintings of Picasso, Matisse or Rembrandt, and together they would pore over maps of countries she'd never even heard of.

'After we're married we can go here . . .' Panos closed his eyes and arbitrarily pointed to an exotic place in the middle of the Pacific Ocean. 'Or here, now this terrible war is over,' he said again, pointing to Paris, Vienna and Rome.

'Athens!' she said with excitement. 'Can you take me to Athens? Show me all the places you know?'

'Of course,' Panos said and kissed her tenderly on the forehead.

Anastasia proved to be an adept student with an insatiable thirst for knowledge. She started to devour any novel that sparked an interest in her; the poems of Konstantinos Cavafy ignited her romantic and erotic curiosity. Above all, what she loved most about Panos was that in him she had found someone who allowed her the freedom to continue with her work and made no objections to her days at *Kyria* Thecla's workshop, even if his mother had plenty to say about it.

'Do you intend to allow your wife to work after you are married?' she asked Panos, making no attempt to hide her contempt.

'If that is her wish, why shouldn't I?' Panos replied.

'Because after you marry she should stay at home and raise your children.'

'But we have *you*, Mother, to help with that!' Panos teased, knowing that his comment would infuriate his mother further and possibly silence her. 'Besides, Maroula and Penelope are there to help with bringing up children, so don't worry yourself too much about it,' he concluded, putting an end to the discussion.

Even though she had become engaged to Panos, Anastasia's plans for the future and the opening of a shop were still very much alive, and while Hatiche and Leila were visiting for the engagement she never ceased to discuss it with them. Mother and daughter had stayed on in Nicosia for several weeks, urged by their friends not to return to the village just yet.

'After I'm married we can seriously think about starting to look for a shop in town,' she told Leila. 'Panos has promised to help us.'

Anastasia had started to take Leila to the workshop with her during her visit and as *Kyria* Thecla was always in need of extra hands she was grateful to have the Turkish girl helping out.

'Why go back to the village on your own?' Maroula had

said to Hatiche when the latter insisted that she needed to return home in order to work. 'Stay a while longer with us, and since Leila is going to work with Anastasia you won't be out of pocket. We all miss you, and look how happy Orhan is to have you here.' Maroula's wish was for her friend to give up the village altogether and come and live with them in Nicosia, but her powers to convince didn't seem to work. Hatiche's home was in the village. She was born and raised there and that's where she and her beloved Hassan had brought up their children, had their workshop, had their life. She belonged in the mountains, not in the city, no matter how much she missed her friend.

'Leila can come and live with you when the time is right, if the girls set up their business,' Hatiche told Maroula and Anastasia, 'but I am happy in the village, and if you can all come and visit me a little more often then I'll be even happier.'

'I have promised I'll come and stay with you before I get married,' Anastasia said, giving Hatiche a hug, 'and you know I always keep my promises!'

'*Inşallah*,' Hatiche replied. 'It won't be long before the summer is here again and I shall be holding you to your promise, *askim mou*.'

11

August is the month when everything stops in Nicosia. The heat is unbearable, the commercial quarters of the city quickly empty of people and become deserted as a ghost town.

Those who can, try to escape to the cool of the mountains and one of those was *Kyria* Thecla, who traditionally closed her workshop for the two hottest months of the year, giving herself and her staff the whole of July and August on leave.

Panos was busy setting up his architectural office and had already been offered a few commissions, so Anastasia reflected that *this* was possibly the last summer she would be able to enjoy being alone with her beloved Hatiche and Leila. By the following summer she would be married and although that didn't exclude visiting the village she knew that from then on her life would be different. Maroula was already dreaming and planning her summer escapes with Anastasia and the numerous grandchildren that she was certain her daughter would soon be providing for her.

'Just imagine how peaceful it would be, you, me, and

the babies up in the village with our friends away from this awful heat.'

'I'm not even married yet, mother,' Anastasia exhaled deeply, 'and you've already got me with half a dozen children in tow!' *This*, she reminded herself, was exactly one of the reasons why she wanted the long engagement.

There had been only one return visit to the village since they had all left and that was for Hassan's funeral, so Anastasia was now excited to be having a prolonged period of time with her beloved friends under happier circumstances. She looked forward to talks with Hatiche *Hanoum* who would always listen and advise her without prejudice and judgement, unlike her own mother these days, plus she would spend time with Leila discussing their plans for the future.

'Why don't you come with me for a few weeks?' she asked Victoria while discussing their summer break some days before they stopped work. 'There's plenty of space in Hatiche *Hanoum*'s house.' Anastasia couldn't think of anything better than to spend a couple of carefree months in the village of her birth, showing her friend around and reliving something of her childhood before adulthood took over her life completely. But Victoria had other expectations and plans for that summer; she hoped that her relationship with Dino might take a different turn and he might be brave enough to talk to his mother about getting engaged.

'Well, let's hope Dino summons up his courage,' Anastasia smiled, 'and when I come back we can look forward to another celebration!'

In her eagerness to get away, Anastasia started preparing for her summer trip weeks in advance. This time she would be going to the village alone: Lambros and Orhan were now too busy with their studies, and her mother and aunt were going to be helping with the bakery and the shop. This suited Anastasia fine, she was ready to have some time away from the entire family. Ever since her engagement to Panos, relationships seemed a little strained. Her mother and aunt were constantly giving her advice, her father and uncle were always busy and irritable, Panos was preoccupied with his new business, and Orhan was withdrawn and moody. Lambros seemed the only one who was himself but even he had his nose buried in books these days. The trip to the village couldn't have come at a better time.

The drive to the mountains in Bambos's bus was the most enjoyable she had experienced so far. Lambros and Orhan had walked Anastasia to the main square to pick up the bus early in the morning before the heat set in to make the walk with all her bags difficult.

'Hello, missy!' Bambos exclaimed, delighted to see Anastasia again as she climbed the stairs into his bus. 'Aren't they coming too?' he asked, pointing with his chin at the boys, surprised to see her travelling alone. 'Why aren't your brothers coming with you?' he carried on, his curiosity getting the better of him. 'How come they send you off on your own?'

'I've escaped at last!' Anastasia replied, laughing, positioning herself in the front seat next to Bambos, so she could have a clear view of the landscape that would soon be unfolding in front of her. She looked out of the window at her brother and Orhan who were still standing on the road waving, and with a beaming smile she blew them both a kiss. At that moment as the bus rumbled away, her heart filled with joy and anticipation. *This*, she told herself as she settled into her seat, sliding under her feet the basket of food her mother and aunt had insisted she must take with her, *this* was going to be the jolliest of journeys and her best summer ever.

No sooner had they left the plains of Mesaoria and started the ascent towards the Troodos Mountains than Anastasia reached for the food basket and began tucking into fresh bread, olives and ripe tomatoes which she shared with Bambos. When she didn't have a mouth full of food she sang along with the other passengers, a common habit among long-distance travellers to pass the time and fend off travel sickness.

On the way they picked up more passengers from small villages and towns, all greeted like long-lost friends. Anastasia, joining in with the rest, revelled in her sense of independence. Here she was, travelling alone for the first time in her life, heading up to her mountains and the forest, to her home, her people, to a place of childhood and innocence. She imagined herself running wild and carefree with Leila as they had done when they were girls, shrieking with delight. They would climb trees and run into ravines, collect flowers from the meadows and fall asleep under bowers of honeysuckle. Come nightfall they would sit in the square to watch the shadow theatre, and walking home afterwards they would marvel at the diamonds that filled the sky. The first time Anastasia had seen the night sky over Nicosia, she fancied that thieves had robbed the heavens.

All through the journey she daydreamed of how the summer would be, smiled with anticipation at the plans she was making in her head and could hardly wait to experience them. But nothing she had imagined while sitting on that bus that day was ever going to match the reality of what happened once she arrived.

12

They reached the village square just before sunset, in that enchanted hour when the sun is still making up its mind whether to depart the sky or linger a little longer. As always, the arrival of the twice-weekly bus and the prospect of visitors never ceased to excite the villagers. Some had arrived to welcome Anastasia, others simply out of curiosity to see what other *xeni* from the city might be arriving. As it happened, that day Anastasia was the only passenger who remained on the bus, all the other travellers having ended their journey on the way. Hatiche and Leila pushed everyone aside and ran to receive their guest with open arms.

'Hoş geldin, Anastasia mou,' Hatiche said in the customary Turkish welcome and wrapped the girl in her arms. 'I'm so happy that you kept your promise.'

'I said I'd come!' she replied, turning to embrace Leila, who was standing next to her mother waiting her turn.

'I'm so glad to see you again,' the girl said, kissing Anastasia on both cheeks.

'And you can't imagine how happy I am to be here—'

Anastasia started to reply but was cut short by an abrupt and deafening outburst from Hatiche *Hanoum*.

'ENVER!' she shouted at the top of her lungs right by Anastasia's ears, in the direction of the square. 'Come!' she screeched again, as loud as she could, looking towards the *kafenion*, the village coffee shop. 'We need you over *here*!'

Anastasia turned her head to see who was the target for Hatiche's shouting and saw a young man sitting at a table under the natural canopy of the vine that provided shade for the tables and chairs. At the sound of Hatiche's voice the young man got up and started to walk towards them as if in slow motion. His head, Anastasia noticed, almost touched the bunches of red grapes hanging down from the vine, causing him to stoop a little. Was it her brain that was moving slowly, dizzy perhaps from the journey, or was the young man indeed moving that way?

'*Quickly!*' Hatiche shouted again and then turned to Anastasia. 'That's Enver,' she told her in a normal voice this time. 'He's Hassan's nephew, he's staying with us for the summer.'

Anastasia watched the young man make his way to them. The light from the setting sun was in his eyes, obstructing his vision; unable to see them, he lifted his hands to shield them from the glare.

'I'm coming, Auntie,' he called out in Turkish which Anastasia understood. Hatiche *Hanoum*'s teaching when she was young had not gone to waste. She watched him as if mesmerized, but he didn't see her until he was much closer and then it was apparently his turn to be struck. He stood looking down at her with penetrating eyes the colour of the sky on a summer's day.

'*Hoş geldin!*' he greeted her politely, his blue gaze scanning her face and then, taking her hand, he gave her the firmest handshake she'd ever felt.

'The bags are up there,' Hatiche's loud voice boomed in their ears again, snapping Enver out of his trance. 'Come on, don't just stand there, help Bambos get them off the roof . . .' Impatience evident in her tone.

'My uncle Ahmet and my cousin Enver just arrived from Turkey. Uncle Ahmet lives in London and my cousin studies in Istanbul,' Leila explained as she led Anastasia by the arm towards the house and away from the square. 'We were expecting them both but not so soon,' she added.

Anastasia was confused. Was she feeling flustered? Was her heart pounding out of happiness to be back home or was it her encounter with those blue eyes that disturbed her so? Either way she was in a state of disarray, her mind a jumble, and flooded with a mixture of irritation and excitement. As they walked, Leila chattered on, asking her a hundred questions which Anastasia not only couldn't answer but couldn't even hear. She was irritated to learn so unexpectedly that she would now be sharing her precious summer with two strangers; but then, even more confusing, she found herself disturbed by the thought that she would soon be seeing the owner of those blue eyes again.

Uncle Ahmet, who was Hassan *Bey*'s younger brother and had emigrated to England at a young age, was sitting under a mandarin tree in the yard, waiting for them with a plate of watermelon and halloumi and a glass of ice-cold lemonade. The minute he saw the girls approaching, he stood up and hurried to greet them. In the distance Anastasia fancied she saw Hassan *Bey* walking towards them, causing her to stop in her tracks. She looked at Leila, and as if reading her mind, the girl squeezed her arm.

'I know . . . they're so alike,' she said and waved at her uncle. 'It brings a lump to my throat to see him every day.'

'Happy to meet you at last, Miss Anastasia,' Ahmet said as he approached them, shaking her hand warmly; the intensity of his handshake, she noticed, could not be compared to the one she had received from his son.

'Where are your mother and Enver?' the uncle asked, looking over the girls' shoulders for a sight of them.

'Mother's gone to pick up some vegetables and Enver's bringing Anastasia's bags,' Leila replied. 'They should be here soon.'

Dinner that first evening around Hatiche's kitchen table, which Anastasia had anticipated with so much excitement, was not how she had envisaged it. Hatiche had made her special dish of stuffed vine leaves and no matter how similar they were to her mother's, something about the way Hatiche *Hanoum* made them was always more to Anastasia's liking. She had imagined the three of them sitting together in that self-same kitchen of her childhood, doors and windows thrown wide open to the night, letting in the sweet-smelling mountain air while they talked of old times. Of days gone by when they shared meals on that very table and when they all lived as one family. She had longed for that return to her past, she yearned for the solidarity of the three women taking a journey together back in time. But instead the two unexpected male visitors who were now sharing their meal had brought conflict and confusion into Anastasia's mind and heart.

Uncle Ahmet was a boisterous, talkative and likeable man with a lavish moustache and sparkling brown eyes. He spoke animatedly throughout dinner but was polite enough to insist on speaking mainly in Greek for Anastasia's benefit, even though she assured him that she was able to follow most of the conversation in Turkish. In contrast to his father, Enver was quiet and reserved. He sat opposite Anastasia, his blue eyes upon her, poised and attentive, listening to everyone but without participating. She wanted to look at him, return his gaze, but found herself unable to do so and instead looked anywhere else but at him.

'Considering you don't live in Cyprus you speak excellent Greek,' she heard herself praise Uncle Ahmet when

Hatiche explained that Enver, unlike his father, spoke only Turkish and English. She made an effort to banish the resentment that kept welling up in her for no good reason towards the male intruders, who she now had to admit were perfectly pleasant.

'Thank you,' the uncle replied, 'but don't forget that I lived here for many years before emigrating; we all had to learn Greek.' He looked at Hatiche who nodded in agreement. 'In London,' he continued, 'Turks *and* Greeks, we are all Cypriots but to the English we are all *bloody foreigners.*' He said the last two words in English and laughed heartily at the description which only Enver understood.

Anastasia couldn't envisage anything about England or London, or anywhere else at that – apart from what she saw in the fashion magazines she loved to look at. Not that long ago even Nicosia was a foreign land to her and the mere mention of those places formed mysterious images in her head, like those she and Panos talked about visiting when they leafed through the world atlas.

'What is it like?' she asked, looking from father to son with genuine curiosity.

'You mean London?' Ahmet replied, leaning forward on his elbows. 'Well, let me see.' He looked across at Enver. 'I'd say it's mainly dark, cold and grey, and,' he reached for his glass of wine and glanced at his son again, 'the sun never shines!'

'Don't exaggerate, Father,' the young man said in Turkish,

a smile starting to play on his lips. 'The sun *does* shine, at least *once* a year!' Hatiche turned to look at Enver with surprise, not knowing what to make of his comment.

'Enver jokes!' her brother-in-law said, erupting into more laughter at the sight of the three wide-eyed incredulous women. 'But it's true,' he went on, 'we don't see much of the sun there, we see more of the rain.'

'I like the rain!' Anastasia said, thinking how she had always loved the change of seasons. 'I look forward to the winter when the rain comes after the summer heat.'

'That's a different matter,' Ahmet replied. 'I don't think you'd like the rain if it was most of the time, and not only in winter.'

'Even in the summer?' the girl asked. 'You mean it rains even in July?'

'Yes, my girl, there is rain even in July!'

The three women sat silently, trying to imagine a place where the sun didn't shine and it rained most of the time. After a pause Enver leaned back in his chair, reached for his glass of wine and looked around the table at everyone.

'Well,' he said cheerfully, 'lucky for me, there's plenty of sunshine where I live now,' and lifted his glass up for a toast, 'and rain and snow, but all at the right seasons!'

'There certainly is plenty of sunshine where you live now, my boy!' Ahmet bellowed and lifted his glass too. 'Let us all drink to the sun!'

*

Enver had apparently been living for several years in Istanbul, studying medicine and returning to what he called his 'cultural roots', his interest in Turkish culture ignited by his mother who was born there. Since her death and Ahmet's retirement, the young man had decided to settle in Istanbul in the hope that his father would join him. But Ahmet was entertaining other possibilities. He had missed his brother's funeral and that weighed heavily on his conscience, so after Hassan's death he started to reflect that he should return to Cyprus to take care of his brother's widow and Leila. His years of living and working in London as a tailor in the Terzi family tradition had provided him with a good income, so now with no family of his own in London he felt it was his duty to take care of his brother's family. There was nothing to keep him in England anymore. His only son was gone and his wife dead and buried; time to come home.

'We can rebuild the shop,' he told Hatiche when he first arrived. 'You and I and Leila can continue where Hassan stopped; maybe the boy might even come back from Nicosia and join us.'

'I wouldn't count on the boy,' Hatiche told him. 'Orhan has other plans and dreams, but there is no reason why you and I can't start something.'

They sat around the table, eating and drinking – Hatiche had gone to town and had also made her most delicious *kleftiko* lamb which had been slow cooking since early morning in the clay oven in the backyard, infused in lemon juice, garlic and the essential ingredient of wild mountain oregano, and no one could get enough of it. During the course of the evening, Anastasia was informed that Ahmet was here to stay while Enver, once the summer holidays were over, would be returning to Turkey to complete his medical degree. To her surprise she wished it was the other way round.

After supper that first evening, the three young people decided to take a stroll in the village to see if there was a performance of the shadow theatre in the square. Anastasia had forgotten how dense and black such moonless nights could be in the mountains and how sweet the air was, a fragrant mixture of honeysuckle and pine hovering in the air. She looked up to the sky and her heart soared with what she saw. She had missed these mountain nights, where the heavens were so densely populated that it would have been impossible to squeeze even one more tiny little star to what was already up there. They made their way up the hill in the darkness and each girl held on tight to Enver's arm as they walked either side of him. He had taken a torch in his pocket for good measure but though the night was as black as carob-honey the young man was loath to use it; he was enjoying the feeling of Anastasia's arm linked through his own and the proximity of her body too much to disturb it by lighting their way.

The shadow theatre was already in mid-performance when they arrived and the mood in the village square was genial. Karagiozis had been getting up to all his usual shenanigans and was reducing the audience into huddles of laughter. Three more chairs were promptly brought out from the *kafenion* for the new arrivals and placed among the crowd.

They sat with the villagers under the Milky Way in the night breeze, surrounded by laughter and giggles, and Anastasia couldn't remember a time she had felt happier than at that moment. Given her earlier irritation she was a little perplexed at her euphoria now, but as she turned her head to glance at Enver she realized that being back in the village wasn't the only reason she felt so glad; the prospect of sharing her summer with him flooded her with added pleasure. She took a deep breath, filling her lungs with the night air, and shifted closer to him.

During supper Anastasia had been reluctant to meet Enver's gaze but now, protected by the darkness, she was able to steal some glances and even let her eyes linger a little longer upon him. She watched him laughing heartily, joining in the fun and enjoying the performance – no matter what language it was performed in, Greek or Turkish, everyone was familiar with the stories of Karagiozis.

Enver was like no one she had ever met before. Panos was a little like Orhan, Orhan was a little like her brother,

her father was very much like her uncle, and *Kyria* Thecla's sons were like each other and not unlike most other young men she came across. In fact, she concluded, all the men and boys she ever knew were like each other. But not Enver. Apart from those azure eyes of his, a colour she had never encountered before, she found herself fixated by the dimples on his cheeks every time he laughed and his golden skin, like ripe wheat. Whenever his bare arm brushed against hers or he turned around to look at her, an unfamiliar shudder went through her spine. Enver was indeed different, totally different from anyone she had ever known, and that difference, she realized, was what captivated her and drew her to him.

Insomnia was not something Anastasia was familiar with nor was she often troubled by unwelcome thoughts when she was in bed. Sleep always came easily to her. Yet that night she had to endure both. She lay awake, her head spinning and troubled, trying to make sense of her confusion. She tossed and turned and sighed and moaned so much that at one point Leila, in the bed next to her, got up and came to see what was wrong.

'I must be tired from the journey and over-excited to be here,' she lied and from then on tried her best to keep her nocturnal fretfulness to herself. At last, with the first rays of the sun creeping through the shutters, she got up and went to sit in the backyard with the chickens. She couldn't work out what was wrong with her. When she thought of the night before and her proximity to Enver while sitting in the square her pulse quickened. The feeling was new, it had an unfamiliar physical effect upon her mingled with something like guilt when Panos came to mind.

Soon afterwards the back door creaked open and out came Enver, rubbing his eyes and looking as tired as she was feeling. At the sight of him Anastasia felt the blood rush to her head and at that moment for the first time she understood what Victoria meant about Dino. She had mocked her friend when Victoria described her flutter of excitement when she was near him, dismissing it as exaggerated romantic fancy, yet there she was now, her heart pounding like a drum, and her face hot and flushed; *this* was a new and disturbing sensation for her. She had never felt *this* in anyone's presence before, and she had certainly never felt it at the sight of Panos.

'*Kalimera*, Anastasia,' he said in Greek. 'You see? I'm not as ignorant as my aunt says I am,' he laughed.

'*Salam*, Enver,' she replied, throwing him a casual Turkish greeting, all the while trying to steady her voice.

'Why up so early?' He looked quizzically at her.

'I like the early morning,' she lied, continuing in Turkish.

'My aunt says she taught you to speak Turkish; is that true?' he asked, impressed by her fluency.

'Yes, she did . . . among other things.'

'You must tell me about them sometime.' He smiled and pulled one of the chairs to the wooden table to sit next to her.

They sat in the garden, chatting quietly and enjoying the thyme-scented early morning breeze as the chickens clucked around their feet, until Anastasia's aunt from their old house next door threw open the kitchen window just as Maroula used to do and called out to them.

'I'm making coffee!' she shouted. 'Come! I have *goulour-akia* just out of the oven.'

The thought of eating anything made Anastasia's stomach lurch; coffee was fine, but food was definitely not. This happened when she felt disturbed or nervous, though very rarely. What on earth was wrong with her, she fretted; it wasn't like her to reject the offer of sesame *goulourakia*, nor was it in her character to wish that her aunt wasn't there. All she wanted was to continue sitting alone and undisturbed with Enver in the yard; she had never felt that level of yearning to be with someone. She enjoyed Panos's company hugely and looked forward to seeing him, she loved being with her brother and Orhan when she needed their advice or wanted someone to listen to her woes. But this was different, this was beyond wanting to satisfy her own vanity with the knowledge that someone, whether it might be Panos or Orhan, adored her or found her inter-esting and fun. This was an altogether visceral emotion making her stomach clench, travelling to her heart to make it pound, and then reaching her brain, causing her head to throb. She was used to thinking things through, using her brain to understand her emotions not be hijacked by them. *This*, whatever it was, was physical and she was gripped by it.

She looked at Enver as he talked animatedly, smiling broadly with those impossibly sweet dimples, giving him a look of boyhood innocence. And then, there were his eyes. What was it about his eyes that disturbed her so? It was as if there was nothing she could hide when they were upon her. In contrast to what she was brought up to believe – that blue eyes are to be feared, for they can put a curse on you if they so wish – Enver's eyes were as pure as a cloudless sky on a summer's day.

When she was little her mother always pinned a little blue glass charm inside her undergarments, the so-called *mati*, to fend off the curse of the evil eye and keep her from harm, and when she was older Maroula insisted that she hang the blue *mati* on a gold chain round her neck along with a gold cross given to her by her grandmother on her baptism. When Anastasia looked into Enver's blue eyes now, she saw no evil; all she saw was love.

13

Did she really see love in Enver's eyes, Anastasia asked herself, or did she only see what she desired? She had no way of knowing. She only knew how he made *her* feel, which was something like love – a strange unfamiliar sensation that disturbed her deeply. She believed she knew about love; after all, she loved Panos, or why else would she have agreed to marry him? Yet when Enver's eyes were upon her they caressed her with such intensity she felt as if her skin was on fire. Neither Panos's eyes, nor his hands, had ever sent such signals to her brain as to leave her breathless. She was no stranger to loving, she had plenty in her heart for the people she knew – in fact it was her chief motivation in life – but *this*, this kidnapping of her thoughts and senses she had never encountered before, and it was thrilling and frightening all at once.

Enver, at the age of twenty-four, had been in love several times with both English and Turkish girls, but none had ever had the effect that this Cypriot beauty had on him. From the very first moment he met her he was captivated.

She drew him to her like a magnet and apart from her obvious good looks he sensed something else, something he had never felt with any other girl who came his way. There was a hint of rebelliousness about her which excited him; she was like a graceful gazelle, with eyes warm and sweet as mountain honey that spoke to him more than words ever could. No sooner had he met her than he wanted to take her in his arms and kiss her lips, which her eyes were inviting him to do. He too had stayed awake that first night after they met in a torment of opposite impulses, scolding himself that he should keep away from the girl. Apart from being a family friend she was a Christian, a Greek. There would be no way she would ever have him, it was unheard of, and besides his aunt had told him the girl was already spoken for and betrothed to be married.

Anastasia and Enver both knew, both recognized and accepted silently and secretly to themselves, that their attraction to each other was mutual and momentous and had been simultaneously consumed by the same disturbing feelings for each other. Romantic love or erotic attraction, whatever this was, did not concern them. All they knew was that what they felt was both real and utterly impossible.

During the days that followed the two young people spent most of their time trying to avoid each other lest anyone pick up on the chemistry between them. Enver feared he couldn't be responsible for his own behaviour if he came near Anastasia, while for her part, she knew that her actions would soon give away her feelings if she stood too close to him. She fretted about it privately and alone, not knowing who to turn to. Her usual modus operandi would have been to seek advice from her beloved Hatiche *Hanoum* or speak to Leila, or to confess to Orhan if she was in Nicosia. But for once she was alone, and what's more she had no desire to share her feelings with anyone. Apart from anything else, what could she say? *I have fallen in love with a man I don't know, who is not my fiancé and who is a Muslim and a Turk?* All three statements would be contradicting every principle she had believed in so far in her young life. Wasn't she the one who had argued with her parents that she could never tolerate a union with a man she didn't know, and that desiring someone purely on first appearances was abhorrent to her? Wasn't she the one who had told Orhan that a union between a Christian and a Muslim was impossible, and wasn't she the one who accepted Panos's love because she had come to know and like him? She was a hypocrite, she rebuked herself; yet what she felt now for the first time in her life was too powerful and too all-consuming to allow for any feelings of remorse.

That summer which she had longed for and looked forward to for many reasons was turning out to be anything but relaxing for Anastasia. Now all she wanted was to spend time on her own to decipher her emotions and put order into her thoughts. But as privacy was not a concept understood too well by the Cypriots her apparent wish to be alone started to trigger reasons for concern, and drawing attention to herself was the last thing she wanted to do.

Lying in her bed at night was the only time and place that Anastasia was able to think in peace. Finally, after sleepless nights, she came to the conclusion that she had no choice but to accept and acknowledge that the feelings she had for Enver were real, and moreover that as she could do nothing about them she had to keep them in her heart as a precious gift from God. This, she also decided, meant that now she *could not*, nor even *want* to, marry Panos as she clearly did not love him. Enver would be her one and only true love, regardless of the fact that she could never belong to him.

After her decision Anastasia felt better, lighter and more at peace. She was less fearful of being in his presence, so she started to spend more time around him and the others. Her decision, and the knowledge that she loved him regardless, comforted her and indicated to her that this must be God's will. He, she told herself, had sent her a love which she couldn't *have* but could *keep* in her heart forever.

No matter how much she had tried to conceal her confusion, both Hatiche and Leila had noticed Anastasia's withdrawal, so when she regained her composure and was her old self again they both breathed a sigh of relief.

'I think she must have been missing her fiancé, it's still early days,' Hatiche told Leila after Anastasia breezed into the kitchen one morning and greeted everyone with her usual smile before joining Enver and his father out in the yard.

'I know, Mother,' Leila replied. 'If I was engaged I wouldn't have left my fiancé for so long.'

'I think you youngsters should arrange to do something nice today to take her mind off it,' Hatiche suggested.

'I've been talking with Anastasia's cousins about taking a hike up to Kato village, where there is a *panigiri* today,' Leila suggested. As was customary every year, the closest village to them whose patron saint was the Prophet Elias was celebrating his name-day with a three-day-long fiesta which attracted people from all around the mountains.

'Good idea, you can show Enver around, and explain to him how the Christians celebrate their religious festivals. I don't suppose he's seen any where he lives,' her mother agreed. 'You can take some food and make a day of it.'

It was almost mid-morning by the time they had all gathered in the backyard for their hike. There were seven of them in total. As well as Enver and the girls, Uncle Ahmet decided to come along with Anastasia's three cousins from next door, two boys and a girl, Hambis, Costas and Agathi, all excited about their day's adventure. They set off carrying baskets of food and water for the journey. They took fresh sesame bread and olive bread, freshly laid hard-boiled eggs, halloumi cheese and Hatiche's *keftedes*, her famed meatballs which she had made for their lunch the day before with plenty left over, giant red tomatoes, and black olives.

'We'll pick ripe grapes from the vines on the way,' Uncle Ahmet said with delight, 'like we used to do when I was half the age you all are now.'

Although the sun was already high in the sky, a mountain breeze prevented them from overheating. The climb through the forest was steep but they all knew their way apart from Enver, who was more than happy to hang back and walk by Anastasia's side.

'You're all regular little mountain goats, aren't you?' he remarked as he clambered behind her over a rocky slope.

'You mean mouflons,' his father teased back.

'And what *is* a mouflon?' Enver asked, looking at Anastasia.

'It's what you call a goat,' she replied laughing, 'only different!'

'They're the wild goats of Cyprus, son,' his father started to explain. 'If you were born and raised here like me you'd know all about them. They roam the forest, but they aren't easy to spot.'

'They're very shy creatures. If you're quiet and don't

disturb them you might get to see one,' Anastasia added as they continued cheerfully on their way towards a clearing by a little stream for their picnic.

They sat on the ground, soft with pine needles and ferns, and dived into the baskets of food, hungry and thirsty from their climb. They ate with gusto before relaxing back in the summer breeze while one of the boys, Hambis, delved into his pocket and pulled out a harmonica. Bringing the mouth organ to his lips he started to play a lilting tune which filled the air, drowning the endless drone of the cicadas.

As the day progressed they lay languidly in the warm sun. Anastasia was leaning against a tree trunk while Enver lay on his side propped on his elbow, gazing at her. Eventually Hambis put down his harmonica and closed his eyes as one by one the company drifted into a doze in the afternoon heat.

'Look at them all,' Enver said and shifted a little closer to Anastasia. 'No stamina. Shall we go for a little walk to find some mouflons?' He reached for her hand. As if hypnotized, she obediently started to get up. He helped her to her feet and holding her by the hand led her into the forest. They followed the stream, which led them into a heavily wooded area.

'Over there!' she called out softly, spotting an animal behind a tree. They both stopped in their tracks. She pointed to some rustling leaves in the distance. 'See it?'

She brought her index finger to her lips to stop him from speaking. 'He's behind that tree . . . see?' But the creature had fled to safety before he managed to glimpse it. Enver didn't care, because at that moment the only thing that the young man had eyes for or cared about was the girl standing next to him whom he desired more than he had desired anything in his life before. Taking a bold step towards her, he pulled her with one arm against him and kissed her lips with such intense urgency that it made her stumble backwards.

'*Seni seviyorum*,' *I love you*, he murmured, releasing his grip a little, his breath burning in her ear, his voice throaty and hardly audible. Bringing his other arm round her waist he pulled her closer yet, in an embrace so tight, so powerful she could hardly breathe, her heart thumping, her head spinning. 'You are my destiny.' He murmured more words she did not understand. His head was bent over her face, his eyes blazing with passion, her heart thumping. Standing on tiptoe she looked up, lifted her arms, wrapped them around his neck and pulled his face to hers with as much force as he had done earlier, offering him her parted lips. They stayed locked in each other's arms for timeless minutes – how long neither of them knew – until they heard voices calling for them from afar.

The rest of their day was spent in blissful confusion and delirium.

*

From then on everything changed for Enver and Anastasia. They both knew that life would never be the same for them again. The knowledge of their shared passion gave them wings and made their hearts soar with courage to face the truth which they knew had existed since the day they met.

Creating opportunities to be alone again wasn't easy. After the day of the picnic the first time that they managed to steal away from everyone was the day that was to change the whole course of their lives and of those close to them too.

With the arrival of Bambos's mobile post office, Enver suggested that Anastasia accompany him for a stroll in the village under the pretext of posting a letter.

'Maybe we can go and look for those mouflons of yours too,' he suggested, darting a glance at her as they drank their early morning coffee together with Ahmet in the backyard. Hatiche and Leila had left early that morning to catch the farmer from the nearby village, who was still delivering fresh produce from his farm.

'Good idea,' his father encouraged. 'I spotted one the other day quite near the village when I went for a walk.'

'You never know . . . I might be lucky second time around,' Enver said and gave Anastasia a dimpled smile that melted her heart.

No sooner had they finished their coffee than they left the house before the two women returned, to avoid having to explain where they were going. They made their way straight into a large orange grove, which in turn led deep into the forest thus bypassing the square: it would most certainly have caused unwanted village gossip if they were seen heading into the woods alone together.

They walked side by side for a long while between the densely planted orange trees laden with not-as-yet ripe fruit. They held tightly on to each other's hands until they reached the start of the woodlands, and only when they felt they were safe and protected by the deep forest did they stop. Enver bent his head to look into Anastasia's eyes and cupping her face kissed them both in turn, then softly kissed her lips. She looked down at her hands and removed the gold band on the third finger of her left hand that tied her to Panos and placed it in her pocket. Then, taking hold of her arms, Enver gently pulled her down onto the soft pine-scented ground and there among the plane trees and pines, to the sounds of birdsong and the mountain breeze rustling through the leaves, they made love for the first time, with no conscious thought or awareness other than of each other and the pleasures of the senses. Anastasia had never imagined that anything could be so all-consuming as this act. Any pain she might have felt from losing her virginity was overshadowed by the joy of his love and the flood of pleasure that engulfed body, mind and heart all at once.

Neither of them felt any remorse. This was indeed their

destiny. Nothing mattered to them anymore, *nothing* at all, not religion, nor culture, nor language nor moral judgement. The only thing of any significance for them now was their love and each other. Nothing would come between them.

14

London, 2008

'Ah, Anastasia, Anastasia,' Lambros sighed, looking at Stella, 'she was born a rebel and lived like one . . .'

The old man reached for his coffee and sat back in his chair. 'She had a great future as a businesswoman, you know. A talented seamstress, which I suppose would have made her what you now call a fashion designer like young Erini. But she didn't do it, she ruined it all.'

'What do you mean, ruined it all, Papa?' Stella looked quizzically at her father.

'She went and fell in love with a Turk, that's what.'

'Papa!' Stella raised her voice and darted a disapproving look at her father. 'How can you say that? Your best friend was a Turk! How was it so wrong?'

'Yes, but you don't understand, Stella *mou*, it just wasn't done then, nobody married outside their religion – it wasn't like it is here and now in Europe. Christians and Muslims couldn't mix their blood together. Right or wrong, that's how it was.'

'Wrong!' Stella swallowed hard to stop herself from saying more. She had no wish to plunge into a debate with her father just then. She wanted him to tell her more about the past. 'Is that why you hardly ever talk about your sister?' Stella asked, encouraging him to go on. 'Is that why I know so little about her?'

'Yes, at the beginning it was that, and there was all the political stuff too that made things difficult, but not for me. For me it was about the rift she caused between us all.'

'What exactly happened, Papa?' Stella asked, curiosity getting the better of her and seizing the opportunity to ask Lambros more, now that she had found him willing to talk. She had wanted to ask her father about this family skeleton for many years, but he had refused to talk about it. Her aunt Anastasia had always been something of a mystery. But perhaps now at last she might be able to piece some of the story together.

'Well, you see,' Lambros continued, 'after my sister decided to do what she did, she broke your *yiayia*'s heart, brought shame to the family and divided everyone in half.'

'What does that mean, Papa, divided everyone in half? I don't understand!'

'You know what I mean, it's a Greek expression; she came between us all. Our family was all against it but the Terzi family seemed to be OK with it as the boy was a Turk and a member of their family; at least I think they all were. I never found out what Orhan thought about it.'

'From what you tell me, Papa, he was very religious; do you think that's what upset him? If the Christians were against it why wouldn't a very pious Muslim be opposed to the match too?'

'Orhan was very close to my sister . . . now when I try and make some sense of it all I wonder if he was sweet on her himself. But you see, Stella *mou*, he would never have admitted such a thing. We grew up together, we were family and he was honourable and, as you say, very religious so her actions must have been as upsetting to him as to all of us.'

'If only you could have seen each other and spoken about it—' Stella started to say but Lambros fervently cut into her sentence.

'Exactly! *That* is why I can't forgive myself, I rushed to judge him too quickly. None of this was his fault, but that's another story.'

'Oh, Papa, it's so sad.' Stella reached for her father's hand. 'It's such a sad story, but she only fell in love, was that really such a crime?'

'You might not think that now, my girl, but remember those were different times,' Lambros replied. 'Falling in love was drama enough then, but that wasn't all, there was everything else too . . .'

15

Cyprus, 1950

Once Anastasia and Enver had decided that nothing in the world would separate them they went to Hatiche. The two lovers told the older woman what had happened and asked for her blessing. She listened with a troubled mind, for she knew this could not end well, no matter how much love the two young people had in their hearts or how much was shared between their two families. She loved Anastasia like her own, and Maroula like a sister, but she knew only too well that her friend would find this unacceptable and see it as a betrayal. Greeks and Turks had lived harmoniously in the village for generations but there was always one factor that set them apart and that was the dividing line that both communities would never compromise on or renounce – their religion. The Constandinous and the Terzis were no exception. Even if the political unease that was on the rise on the island at that time was creating discord between Turks and Greeks, mainly fuelled by the British colonial rule, both families had refused to allow conflict to come between them, much to the disapproval of certain members of their community. However, when it came to their faith, that remained non-negotiable for them all.

'You know me better than my own mother,' Anastasia had said to Hatiche, seeking her approval.

'That may be true, my girl,' a pale and troubled Hatiche told her, 'but your mother is my dearest friend and I know how she will feel about this. You are Christians and we are Muslims – I don't need to remind you again that the two faiths don't mix.'

'You know that I don't care for conventions or what people say and that I always follow my true beliefs. My mother should know that by now and if not, she should be prepared for the consequences.'

'Your family care deeply for their religion and their conventions, as we do ours. We have managed to keep the two separate from our friendship all these years, Anastasia *mou*, we have respected our differences and that is what kept us united as friends for so long. Do you not care for that at all? Are you prepared to stand in front of your parents and defy *them* and your faith?'

'If need be, yes!' Anastasia replied without hesitation.

Hatiche had no answer to that; the girl was obviously set to follow her heart despite the certainty of hurting her family and the young man she had vowed to marry.

'And Panos?' she finally asked. 'Do you not care about him either?'

'Yes . . . I do,' she said a little more hesitantly this time, 'but clearly I can't love him, otherwise how can I love Enver with every inch of my being? It will be a worse betrayal to marry Panos if I do not love him!'

Once again Hatiche had no reply. The girl had made a valid point. But what a terrible mess this was going to be. She felt helpless, unable to decide how to deal with this dilemma, so she did what she always did when she needed help: she turned to the coffee grounds. The next morning, after everyone had breakfasted she swiftly collected Enver's and Anastasia's coffee cups and, turning each upside down in its saucer, put them in a safe place until she was free to read them alone and at her leisure. What Hatiche saw in both cups was so confusing and troubling that for the first time she could not be sure of their meaning. So as soon as she had finished, with a sense of unease she took the cups to the sink, washed them, wiped them, put them away in the cupboard and never spoke to anyone about what she thought she saw. Destiny, she realized, would have to take its course and there was nothing she or anyone else could do to prevent it.

The weeks passed and still nobody in Nicosia was informed of the situation. Panos, in touch with Lambros and the rest of the family, assumed all was fine and was therefore oblivious to everything that was going on in the village. He continued to write to Anastasia but his letters lay unopened on the top of the bedroom dressing table, much to Leila's disapproval at first, although after her initial shock she too started coming round to the idea of Anastasia and Enver's romance.

'I know it's not allowed,' she told her friend, 'but there's a first time for everything, and if you two love each other so much it's only right that you should be together, as I keep telling my mother who is worrying herself sick about it all.'

Poor Hatiche was caught up in an impossible situation. She wanted to send word to Maroula but she also believed that it was Anastasia's responsibility. She repeatedly urged the girl to talk to her family, to no avail. Anastasia and Enver were basking in the warmth of their new-found bliss, apparently indifferent to the havoc they had already set in motion. A mixture of defiance and cowardice prevented Anastasia from returning to Nicosia to confront her family and Panos. She wasn't refusing, she kept telling herself, she would do it in her own way and in her own time, but what eventually forced her hand to confront reality and the wrath of her people came suddenly and very unexpectedly.

It was early September – and two months had passed since she and Enver had made love for the first time in the forest – when Anastasia decided she had no alternative but to speak to Hatiche *Hanoum* again. She found the older woman sitting with her sewing in the backyard in the shade of the mandarin tree, deep in thought, her feelings a confusing combination of pleasure and displeasure. On the one hand Hatiche was worried sick about what Maroula and Andreas would say about this unfortunate situation, fearing that they might put the blame on her, but on the other hand she lacked the heart to condemn the young lovers entirely. She knew all about the joys of early love and remembered well her own feelings when she had first fallen for her Hassan all those years ago; and, if she was honest, she was also secretly delighted that Anastasia had fallen for a Turkish boy. Ever since she had held her in her arms minutes after she was born, Hatiche thought of the girl as her own, and now she would truly belong to them. But then her thoughts would turn again to Maroula and Andreas and her heart would sink. These people loved her, had taken care of her and her family in their hour of need, they trusted her; what she was now thinking, and plotting, amounted to a betrayal. No matter how much she considered the girl as another daughter, she tried to reason with herself, Anastasia was Maroula's daughter. She didn't belong to her, despite all the love she felt for the young woman.

Anastasia crossed the yard to where Hatiche was sitting and stood quietly under the orange tree for a moment, then drawing up a chair she sat down beside her. She looked the older woman in the eyes, took a long deep breath and spoke in a strong steady voice.

'I am three weeks overdue,' she stated with shocking confidence. The words scalded Hatiche like boiling water, causing her to drop her needlework on the floor. She brought her hand to her mouth and gasped.

'Are you sure?'

'I have never missed a period, not even by one day, since I was eleven years old,' Anastasia replied, her eyes shining like stars. 'So yes, I'm sure!' she said. She knew all about being pregnant, she had seen and heard enough women talk about it. Even though it was something she had dreaded and wanted to postpone for as long as possible, not wanting to be plunged into the treachery of motherhood before enjoying life, *this* was different. That was then, and this was now. *Now* she was carrying the fruit of her union with the love of her life and she welcomed it as the best gift she could ever have been granted.

'Your mother *must* be told, Anastasia,' Hatiche replied sternly after regaining her composure, determined that now they all had to face the consequences whatever they might be. 'I have held on to this secret of yours for too long, I cannot do it any longer,' she continued with a stony face. 'I had hoped that giving you time might bring you both to your senses and you would realize that this love of yours could not be. If you had kept quiet no one would have been any wiser, but now? Now it's gone too far and there is no way back.'

'Now I'm counting on your support and understanding!' Anastasia replied. 'You always understood me better than anyone, better than my own mother. I don't have to think too hard to know what she, or any of the family, will say about this . . . but I had hoped that at least *you* would be on my side.'

'It's not about taking sides or understanding, *askim mou*,' Hatiche replied a little more gently. 'I can see you love each other, but this is going to hurt too many people. It is not a *blessed* love; in the eyes of our two families and our faiths, in the eyes of God, your union is wrong . . . a sin.'

'How can love be wrong in God's eyes?' Anastasia persisted. 'God *is* love.'

'You *know* that both of our religions forbid this,' the older woman pressed on, her voice hardening again, 'and what about your child? What religion would that child have? Or will you bring it up to have no religion?' Hatiche *Hanoum* shook her head in despair. 'God is merciful, my girl, but this? I pray that he forgives you.'

'There will be no need for forgiveness,' Anastasia said. 'I will follow Enver to the end of the world to be with him and if that means taking his religion, so that our child is not without, so be it!'

Hatiche looked at the girl in disbelief.

'You mean . . . you mean,' she stammered. 'You mean you are willing to convert, that you are willing to become a Muslim?'

'Yes, Hatiche *Hanoum*, I am willing to do that and more, if it means I can be Enver's wife and bring up our child together. After all, there is only *one* God, isn't there?'

16

London, 2008

'So you see, Stella *mou*,' Lambros said, taking a deep breath as he stood up to stretch his legs, 'my sister did the unthinkable! She married a Turk and converted to Islam and became a Muslim at a time when it was unheard of. It was considered a sacrilege by everyone. She brought great shame to our family.' Lambros started to walk around the table to ease his joints from sitting down too long, all the while continuing to speak. 'It might not seem so radical now, but then? Imagine your grandmother's reaction. She took it very badly and she blamed Hatiche for not stopping her.'

'Did Anastasia go to see everyone and explain?' Stella asked, riveted by this tale of insurrection and defiance, and of the kind of love that has apparently ceased to exist in the twenty-first century. Does anyone love with so much passion and commitment anymore? she asked herself, reflecting on her own life, which although happy and seemingly content had never known such devotion. She too had married young although not as young as her aunt, a fellow student she had met at university, and so far they had a good marriage that she hoped would last as long as her parents'. Yet she also knew that if she hadn't married Steve, she might have married Keith, or even Tom; she had dated them in turn and they were all nice and as good-looking as each other and she was in love with each of them for a while. But she couldn't ever imagine a love so intense, so all-consuming that it would make her forsake her family and change the entire course of her life. That apparently belonged to a different era.

'So, Papa,' Stella persisted, 'did she go and talk to them? What about Panos, how did he take it?'

'Well, my girl, this was the problem,' Lambros replied. 'She didn't go and see anyone, nor did she explain. She just left with her young man and sailed to Istanbul; none of us ever saw her again and she left poor Hatiche to explain and pick up the pieces!'

'*What?*' Stella gasped. 'She went to Istanbul? Why? You've never told me that before, Papa. Why didn't any of you tell us about this?'

'Because, my girl, we never talked about Anastasia after she left, we all avoided the subject of your aunt.' Lambros sat down again, rested his chin in his hands and sighed deeply. 'We behaved as if she had died. A terrible thing to do, and I think about it all the time now. That, and what happened with poor Orhan. What Anastasia did must have hit him hard too . . .' Lambros looked at his daughter, his eyes full of sadness. 'They were always very close, you know, those two . . .'

Stella reached for her father's hand. 'We do such terrible things in our ignorance, Stella *mou*,' he sighed. 'We think we know what's right and wrong but it is all nonsense . . . we don't!'

'Ignorance and prejudice are two very dangerous things,' Stella murmured, and leaned forward to hear more.

'My sister did wrong, I will admit that. She wasn't blameless, but she was young and foolish and maybe if she had handled it differently or had been given better advice it might not have caused all the upset and drama that followed. There was too much blame put on the wrong people, I see that now. But then . . . then, we were all blinded by what happened and we all rushed to judge and condemn.'

17

Cyprus, 1950

Enver was delighted by Anastasia's decision. 'I never imagined or dreamed that you would do this for me, my love,' he said to her after she had spoken to Hatiche. 'I've been tormenting myself knowing that I must leave soon and that you wouldn't want to come with me.'

'You and our baby mean everything to me, and I would do anything for us to be together,' she told him, repeating what she had told Hatiche earlier.

'I only have two more years to go at the university and then we can come back here if you want.' He held both of her hands tightly. 'But I know you will love living in Istanbul.'

'If I'm with you I don't care where I live. Istanbul will suit me very well, I'm sure,' she said and fell into his arms.

As the days progressed and Hatiche could see that Anastasia was still making no effort to contact her family in Nicosia, she decided to take action and sent a note, via Bambos, summoning Orhan. At a loss as to what else she could do, fearful of breaking the news to Maroula herself, she hoped that her educated and wise son might know how to handle this most delicate predicament. She tried seeking advice from Ahmet but it didn't help: his view was that if the young people were in love then it should be no one else's business. Hatiche believed her brother-in-law had been living in England for too long to see the gravity of the situation.

'It has happened before, it's not the first time, Hatiche,' Ahmet said, trying to soothe her misgivings. 'There's a mixed couple in our community in London, he's a Turk and she's a Greek and he's become a Christian. It's not the end of the world!'

'It might not be the end of the world in your London, Ahmet, but mark my words, it is here,' she told him with dread in her heart.

Anastasia and Enver's world was about to begin, but for their two families Hatiche knew it was going to be the beginning of the end. She knew this to be true because there was no denying that if the reverse was happening, if her Leila wanted to marry a Christian, she too would believe that her world was collapsing. These things were not taken lightly in their community.

Lambros wanted to go with Orhan to the village but as the teacher-training exams were upon them and the workload was heavy he couldn't afford to take the time off.

'It's not fair, you get to have a little break and I have to carry on working in this heat,' he moaned, longing to sneak away for a few days too.

'I'm only going for a short time,' the other boy replied. 'So stop complaining. You'll at least be ahead with your revision and I'll have to catch up when I come back.'

'Yes, but you'll return refreshed.'

'I'd rather be staying here, but my mother has never sent for me without an explanation before. It sounds like an emergency.'

They chatted as they walked to the bus terminus together, very much as they had done when they took Anastasia to the bus at the beginning of the summer.

'Maybe you'll bring her back,' Lambros said. 'She's been there long enough, I think. It's time she got back to work too, don't you think?' he added with a smile this time.

'Do you blame her?' Orhan retorted. 'Who wouldn't want to be away from this heat?'

'My point exactly!' Lambros laughed. 'She's had it too good!'

The bus was almost ready to leave by the time the boys arrived at the square and Orhan hurried to climb into it.

'Is it his turn to be left behind now?' Bambos laughed as Orhan looked for a seat in the crowded bus. 'Off to collect the sister, are you?' he added, curious as always.

'Something like that,' the boy replied, choosing a seat by the window.

Like Anastasia a few months earlier, Orhan enjoyed the journey to the mountains, and his concern about what might be worrying his mother was eclipsed by the anticipation and excitement at the prospect of seeing Anastasia again. They had not been separated for this length of time before. Even when they lived under different roofs in the village the proximity of their houses meant that they saw each other every day. These past summer months without her had seemed like an eternity to him.

He couldn't imagine there was any serious problem that had upset his mother. At the most, he thought, she might have found a husband for Leila and wanted his approval. So he settled back and indulged in daydreaming about the reunion with his beloved. Orhan was still very much in love with Anastasia and although her betrothal to Panos had pained him a great deal he was resigned to the fact that since they couldn't be together as man and wife he would continue to love her secretly and enjoy her friendship. Besides, he knew she loved him too, and as she had always let him believe the only factor that kept them apart was their faiths, just being close to her was enough for him.

The girls were in the square waiting to welcome him. His heart skipped a beat when he saw her standing under the canopy of the big plane tree with his sister. They stood in the shade, arms linked, waiting for him to step down from the bus before they ran to embrace him.

'We missed you!' Anastasia and Leila chimed, and threw their arms around him.

She looked different to him. More beautiful, fuller, healthier, eyes shining with excitement. *Mountain air does wonders*, he thought, and returned their hugs and joyful greetings.

'Where is Mother?' he asked, suddenly anxious that she was nowhere to be seen.

'She's at home waiting for us, getting supper ready,' Leila replied.

'Is she well? Anything wrong?' Orhan asked. It wasn't like his mother not to be there to greet him.

'Oh yes, she's fine. Uncle Ahmet and Enver are here too so she's with them,' Leila went on cheerfully as the three started towards the house. As they walked down the hill, Orhan saw his mother sitting under one of the trees talking with his uncle and cousin, who he hadn't seen for years. As a boy he had met Uncle Ahmet when he came to visit the family, but the only time Enver had visited the village with his mother for a summer holiday Orhan was still very young, so he had no memory of this cousin.

'*Hoş geldin*, my son,' Hatiche cried, hastening to take him in her arms and kiss him on both cheeks before turning to the men standing by her side. 'Remember your uncle Ahmet and cousin Enver?' she said and felt a tightening in her throat, recalling the reason why she had summoned him. She knew of Orhan's strong religious and moral beliefs and hoped he would be able to give her some sensible advice. Hatiche had no idea of the devastating effect the news might have on him, nor could she ever have understood the reason why.

She left him to wash and rest for a while, then she made coffee, which they drank all together under the mandarin tree. After a while Hatiche asked Orhan to come with her to the kitchen because she needed to talk to him.

Not a single word left his lips all the while she spoke. When she had finished, Orhan got up, looked at his mother, nodded silently and, to her confusion, left the house. He went out of the back door into the yard and out of the gate, continuing at a normal pace while he was still in full view of the family and then, once he was far enough away, he started to run towards the hills until he was deep in the forest. Then he let out a scream of despair so loud, so heart-wrenching, that it caused the birds in the trees to fly away in alarm. He did not return to the house until he was sure he had regained his composure.

The misery that engulfed him on that first day after he arrived at the village was more than he could bear, yet he had no option but to endure it and be strong. No one must know his pain. He had no solution or advice for his mother. If Anastasia was set on changing her religion and willing to forsake her family along with everything that was sacred to her, including him, then he had nothing much to say.

'She's betrothed to be married, and has given her

promise to another man,' was the only comment he had made to his mother after he returned from the forest in an effort to distract from his own personal turmoil. 'Her actions are unforgivable.' But the words that pounded inside his head were, *If she is willing to change her faith for him, why not for me? Why is his love greater than mine?*

He had held Anastasia in such high esteem, he had put her on a pedestal of virtue and honesty, and her fall pierced his soul. He took her actions as a personal betrayal. Meanwhile the girl, unaware of his feelings, was eager to confide in him and seek his advice, as she always did. She was eager to tell him of the great love she had so unexpectedly found and had been blessed with but his sudden frosty distance towards her, so uncharacteristic, perplexed and confused her. Unsure of what to think, she interpreted his behaviour towards her as a condemnation of her actions. She had expected this reaction from her brother and her parents but not from him. She had hoped that as her best friend he might let her explain, try to understand, even approve of her determination to be independent, join her in solidarity against what she was sure would be her family's reaction; but he remained unapproachable.

As much as Orhan believed that Anastasia had given him a sign of her love for him, he had been grossly mistaken. The girl had only ever loved him as a brother, a dear friend and confidant.

*

That night Orhan joined the company for the evening meal. He sat quietly and solemnly watching Enver bending lovingly towards Anastasia and wishing he was anywhere but there; his humiliation was too much to endure. Only his mother was aware that her son was in some kind of turmoil, yet she was at a loss as to why he would be so upset. This was indeed a difficult and troublesome situation, Hatiche told herself, but since they could do nothing about it they would have to accept it, and she wished that Orhan would be a little more lenient and stop being so disapproving.

The next day, on the pretext that he must return to his studies and unable to endure staying in the same house with the two lovers any longer, Orhan left for Nicosia. He kissed his mother goodbye, avoiding everyone else, and left the house. As Bambos's bus was not due to stop in the village for three more days, he walked the ten miles to the next and bigger village to catch the bus back to town from there.

18

On arriving back in Nicosia, Orhan found the house empty. Maroula and Penelope were at the shop and Lambros at the college. Breathing a great sigh of relief, he took himself to the bedroom, pulled out his old suitcase from under the bed, packed all his books and clothes and then, sitting down at the desk, he started to write a note to Lambros. Anxious to finish it before anyone returned home, he quickly sealed the envelope, propped it up against the desk lamp and with a heavy heart left the house quietly and hurriedly, never to return. He knew it would be impossible for him to live among Anastasia's family any longer, no matter how much he loved them, no matter how much it would break his heart to do this to Lambros. He knew the pain in his heart from the constant reminder of Anastasia's betrayal would be too much to bear. Dedicating himself to God, taking solace in his faith, was the only way forward for him from now on.

He stepped out into the garden, closed the gate behind him, crossed the dusty street and scrambled into the dry moat, dragging his suitcase. Then he climbed the Venetian wall as he had done so many times and entered the garden surrounding the mosque. He found his mentor and adviser there at prayer. Without asking any questions, the old imam invited him to his family home. From that day onwards Orhan's life would be dedicated to the reading and the teaching of the Quran. He would be a scholar, and teacher, not of children as he and Lambros had so ardently been preparing for, but of his religion.

Lambros picked up the envelope on the desk with curiosity and ripped it open with his thumb. He read the note quickly, leaning against the wall. He stood for a few minutes holding the paper, blinking in disbelief. Then slowly he walked to the edge of the bed, sat down and started to read again. He was unable to make any sense of it.

My dear beloved friend,

I am leaving your home which was my home too for all these years. I cannot tell you the reason why. I know you will be upset and I don't blame you, but I want you to know the gratitude I feel towards your family, and my feelings towards you and our friendship cannot be expressed by mere words. As much as I love you all, I have no option but to leave because it's impossible for me to live amongst you any longer. Perhaps someday I will be able to explain but now I must go.

> *God be with you all,*
> *Your friend always*
> *Orhan*

Lambros held the note in his hands in utter disbelief. At first, standing by the desk and reading the words quickly, he thought this must be a joke, a trick to tease him about all his complaints at not being able to go to the village with Orhan. As if paralysed, he continued to read the note over and over again. Suddenly he jumped to his feet, dropping it on the floor, and ran towards the wardrobe which the two boys shared. Frantically he started searching for signs of missing clothes. All of Orhan's possessions were gone. He ran back and peered under his friend's bed to look for his suitcase. Distraught, he collapsed back on the bed and, picking up the note, started to reread the words carefully. This time the blood rose to his head; tears of confusion blurred the young man's eyes. What was the meaning of *this*? How could Orhan, his most beloved and faithful friend, do this? How could he leave like a thief with no explanation as to why? He could make no sense of what he was faced with. Orhan would never have done this without an explanation, not the Orhan he had known all his life, their loyalty to each other was unquestioned. To Lambros this untimely exit, this sudden secret flight, felt like a kind of betrayal of their friendship, their brother-hood. He sat in the room holding the note in his trembling hands until the light started to fade and he heard his mother's voice calling for him.

'You'll ruin your eyes with all this reading,' Maroula called from the kitchen, imagining her son was still studying. She was preparing the evening meal with Penelope and decided that it was about time Lambros took a break.

'Time to eat soon, my son, wash your hands and come,' she called.

He could hear his mother and aunt chatting in the kitchen as he continued to sit motionless in the bedroom; he couldn't bring himself to face either of them, let alone break the news he'd received in Orhan's note. Instinct told him to prolong his silence: not speaking about it was to deny that this had happened, that Orhan had gone. He knew that the moment his family read the note, the collective response, especially from his aunt, would be explosive and he couldn't face the inevitable eruption of anger. He could just hear Penelope spit out her words. *They had opened their home and their hearts to the boy, they had given him refuge and this is the way he repays them? What an ungrateful wretch he was.* Lambros always knew how his aunt felt about his friend and he did not ever want to hear it, much less now, when he had his own feelings to deal with.

His thoughts were a muddle; gradually, as his initial state of shock started to subside and the anger that rose in him seemed to fade, it was replaced with a combination of other emotions: bewilderment, irritation, curiosity, and then, finally, concern. He sat alone for several more minutes in the dimness of his room, trying to compose himself before facing his mother and aunt. One word kept rising to his lips – *why*? Doubts and fears swirled in his head. He knew his friend well and there had to be a reason for his action, there *had* to be something terribly wrong, but *what*? Was his friend in trouble, and if so why did he not turn to him for help? What could possibly have provoked Orhan to commit such a drastic act? They had lived side by side, had shared everything since they were born. The only thing that had ever *separated* them was that one was a Greek and the other a Turk, but that had never *divided* them. So *why*? The question pounded in his head.

'Lambros! Are you coming?' His mother's voice echoed again from downstairs in the hall.

Stunned silence hovered in the kitchen. Maroula stepped backwards and collapsed onto a chair; she picked up the note and started to read it again. She looked up at Lambros, tried to speak but no words emerged, bewilderment etched on her face, her eyes wide as an owl's.

'Well!' Penelope hissed, the first to break the silence. 'I always had my doubts, I did warn Savvas, but—'

'*Doubts?*' Lambros retorted sharply to his aunt, putting a stop to anything else she was about to add. 'There were never any doubts,' he said, quietly this time.

'We need to find out what happened,' Maroula finally

managed to say, her voice barely audible. 'Something's wrong. Very wrong.' Her voice trailed away. 'We must find out what has happened.' She looked up at Lambros again, eyes pleading.

'Did you see him after he came back from the village?' Penelope asked.

'No, he left before I got home. I found the note,' the boy replied, trying to piece together the sequence of events.

'So, he must have left the village early this morning.' Maroula looked at her son again. 'Something's very wrong, Lambros *mou*, something happened there. Why else would he not stay? Even for a day!'

'If something was wrong, wouldn't Anastasia have come back with him or sent word? What could possibly be wrong?' Penelope added. 'No! The boy obviously decided he didn't want to live here anymore.' She looked around the room at the others. 'Ungrateful, that's what I call him!'

Lambros stormed out of the kitchen in a fury, refusing to be drawn into any discussions with his aunt.

'We must go to the village at once,' Maroula said, following Lambros out into the back garden. 'Something is going on . . . this is a bad omen, my son.'

Orhan's abrupt departure from the village had left everyone upset and bewildered and Anastasia interpreted it as a personal condemnation of herself. If Orhan, her faithful and dear friend, found her actions so abhorrent, so unforgivable that he was compelled to flee without so much as a farewell, then God alone knew how the family in Nicosia would react. The prospect of facing them all filled her with horror and fear. She could not confront any of them. She pictured with panic her father's wrath and her mother's accusations of betrayal; she vividly envisaged the hysterical scenes of sorrow and lamentation that would most certainly take place when she announced her decision. And then there was Panos . . . *No!* the voice in her head cried. *No!* She could not see any of them. She felt bad for Panos because he was a good man, but what she felt for him was not love. She felt bad for her family, but despite her attachment and loyalty to them all, her commitment to Enver and her unborn baby went deeper.

Rationally, she knew her actions were contrary to all her earlier beliefs. She was aware that the way she felt now had nothing to do with logic and everything to do with emotions. For the first time in her life, her heart and her body spoke to her louder than her mind. She saw only one course of action open to her now and that was to leave as soon as possible, forsake everything of her old life. She knew it was cowardly, but she didn't care; she had to start anew with the man she loved and sail for Istanbul as soon as possible. If she stayed they would try to stop her and the guilt would be too heavy to bear. She couldn't risk her future for that. From now on, Enver and the baby she was carrying in her belly were her only concerns.

'How can I face your mother, my girl, what will I tell her?' Hatiche pleaded tearfully. 'It will break her heart and I don't want any part of that.'

'Her heart will be broken whether she sees me or not.' Anastasia's reply was unyielding.

'But at least that way you can explain,' Hatiche insisted.

'Explain what? That I am carrying an illegitimate baby in my womb? The baby of a Muslim boy they don't even know? How will that make it better?'

Once again Hatiche could think of nothing more to keep her. Anastasia had made up her mind; her future was no longer in Cyprus and Hatiche was powerless to persuade her otherwise.

The very next day before leaving, Anastasia took her engagement ring, wrapped it in a white lace handkerchief and placed it on a bedside table in Leila's room; then, the two lovers took the bus from the village to Limassol and boarded a ship for Istanbul. By the time Maroula and Lambros arrived, Anastasia and Enver were already gone.

19

Anastasia's sole experience of travel had only ever been on Bambos's bus from the mountains to the plains and back again. The sea was a mythical place for her, a place and an element she had learned about as a child at school and then later from Panos, but she had never feasted her eyes on the blue wonderment that was the open sea. Boarding a ship and finding herself surrounded by its vastness was as if she had sailed into another universe and was floating in the sky between heaven and earth. She stood leaning over the rail, gazing in awe at the horizon, the wind blowing wildly in her hair, the salty spray making her face tingle.

'This is more enchanting than I could ever have imagined,' she told Enver, who held her tightly lest she topple over in her excitement. 'I thought only the sweet mountain air was worth breathing,' she shouted over the noise of the engine, and took in a deep breath to fill her lungs.

That night in their cabin Anastasia and Enver lay in each other's arms on the narrow bunk, imagining their new life together. She felt woozy and slightly nauseous, not only from her pregnancy but with all the excitement and stress of the day, yet happier than she had ever felt.

'You will love my little apartment, *askim*,' he said, stroking her hair, her head in his lap. 'You'll see, it's right in the centre of Istanbul, close to the Blue Mosque and Agia Sophia and a short walk to the palace of Topkapi.'

'Will you take me there?' she said and closed her eyes, trying to imagine.

'Of course, *canim*! I'll take you anywhere you like. So much to see. The Bosphorus is more enchanting than any sea,' he said, and leaning over her face kissed her on the lips.

'Tell me about the Bosphorus,' Anastasia whispered as if she was already dreaming. This was one place she recognized from the maps that she and Panos had pored over just a few months earlier, which now seemed to her like a lifetime ago.

'Well, let me think,' Enver replied. 'The wind that blows on the Bosphorus is sweeter than the wind of any sea or ocean. I shall take you there every day to breathe in the air and keep you and our baby healthy and strong. It has therapeutic qualities; I know that because I'm a doctor,' he added and gave a little laugh.

'Will you take me there in a boat?' Anastasia asked again sleepily and wrapped her arms around him.

'I'll do just that!' he replied, pulling her closer. 'I will take you on a boat and we shall glide on the blue waters that run through the middle of the city. You will see beautiful palaces and mosques, and rich ladies waving from the balconies of their wealthy homes, fishermen with their fishing rods and children sitting by the shore.'

Enver's low voice, like a lullaby, carried Anastasia's mind into a new and unknown place, lulling her into a sleep filled with dreams of a world that was strange to her.

While the ship that carried the two lovers sailed towards Turkey, Maroula and Lambros were travelling in Bambos's bus to the village to discover what had happened. They had no time to notify anyone of their arrival so neither Hatiche nor any of their family were waiting to greet them at the bus. On disembarking, both mother and son sensed a strange atmosphere in the square. It felt unusually quiet, with none of the customary noisy banter that prevailed in and around the *kafenion*, and Lambros was sure that when he greeted some of their fellow villagers they avoided eye contact with him. Neither he nor his mother could have ever guessed the reason why, or what the rest of the village had gradually become privy to.

The return to the village would normally have been full of excitement and happy anticipation at meeting family and friends. Instead, as they walked towards Hatiche's house their hearts were filled with misgivings at what they might encounter. The events of the last forty-eight hours had left them confused and fearful. They walked hurriedly and in silence down the hill, and at the turn of a sharp corner they came face to face with Xenia, Maroula's cousin, approaching them. The woman stopped, gave a cry and dropped the basket she was carrying. She crossed herself three times as if she had seen a ghost and then threw her arms around her cousin.

'Ah, Maroula *mou*! Ah my dear, dear cousin, where have you sprung from?' she said, pale as a sheet, looking from mother to son. 'Come, come, both of you, come with me first,' she said, knowing where they were heading, all unaware of what they were about to learn.

'What in God's name is going on, cousin?' an ashen-faced Maroula asked, gripping Lambros's arm to steady herself as her knees started to tremble. 'What has happened? Speak, woman, tell me what in the name of God the matter is! Who has died?'

'Come with me, cousin, follow me . . .' the other woman replied mysteriously and hurriedly ushered them towards her house. 'No one has died, but first we go home then I will explain.'

Maroula sat stiffly on a chair in the *iliakos* of her own old house, holding Lambros's hand tightly, her fingernails digging into his palm, every muscle in her body tense, listening in disbelief to the story that was unfolding. Her cousin went on to tell them that once the lovers' elopement became common knowledge in the village, her one concern was the shame her niece's action would bring to their whole family, and that she was sick with worry imagining how Maroula and Andreas would take the news. She had been very troubled about this and had been considering taking the bus to Nicosia to speak to the family herself, so she was now greatly relieved that they were both here; it was her duty, she said, to inform them before they heard the tidings from others.

When she eventually stopped talking, Lambros, enraged by what his aunt had told them, leapt to his feet and turned to make for the door, but his mother, still holding on to his hand, pulled him down.

'Sit!' she ordered him. 'Sit down!' she repeated, her voice stern as a headmistress's. 'I need to think,' she murmured.

'What is there to think about?' the young man shouted. 'Don't you see, Mother?'

'I see only one thing,' she replied, and her tears started to well up. 'I see that your sister has forsaken her family and has betrayed her own people.'

'But don't you see? They should have stopped her! They are all to blame!' Lambros's anger was getting the better of him. 'Hatiche *Hanoum* should have known better!'

'Perhaps,' Maroula said and stood up, 'but who has ever been able to stop your sister?'

'And Orhan? What did he do? He just left like a coward,

like a thief in the night instead of telling us. What kind of a friend is he?'

His mother suddenly stood up, cutting Lambros short. 'I have to see her,' she said and started towards the back door. 'I have to speak to her . . . alone.'

She looked her son in the eye. 'You stay here,' she repeated sternly, then before stepping outside she turned to look at her cousin.

'You said . . .' she hesitated a second. 'You said that no one had died, but . . .' Maroula took in a deep breath. 'But you are wrong, dear cousin, you're wrong. I have lost my one and only precious daughter. So you see? She might as well be dead!'

The kitchen door was wide open to let in the air, but the second door, made of mesh to keep out the flies and insects, was closed. Maroula gave it a push and stepped into the cool of the room. Hatiche was sitting alone at the kitchen table, her head in her hands, leaning on her elbows, a Turkish coffee cup in front of her, overturned and resting in its saucer, waiting for the grounds to dry so she could read them. The creaking door made her start and as she turned towards it, her face appeared pale and drawn. Fighting back her tears, Maroula walked in and pulled up a chair across the table from her.

For the first time in their lives the two women did not kiss or embrace, but rather sat in silence looking at each other, unable to find the words that they both needed. In all their years together, in all their long friendship, they had never been short of words. They always had so much to talk about, they always knew how to soothe, comfort and encourage one another. Now they sat facing each other across the table, each mute and mournful, the unrelenting call of the cicadas in the trees out in the yard the only sound filling the room. How many times had they both sat in that very kitchen drinking coffee, chatting and laughing, with that same deafening summer sound in their ears, or the winter wind rushing through the forest outside and the crackling of the logs from the roaring fire in the stove? How many times had they sat there with the children at their feet, preparing a feast for their families or reading the coffee grounds? There had been countless such times when they had sat united at that very kitchen table, incapable of ever imagining the fury and anguish that they now both felt in their hearts.

'I tried to reason with her.' Hatiche, suppressing a sob that rose to her throat, was the first to break the silence.

'You obviously didn't try hard enough,' Maroula replied, her voice wavering.

'You don't know that.'

'If you had, she wouldn't have gone. She always listened to you.'

'I begged her to come and speak to you . . .'

'But did you beg her not to change her religion?'

Maroula looked at her with steely eyes. 'Did you tell her she was committing a sin? Did you stop her? Did you beg her not to leave? You knew how I'd feel.'

'What would you have done if it was the other way round?' Hatiche looked into her friend's eyes. 'What if Leila came to you and said she wanted to become a Christian? Would you have stopped her?' Maroula didn't know how to reply to that. She reflected for a minute, but confusion clouded her mind. She had never entertained such a thought about *any* of them. The concept was unthinkable. Maroula was a deeply religious woman and although she never discussed her beliefs with Hatiche, out of respect, she considered that Christianity was where true faith lay, so perhaps if she was faced with such a dilemma she would probably have encouraged Leila to embrace it. But then again, she thought, she didn't have the same kind of influence on Leila as Hatiche had over Anastasia. Hatiche had the power to prevent this calamity and in Maroula's mind, her friend was guilty because she knew what Anastasia's actions would mean to the family, yet she hadn't stopped her. Her daughter had committed a mortal sin. Now they all had to live with the consequences. As far as Maroula was concerned, Hatiche was to blame for this.

The two women had spent their lives ensuring that their faiths did not interfere with their attachment to one another but now they were both faced with the greatest challenge to their friendship. For the first time they were confronting the inescapable difference in their religious beliefs and the equally unavoidable fact that, for both of them, faith went deeper than either had ever expressed, and apparently even deeper than their long friendship, precious as it was.

They parted that day not as enemies but also not as the ever-faithful friends that they had been since they could both remember. Maroula put the blame on Hatiche for what happened, and Hatiche blamed Maroula for being so unyielding and obdurate in her judgement.

'The girl didn't commit a crime,' she told Ahmet after Maroula and Lambros left the village. 'Why is a Christian more blessed than a Muslim?' she asked, her voice rising defensively. 'Why is their religion more sanctified than ours?'

'Be truthful, sister-in-law,' Ahmet replied. 'Look into your soul and ask yourself how you would feel if one of your children had forsaken their faith? What if your Orhan had converted to Christianity, or your Leila wanted to marry a Greek? Eh? What would you be saying then?'

Hatiche, like Maroula earlier, had no answer for him. She had to accept that the division between them, which the two families and many others had tried so hard to ignore, was greater than the personal ties they shared. Ahmet was right, it was indeed more important than any friendship. Their religion was sacrosanct, and it set them apart no matter how much they professed it did not.

If Anastasia had fallen pregnant before marriage to Panos, or to any other boy from the Greek community, the clandestine pregnancy would have been covered up, as they very often were, by swiftly arranging the marriage for the sinful couple and putting a stop to gossip. Many a baby was born a couple of months earlier than the usual nine and no one took much notice. But Anastasia's actions were unforgivable and had brought shame and sorrow to all her family. No one could hide or ignore what she had done. Now they all had to live with the judgement of their people and the shame she had brought upon them. From that time onwards the family would be stigmatized and disgraced. Anastasia's actions would bring sorrow into her mother's heart and cause her family to stay away from their beloved village.

20

Istanbul, 1950

Anastasia found Istanbul as exotic and exciting as Enver had promised her it would be. His two-room student's apartment was on the top floor of a well-maintained ancient building on a cobbled side street in the district of Sultanahmet, in the heart of the old city. Anastasia fell instantly in love with it, especially the bedroom: a perfect love nest tucked away high up in the attic, its low sloping ceiling a hazard for Enver, who was forever banging his head on the beams, much to her amusement.

'I'll have no brains left if I go on like this,' he would joke.

'It would be much safer if you lay down here in bed with *me*!' She beckoned to him, falling back on the cool cotton sheets as he dressed for the day. The autumn term had now begun, and he often spent most of his day at the university.

She would lie in bed and gaze over the rooftops of Istanbul through French windows which opened onto a little balcony. A spiral staircase from the corridor just outside their front door led to a little roof terrace where she would go every morning to water her pots of basil and geraniums and watch the seagulls circle the sky. She would sit on the terrace and let her eyes wander from the domed roofs that stretched across the city to the Blue Mosque with its soaring minarets and further on to Agia Sophia, the Sea of Marmara and as far as the Bosphorus. Some days she would take the Holy Quran with her in order to learn more about her new religion, sitting in the breeze that blew from the sea. As soon as they arrived, Enver arranged for them to be married, though not before Anastasia had converted to Islam in a short, simple cere-mony. The only condition that was required of her was to pronounce with conviction and understanding the meaning of the Shahada, the testimony of faith, which declares that 'There is no true deity but Allah, and Muhammad is the Prophet of God.' After that, the imam was able to declare them husband and wife, and as Enver had no family in Istanbul, he invited a handful of his fellow medical students to mark the day and celebrate with them in a nearby restaurant. Two of the young men who were married brought along their wives, who were almost the same age as Anastasia. The camaraderie between them, Anastasia observed, was hardly different from the friendships she had enjoyed in Cyprus and she wondered if she would perhaps find a new friend in one or both of the wives. Would they accept her, she wondered, for she was not Turkish and in addition didn't share their affluent middle-class background. Both these young women were married to future doctors and although she was too, their obvious air of education and prosperity intimidated Anastasia.

During their voyage from Cyprus, before they arrived in Istanbul, Anastasia had asked Enver to think of a suitable Turkish name for her, knowing that her own would instantly give her away as a Christian. They were taking a stroll up on deck, watching the dolphins leaping as they raced the waves at the bows of the boat when she asked.

'Alev!' he had told her instantly with no hesitation. 'It's the perfect name for you, I've been thinking about it too. It means *brightness* and *light* and that is what you are, my love,' he said and kissed her full on the lips.

During their first couple of weeks as a married couple and before returning to the university, Enver took it upon himself to show his new bride around the city and help her to find her way around the neighbourhood.

'You'll have many hours on your own when I'm not here, so you must learn to be independent,' he had said, taking her by the hand as they entered the numerous bazaars around the city. 'Here, my love, you will find anything your heart desires, and you can reach any of them easily from our apartment.' In fact, Anastasia discovered, there were plenty of interesting places near their apartment;

as soon as she became confident enough to go out alone on foot or by the tram which Enver had showed her how to use, and before her belly grew too big, she started to explore and venture further than the nearby streets. The ancient city excited her curiosity and now, aside from the Quran, she wanted to read and learn about the history of the place which was to be her new home. As she explored further afield, she discovered that there were many Greeks living in Istanbul who had been there for generations, who owned grocery shops and bakeries as her own father and uncle did in Nicosia, or patisseries and general stores selling all manner of things. It was in one of these stores, which doubled as a bookshop in the European district of Beyoğlu, that she came upon a history book simply entitled *Byzantium*; this was to become her constant companion now that, as Enver had warned her, she was finding herself often alone. She had expected that she might have many hours of solitude, but her sudden change of circumstances when Enver returned to his studies made her feel quite melancholic. To fend off any sadness she often found herself wistfully reminiscing about their heady days of passion in the village, but then she would look down at her belly and her heart would fill with joy; she would soon have her baby to keep her company.

'I have learned in my book,' she told Enver once she started to absorb the city's history, 'that Istanbul used to be Greek.'

'Well, strictly speaking,' he replied, 'it belonged to the Eastern Roman Empire.'

'Yes, but it wasn't always so,' she challenged him, emboldened by her new-found knowledge. 'In ancient times it was Greek; apparently a king called Byzas was the founder and that's why it was called Byzantium.'

'The Emperor Constantine was a *Roman* emperor, not a Greek,' he argued. 'In any case this was all a very long time ago. The Ottomans ruled here for centuries, and this is now modern Turkey, my love.'

'Yes, but the language used to be Greek. Everyone spoke it then,' Anastasia insisted, glad to be able to discuss these matters with him.

'It was a common language in all the empire, not just here,' Enver replied, putting an end to her history lesson while Anastasia made a mental note to check her facts again. She was well aware how much more educated and knowledgeable than herself he was – after all, he was going to graduate as a doctor before long, and she was a mere seamstress with little education apart from what she had learned in her old village primary school, even if she had always been the best pupil in her class. But the more she learned, the more confident she felt in discussing the ancient city's history with him.

During those talks she was surprised to discover that although she had rejected her homeland, she could feel a sense of pride here in the city's historic past. These Greeks, she realized, these inhabitants of Istanbul now, were the descendants of those Byzantines of long ago; in fact, she concluded, so was she, since Cyprus too had been part of the same empire. Book in hand, she enjoyed learning about her new country.

As time went on and her belly grew bigger and the warm autumn gave way to early winter, she began to spend less time exploring and more time reading, although if she felt robust enough her feet would often lead her to Beyoğlu. This district, which was also known by its ancient Greek name of Pera, meaning '*across*' because it was divided from the old city by the Golden Horn and connected by the Galata Bridge, was an area that Anastasia found herself returning to time and time again. She would cross the bridge past all the fishermen casting their lines in the early morning after Enver left for university and she would make her way up the hill to Pera. Galata Bridge was one of the first places Enver had taken Anastasia to visit after they arrived, to show her the Bosphorus and to take the ferry ride that he had promised her.

She was now quite familiar with Pera, and with time she had also come to know some of the proprietors of the Greek shops, especially one particular fabric shop that sold textiles and tapestries, where she was befriended by the shopkeeper's daughter, a girl named Myrto, around the same age as Anastasia. Surrounded by all the familiar rolls of fabrics, textiles and colourful yarns, her dressmaker's passion began to occupy her thoughts again. As her belly grew steadily bigger her old clothes became increasingly tighter, so she set about making herself a new wardrobe with an old Singer sewing machine Enver bought for her. One day, while chatting with Myrto and browsing through the stock on display in the store, she was delighted to discover among the tablecloths several fine examples from her native Cyprus, the famed Lefkara lacework. These exquisite geometric needlepoint designs that were stitched with satin thread on linen were something Anastasia often tried to imitate but without too much success. The craft was particular to the village of Lefkara and was passed down over the generations from mother to daughter. Everyone in Cyprus knew about it, and every girl hoped she would possess at least one item – a tablecloth or a bedspread – as part of her dowry trousseau.

'We have a few merchants who travel from Cyprus to sell their handiwork,' Myrto explained after Anastasia asked how they had come to stock this precious trad-itional lace. 'There's one salesman called Mr Costas,' she continued, 'who comes with a suitcase full of Lefkara linen and embroideries to sell. He's a good friend of the family now and he even stays with us sometimes when he is here. He is like you,' the girl went on, 'he's a Cypriot.'

From that day on, Anastasia began to visit the shop more regularly. The two young women would chat and sometimes drink coffee made by Myrto's mother, who often worked in the shop and who was as skilled at reading the coffee grounds as Hatiche *Hanoum* used to be. It was a pleasant yet bittersweet time for Anastasia, reminding her of the old life that she had left behind. Both Myrto and her mother liked the Cypriot girl, who aroused their curiosity but who would give nothing away about herself and her circumstances. '*If she won't tell us anything, I'm sure to see something in her coffee grounds,*' Myrto's mother would tell her daughter after Anastasia left the shop. But try as she would, she saw nothing that led her to the truth. The truth of course was unthinkable and, if they knew it, would have shocked, dismayed and disgusted them. Anastasia would no longer have been welcomed there. For a Greek Orthodox, conversion to Islam would be to commit the unforgivable sin.

After the fall of Constantinople to the Ottomans, these Byzantine descendants had clung tenaciously to their proud heritage and religion for centuries. Anastasia's arrival coincided with a time of growing antipathy towards the community, but the Greeks were adamant that the city belonged to them as much as to the Turks. As well as the Church of St George, the most holy of all Greek Orthodox churches and the official seat of the spiritual leader of all Eastern Orthodox Christians, the Patriarchate of Constantinople had existed there for centuries, so didn't they have every right to be there too? These were troubled times in the history of their beloved city. Antipathy towards the

Christians had been present for centuries; even though they had been given an option by the Ottomans to be left alone and be accepted by changing their faith, no Greek worthy of respect and decency would ever have consented – perhaps over the centuries some did, but they were the unmentionables to these remaining Christians living in Istanbul now. So Anastasia understood all too well that to reveal her circumstances to her new friends was not an option, and as most of the Turkish women she met through Enver seemed reluctant to embrace her as one of them, her isolation increased, especially during the latter part of her pregnancy.

Winter arrived suddenly in Istanbul and brought Anastasia's freedom to an abrupt end. Gone were her excursions to Pera and her visits to her Greek friends. Her heavy belly and the snow which fell suddenly and unannounced made it impossible for her to venture out into the streets, nor did she feel any inclination to do so. She found the Istanbul winter brutal. She was no stranger to the cold – in Cyprus winters in the mountains were long and sometimes harsh, but they were also bright and crisp, and when the snow stopped falling the sky was clear and blue, beckoning you out into the crisp air. Here in the city, unless she had to go out for provisions, she could hardly bring herself to set foot outside the apartment. She couldn't face mingling with the rushing crowds who pushed past her, wrapped in their heavy overcoats, down the darkened streets, jostling each other at the tram stops and hurrying to the safety of their homes. She felt excluded, shut out and alone.

When she first came to Istanbul Anastasia had promised Leila that she would write regularly, yet she remembered to send a letter only once in a while, if that. The excitement and elation of her new life had at first got in the way of thinking about anyone else. Now, finding herself house-bound and isolated, she had plenty of time to write. *'The cold is bitter here,'* she wrote to Leila and her mother. *'The icy north wind goes right through your bones and the snow is not like white mountain snow. Everything looks grey and I don't see a soul apart from Enver from one day to the next . . .'*

Alarm bells rang in Hatiche's ears. She was worried for the girl and made sure that they both wrote back to her regularly with news of the village.

Childbirth on the first of May 1951 came easy to Anastasia. In contrast to her mother's struggle to bring her into the world, her labour only lasted a matter of two hours before a baby boy was safely delivered by a midwife from Enver's hospital. It took a single glance for Anastasia to fall wholly and utterly in love with her son, whom they named Hassan, after the dear departed Hassan *Bey*. As a second name Anastasia insisted on giving the boy her father's name – Andreas.

'Maşallah,' Enver said when he took the boy in his arms.

'I thank Allah for granting us such a healthy baby and I pray he grows up to be as good a man as my uncle was.'

Hatiche and Leila received news of the birth by way of a letter from Anastasia, who, despite her relief to see the end of the long hard winter, was reluctant and anxious to venture out into the world with her new baby after months of isolation and confinement.

'*I feel so scared to take him outside, I feel he will be harmed,*' she wrote to them. '*The city seems so hostile.*'

It was in response to such a letter from Anastasia, in which loneliness seeped through the lines, that Hatiche with mounting concern wrote back to tell the new mother that she and Leila intended to come to visit her. Her heart ached for the girl, knowing that this was a time when she should have her mother by her side but that she had not been in touch with her family since she left.

Anastasia, longing for company and support, received the letter and news of their visit with great excitement and relief. The reality of living in a strange city away from everyone she had ever known and loved was taking its toll on her. Her love affair with Istanbul was gradually diminishing while her homesickness steadily increased. Enver was absent more than he was present these days, involved with his studies and work, and her only joy and occupation now was her baby boy, looking after their little flat, and the letters she exchanged with her friends in Cyprus.

Once Hatiche had made the decision to visit Anastasia,

she found herself in a dilemma; she felt that Maroula should know about the baby, but the two old friends had not met since the last time they had sat in her kitchen and exchanged harsh words with one another. She was troubled by what her next step should be; she felt strongly that Anastasia should be in touch with her own mother, but if this was not to be, then it was her proxy mother's duty to go and visit mother and baby in Maroula's place. *'It's time we came to see you and meet the baby,* askim mou,' Hatiche wrote. *'Ahmet also wants to come to see his grandson, but he must stay behind and take care of the shop.'* Enver's father, true to his word, had moved back to the village and had revived his brother's tailoring shop; together with Hatiche and his niece they were once again making a living from the family business.

Over the past months Anastasia had begun falling into a kind of melancholia, but now, with the pending arrival of these two much-loved women in her life, she was once again infused with a new sense of energy and purpose. Some days before they arrived she started to spring-clean the apartment and transform the little sitting room into sleeping quarters for Leila and Hatiche.

'I know we shall be cramped for a while, but we'll be fine,' she told Enver who was not in the least concerned, knowing he would be out all day and return home only in the evening. If anything, he looked forward to having meals cooked by his aunt and not having to worry about

Anastasia being left alone all day. He was aware that she had been feeling lonely and isolated but there was very little he could do about it. Besides, that was a woman's role, wasn't it? His own mother had had to stay at home and look after him while his father went out to work; didn't all women do the same? He knew Anastasia was a free spirit – he had liked that about her – but now she was a mother and she had new duties. Now, he told her, she was going to be bringing up their son and if God willed it a few more. His own mother had been in a similar situation when his father took her to England away from her family after they married in Cyprus. At least she could speak plenty of Turkish, he told her, unlike his own mother who possessed not a word of English and was frightened even to take a bus on her own. *She* could find her way around town with no problem.

By the time Hatiche and Leila arrived in Istanbul, baby Hassan was already two months old and the summer was at its breathless height. The three women were beside themselves with joy to be united again, and it took only a glance into the cradle for Hatiche and Leila to fall in love with the baby.

'Oh yes!' the older woman said, looking up at Anastasia with tears in her eyes as she held the boy in her arms. 'I think he too has been here before, just like you, *askim mou!*'

Baby Hassan was a healthy, beautiful boy with big bright eyes the colour of deep amber just like his mother's, and he thrived under the love and nurturing of the three women. The nursing mother, too, seemed to blossom under Hatiche's supervision and cooking; her appetizing food helped Anastasia's milk to flow in abundance and the baby to grow bigger and stronger day by day. As both mother and baby grew more robust, Anastasia's old appetite for life and interest in exploring the city returned and she set about showing her guests the sights of Istanbul, as Enver had done with her on their arrival. However, much as she longed to take them to Pera, she dared not. She could not afford to give herself away, so she kept closer to home. Besides, there was much to see within walking distance from the apartment, and the heat and the new baby were enough to deter them from venturing too far. She had not seen Myrto and her mother for a long time and would have liked to visit them and show off her baby boy, but *that*, she decided, would have to wait until Hatiche and Leila left.

The many bazaars and street merchants dotted around the city that sold goods, from exquisite Turkish, Persian and Egyptian carpets to silver and gold to exotic spices and perfumes, kept them busy for days and they didn't know where to look first and what to buy to take home.

'I have wanted to replace that Turkish carpet in the sitting room and covers for the divans for years,' Hatiche told them as a vendor rolled out a crimson Bakhtiari rug from Iran for them to inspect. 'This is my chance! I could never find such quality in Cyprus!'

Now that the family business was beginning to prosper, Hatiche could once again afford to be generous to herself and her daughter. 'This is where we shall find pieces for your dowry, my girl,' she told Leila as they browsed from shop to shop, bartering with the shopkeepers.

They found the city fascinating, enormous and daunting, all at the same time. There were grand houses and palaces the like of which they had never seen before, as well as shanty towns of incomers from the countryside living in old wooden houses overlooking the Bosphorus. The mosques too were particularly imposing, more than any mosque they had ever entered into in Cyprus.

'How Orhan would love to pray here and be with us,' Leila commented the first time they entered the Blue Mosque and stood beneath its gravity-defying dome. 'Perhaps he'll come and visit you some day,' she said to Anastasia, not knowing what torment that would bring to her brother.

'He has done us all proud,' Hatiche said about her boy when Anastasia asked after him. '*Maşallah!* I am a lucky woman to have such a son,' she continued, full of pride. 'He's training to be an imam now, you know.'

That was the first Anastasia had heard about Orhan's change of direction; she had assumed that he and Lambros were still studying together and would be graduating soon.

'He didn't finish his studies? But why?' Anastasia was

incredulous, knowing how dedicated to teaching he and Lambros had been.

'He decided to leave before graduating to concentrate on his religious studies,' Hatiche explained. 'He can still teach in the Turkish school but mainly he teaches at the mosque.'

The two women stayed in Istanbul for nearly two months, by which time Hassan was older, stronger and thriving, and Anastasia had regained some of her old peace of mind. She had become used to having them around and when at last they had to return home, their absence left a gap in her life.

Their presence had been like a warm loving embrace and although she tried not to think about it, she now had to admit that she missed her mother and father, she missed her brother and she missed Orhan – the best friend she had ever had.

She still loved Enver, she told herself, he was a good provider, handsome and intelligent, and he was the father of her son, but he was not the friend she had hoped for and thought she had fallen in love with. Her friendship with Orhan had informed her ideas of what a husband should be; their relationship had been her model of a perfect union, though without that extra spicy ingredient – that of sexual attraction – which she never felt for Orhan but had felt so overwhelmingly for Enver. Her youthful imagination had conjured up a husband who would be a soulmate, an equal, a companion and a lover, but Enver was no longer that romantic ideal. He continued to be a lover, even if not as ardent after she gave birth, but his status, education and intellect set him above and apart from her and he treated her that way. He was a good husband who provided for his family, but he was not a friend, he was a patriarch, and by no means an equal. She sometimes caught herself thinking with a sinking heart that she had done exactly the opposite of what she had once intended – she had married someone she hardly knew.

Having Hatiche and Leila with her brought back bittersweet memories that made her heart ache and left her eager to learn news of the family and the village. But of course, Hatiche had nothing to give her except news about Orhan. Until her visitors came to Istanbul, Anastasia knew nothing of the catastrophic results her actions had created between the two families, nor did she know about Orhan's sudden departure and estrangement from Lambros, as all connections with her family had been severed. She had assumed everyone's anger and disappointment would have been aimed towards her, never imagining that any blame might have been transferred to others.

'It's complicated, my girl,' Hatiche told her. 'Yes, your mother was heartbroken and angry with you, but she was equally angry with me.'

'But why? It had nothing to do with any of you,' Anastasia replied, perplexed at what she was hearing.

'Think about it, Anastasia *mou* . . . just take a moment to consider, did you really believe there would be no consequences to what you did?' Hatiche looked the girl in the eyes and held her gaze. 'You are your mother's daughter, not mine. What you did, what happened when you stayed with me in the village, was as if I took you away from her.'

'But you didn't take me away, it was all my own choice. I can understand their anger at me, but not at you . . .' Anastasia's voice faded as she tried to make sense of what the older woman was saying.

'You excluded your mother, but you entrusted me, you abandoned your family's religion and you embraced mine. If Leila had done that I would feel the same as Maroula, I don't doubt it.' Hatiche's words fell heavy on Anastasia's shoulders; she hung her head with regret.

'I hope someday Maroula might forgive me, but I don't blame her if she doesn't,' the older woman sighed. 'But my biggest sadness in all of this mess is the rift created between Orhan and Lambros. Perhaps your mother was right, I could have done more to stop you. But those boys? They had nothing to do with it.'

'Why?' Anastasia asked, looking up in surprise and alarm at Hatiche. 'What happened between the boys?'

'Orhan doesn't live with your family anymore. After

your elopement, he left, and he has not been back to see Lambros or the family since.'

'Why?' The word rushed out of her mouth in confusion again. 'Is Lambros angry with Orhan? What possible reason could he have?'

'I don't know, Anastasia *mou*, everyone was angry with each other. I told you, it is a very difficult complicated thing that you did. I believe that Orhan chose to keep away because he couldn't bear the anger of your family, but then again, I don't know. As you know he is a very honourable young man.'

Anastasia looked from Hatiche to Leila, lost for words, and then, letting out a muffled sob, she covered her face with her hands and started to cry. Her tears flooded her eyes and soaked her face, she cried silently and sorrowfully, unable to stop. Hatiche got up and took her in her arms and rocked her like a baby for a long time. Anastasia cried until she had no more tears to shed. She cried for the loss of her mother and her father, she cried for her brother and her beloved Orhan, and for poor Panos who had only ever shown her kindness. She cried for all the pain she had caused everyone, and then she cried for herself and Enver and their fading passion. Then, when the tears stopped, she got up, picked up her baby boy who had just woken and was happily gurgling in his cot, kissed him tenderly on his downy head and put him to her breast. She looked down at his tiny hand wrapped around her fingers as he fed, and she vowed that she would bring him up knowing about those people that she had so thoughtlessly hurt in her haste for love.

21

London, 2008

'After my sister eloped, the whole family went into a kind of mourning,' Lambros told Stella, following her into the kitchen where she went to fix them both a little food. It was Saturday late afternoon, and she had come for her customary weekly visit, only that day Spiros was joining them.

'Glad your brother is coming,' Lambros had said. 'It seems that lately it's always just you and me.'

'Oh, you know Spiros, Dad, he's forever busy, but he always asks after you and wants to know what we've talked about,' Stella said in her brother's defence. 'I think he just doesn't know how to organize himself. He'll be here soon.'

They had been talking for a long while out in the garden and the afternoon was starting to fade into early evening.

'Did you find out where Orhan went?' Stella asked, laying out some bread, cheese, tomatoes and olives on a platter to take into the garden.

'No, he just disappeared,' Lambros said, filling the jug with water to take outside. 'He dropped out of college and vanished into thin air.'

'Did you try and look for him?'

'No, I didn't, and that is what I mean about people and our stupid pride. I took it upon myself to decide that Orhan was a coward and that it was his duty to come and explain to me what happened, not mine to ask him. Ask me now if I regret it and I'll tell you.'

'And do you, Papa? Regret it?' Stella turned to look at her father.

'Yes, without a doubt, I regret it every single day. Then, I thought it was a matter of honour. It was as if my sister had been kidnapped and Orhan was responsible – my stupidity.'

Stella walked out into the sunshine, Lambros still following behind, and laid the tray of food on the garden table.

'After I graduated from the teachers' training college I was lucky to get a job teaching in a village school,' he continued, as Stella started to serve him some food. 'It was a strange turbulent time then. The British were in Cyprus, they'd been running the island for decades and people were fed up. It was the 1950s and the rebellion started looming around the time I got my first job.' Lambros's eyes took on a faraway look as his memories returned in a rush. 'Everyone wanted the British out, some more, some less, but on the whole people had had enough of their colonial rule, and of course the English didn't like that, so they retaliated by starting to turn Turks against Greeks and vice versa, a way of control. You know what they say, the divide and rule tactics . . .' Stella nodded and stretched across to put some food on her father's plate.

'Eat, Papa,' she said, seeing how he was reliving his past and deeply involved with his story. 'You've been talking a lot, you must be hungry.'

She knew about the struggle for independence from the British – her parents had told her about it many times – but what concerned her now were the friendships that had suffered as a result.

'I'm never as hungry as I used to be, Stella *mou*,' he mused, popping an olive into his mouth. 'Since your mother died I don't have the same appetite, she was such a good cook.'

'I know, Papa, we all miss her cooking but it must be hard living on your own after all these years.'

'Living alone is not a problem, I'm fine with that,' he said, pouring himself a glass of water from the jug. 'What's hard is that I miss her, and the older I get the more I miss the past, the people, I mean, but then again most of them have gone now.'

'Do you think Orhan is gone too?' Stella asked, reaching for his hand. 'Did you ever find out what happened, why he left so abruptly? From what you say about him it was out of character.'

'I believe it was because he couldn't face the family's anger. About, you know, what my sister did . . . He probably felt responsible, somehow.'

'Because of the religion, you mean?'

'Perhaps, yes, he was so devout himself, perhaps he thought we'd all blame him. I don't know.' Lambros closed his eyes, took a deep breath and leaned back on his chair.

'Do you think it's worth trying to find him? Bury the past, try to find out what happened?' Stella said, leaning her elbows on the table towards her dad. 'You never know, he might be thinking the same about you.'

'I don't know, my girl. It was all such a long time ago, so much has happened, we are different people now, and there was quite a lot of bad blood between Turks and Greeks in the years that followed, especially after I left Cyprus.'

'I don't know, Papa,' Stella replied. 'I don't think people change that much, real love and friendship don't die, or at least I like to think so.'

'The trouble is, my girl, during those years of the struggle for freedom from the British, it affected many Greek families who were friendly with Turks. When I was growing up, even though there was already some hostility between the two communities, your grandparents never let it get in the way of their friendship. They ignored any bad feelings that might have been brewing, their friendship with the Terzi family was too strong for that. But after

Anastasia did what she did, then it was impossible. I do think your grandmother would have wanted to make peace with Hatiche *Hanoum* but what with the political situation and Anastasia abandoning the family, it wasn't possible for her, and then it was too late. People talked and pointed fingers, even my aunt Penelope wasn't very sympathetic . . . it was hard for your grandmother.'

'Did you go back to the village again after what happened?' Stella asked.

'No, and I missed it so much. Your grandmother gave our old house to her cousin who was looking after it. We were doing well in Nicosia, we didn't have any need for money, but my aunt in the village was struggling.'

'And Hatiche *Hanoum* and Leila – none of you ever saw them again?' Stella asked, deeply saddened by this tale of lost love and friendship.

22

Cyprus, 1950

After staying briefly with his imam's family, and before finding permanent lodgings, Orhan took a room in Büyük Han, an ancient inn which a few years earlier had been used by the British administration as a prison and had now become a refuge for poor families who had nowhere else to live. The Han was situated within the old Venetian walls, close to the sixteenth-century Gothic cathedral of Saint Sophia which had been converted into a mosque; Orhan would spend most of his day there, returning to the Han only to sleep. The Constandinou family house, though barely two or three miles away, might as well have been the other side of the island; people would rarely cross the town and venture outside the walls without a good reason. Private cars were still a novelty, owned only by the wealthy and the English, so foot or bicycle was the preferred transport. Orhan had even less reason to leave his neighbourhood for fear of coming across Lambros or any of the other members of the family.

Gradually, guided and helped by his mentor, the young man started to settle into his new life; he moved into permanent lodgings close to a smaller mosque where he began to preach. Yet he was still plagued by feelings of guilt and heartache. Anastasia was continually on his mind and he was torn by conflicting emotions. Eventually, with time and prayer, he found it in himself to forgive her and harbour only loving feelings towards her. His spirits would soar whenever her face came to mind until, as the years passed, try as he would to picture her eyes, her smile, her hair, it became harder to recall her features, but he refused to let them fade. His commitment to her memory remained.

Lambros's graduation came as a relief from the sadness and grief that had descended on the family in Nicosia. The young man's academic success lifted their spirits for a while, turning the focus onto him instead of lingering on the calamity and shame Anastasia had brought to them all, but it didn't last long. When Lambros was appointed to a teaching post in a village school on the other side of the island some hundred miles away from Nicosia, Maroula was plunged into gloom once again; now, both of her children were gone. Not only did she miss them more than she could say, her estrangement from Hatiche weighed on her and added to her sorrow. Fond as she was of Penelope, her sister-in-law had never been a substitute for her Turkish friend, and Maroula often found her mind travelling to happier times in the past when they had all lived as one family. When separation was unimaginable and the promise of love and friendship was as real as life itself.

In such a short time she had suffered a double loss; she had lost her daughter *and* her 'sister' – and when Maroula was in that particular frame of mind she imagined herself back in the village making peace with her old friend. She could do nothing about losing Anastasia, she told herself. Her girl had chosen a new life and left without looking back. Perhaps one day she would regret her actions and return; until then they had to live with the loss and hope. But Hatiche was still in the village and she too must surely be lamenting the loss of their friendship. Though she was often troubled by these thoughts, Maroula never shared them with anyone nor took action, as she knew the views of the household, especially of Penelope, who had been the first to lay the blame and her anger on the Turkish family.

'They corrupted her,' she had said. 'Her friendship with Orhan was not appropriate. I always said as much, but no one would listen. That boy turned her head with his preaching.' Although Maroula harboured some silent misgivings about Penelope's theory, her daughter's actions were indisputable and her sister-in-law's words cast doubt in her mind, causing her to alternate between condemning her daughter and blaming the Turkish family.

Lambros's anger was more stubborn than his mother's;

he concluded that Orhan's behaviour proved his guilt, and therefore there was no room for reconciliation or forgiveness. Andreas was the only member of the family who would sometimes quietly express to Maroula in private his regret about the rift between the two families. He did not share his sister-in-law's views about Orhan. The boy was indeed extremely pious with his five times a day *salat*, his dietary rules and observation of the festivals, but he had never preached his religious beliefs to others.

'I think we have to put the blame on our daughter,' he would tell Maroula. 'It's no one else's fault, no matter how much we wish it was,' he would add, wishing he was wrong and that some outside force had pushed her into her actions. And of course, whether or not Andreas realized it, an outside force beyond the girl's control had indeed pushed her to act as she did; it was the force of Eros, which strikes unexpectedly and indiscriminately without taking account of race, family or creed.

'We were never able to control our daughter,' he would tell his wife and shake his head with exasperation.

'That's true,' Maroula replied with a heavy heart. 'The only person she ever listened to was Hatiche, and she should have stopped her. But then again, no one could stop that girl once she made up her mind.'

Lambros's appointment to the village school was arranged relatively soon after graduation and the move came as a welcome diversion from the oppressive mood that hovered over the family home. While in Nicosia he had brooded over the prevailing events and often worked himself into a state of anger towards both his sister and Orhan, but now he was able to escape from the family's unhappiness. As well as the great distance between the village and Nicosia, he would be among people who knew nothing about him or his family, so no judgement could be passed.

On arriving at the village, he soon discovered that as the schoolteacher his reputation preceded him; he was regarded with great respect and reverence, second only to the village priest, not just by the pupils but by the whole community.

The village was newly established, a cluster of some twenty-five or thirty houses which had been built by the British administration to accommodate a group of rural families, mainly shepherds, who had been living a primitive life in mud-brick dwellings scattered all over the surrounding hills, fending for their livestock. When their flocks of sheep and goats had been feeding on land due for cultivation and had started to damage and deplete the terrain, the authorities had to take action. Situated on the side of the mountain against a backdrop of hills, the new village had magnificent panoramic views of the sea, and was complete with a little square, a schoolhouse, *kafenion*, and a small chapel. Any objections or suspicions that the families might have harboured at their relocation were immediately dispersed once they were presented with their new homes. Lambros's arrival was received with delight and he was welcomed with open arms. Most of the villagers couldn't read or write and were grateful that their children would have the chance of an education within easy reach. Previously, any child wanting to attend school had to travel to nearby villages and many didn't bother.

As in most small villages around the island, the schoolhouse consisted simply of one large room that accommodated the entire six academic years. School commenced from the age of six and continued to the age of twelve. The classes were separated into six rows of desks, each representing one year of pupils. Very rarely was there more than one row for any one year: the attendance of children in a small village was never very high.

Although Lambros was spared the burden of large numbers of pupils in his charge, dealing with the different levels of teaching according to ability and age was challenging and kept him fully involved in his work. Nor did his duties as teacher stop at the classroom door. The young man soon discovered that he was expected to act as mentor and adviser, family therapist and parental figure to the children as well as to the adults, who were trying to adjust to life in their new community. Although he was a young man, his experiences in the modern world surpassed any knowledge that these rural people had, though while living among them Lambros was soon to discover the many virtues that their primitive existence had given them. Their acceptance and tolerance of each other, which stood in sharp contrast to the townspeople he had been living with, impressed him greatly.

These people, like the community he had grown up with in the mountains, were mixed, with both Turks and Greeks living together in even greater harmony than in his own village, and to his great surprise he also found out that there were even a couple of cases of intermarriage. He made this discovery on his first day at the school while taking the morning register. First on the list of children's names was a six-year-old girl named Azra, who Lambros mistakenly thought must be mispronouncing the name Anna because of her young age and the lack of her two front teeth. Then to his further surprise he found there was also an older pupil called Ali.

'My father is Turkish,' the boy said in Greek Cypriot dialect when Lambros asked about his name.

'Do you speak Turkish too?' Lambros enquired, curious about this mixed heritage.

'A little,' the boy replied, 'but we all speak mainly Greek.'

The six-year-old girl, Lambros found out later, had a Turkish mother and Greek father, and to his further amazement he discovered that this was not uncommon or frowned upon. Lambros gave this phenomenon a great deal of thought. Given his family's feelings and own experience on the subject, he tried to work out why this community had such tolerant views compared to the rest of the island. He finally concluded that the primitive and basic way the villagers had lived up until now had contributed in bringing them even closer to one another.

Mixed marriages, he was soon to find out, were not the only aspect of behaviour that was apparently tolerated in this community. Fidelity, as it was viewed by the traditional God-fearing communities he was familiar with, didn't seem to apply here either. A few months into his stay in the village Lambros was relaxing with a coffee in the *kafenion* when he noticed one of the villagers, a man named Pavlis, sitting at a table holding his head in his hands, with a glass of *zivania* in front of him and apparently lamenting something. Two men sitting on either side of him appeared to be consoling him.

'Maybe it's time to let her go,' Lambros heard one of the men say.

'You suffered enough, my friend,' the other man added, firing Lambros's curiosity further. Since both men spoke quite loudly he concluded this was not a particularly private matter, so ignoring his newspaper he paid attention to the conversation.

'How many times is she going to do this to you?' the first man said again and reached for the bottle on the table to fill up their glasses. 'She's not worth it, my friend,' he added and swallowed his drink in one gulp.

'Show her the door,' the second man agreed. 'You don't want a woman who's going to keep doing this to you.'

'Says who?' Pavlis suddenly piped up, glaring at his friend through bloodshot eyes, evidently from crying. 'I do want her, damn it!' he burst out and thumped his fist on the table.

'Do you?' both men said in unison.

'Yes, I do!' Pavlis repeated. 'Everyone else wants her, but she's married to me! Why should I let her go?' He reached for his glass, drained it and slammed it hard on the table. 'Besides,' he said, his voice loud enough for all in the *kafenion* to hear, 'I love the devil woman!'

Lambros could hardly believe his ears. Never in his life had he imagined hearing such a public declaration of infidelity without pride or shame, or such a conversation between three men about a woman, and not just any woman, but a wife.

While Lambros sat eavesdropping in the *kafenion* he prepared himself in case he might be asked to intervene in this domestic situation, as people had asked for his help in the past. However, in this case no one approached him and the wife, as expected, returned to her husband after a day or two and all was fine once again.

What had transpired, Lambros found out later, was that Pavlis's wife was a hot-blooded sensual wench who despite being married to poor old Pavlis would also look for her sexual gratification elsewhere once in a while.

This time she had apparently fallen for a younger man and the lovers had run away to the forest. Although Pavlis was unhappy about her behaviour he hoped she would return after a few days, as she always had.

'She has the hot blood in her veins,' he would explain when she lapsed and ran off with a man who took her fancy. 'Nothing you can do about hot blood.' Although Pavlis's wife's behaviour was exceptional, people apparently tolerated it, putting it down to her nature and accepting that it was for herself and her husband to sort out. Pavlis's wife did indeed love him and never deserted him permanently for another man, but what intrigued Lambros most about this story was that it apparently didn't reflect on Pavlis's manhood or stigmatize him; if anything, people treated him with compassion.

With time, Lambros realized that he couldn't judge the people he was living with by his own moral standards or his ethics. These people he had been employed to teach and help had lived for generations in what townspeople would consider to be feral conditions. They had their own rules and moral codes which often failed to conform to anything Lambros had known or understood until then, and if truth be told he decided their way of life was more honest.

When he first arrived at the village he was glad to be among strangers, in a context where there was no fear of being judged; now he had also begun to consider his situation from a different perspective. Judging by what this community tolerated and accepted, were Anastasia's actions so abominable? After all, her overriding motivation had been love. He started to look at the predicament from all sides and then his thoughts turned to Orhan; but try as he would, he could not see why his friend had acted the way he did. His behaviour, Lambros concluded, was inexplicable. The only way to find out what had made this upstanding young man, who Lambros had thought he knew so well, behave so uncharacteristically could be by meeting and talking to him. His experience in the village brought him ever closer to this conclusion and he made up his mind that once he returned to Nicosia he would try to find his friend. His time and work in the village was now coming to an end; he was satisfied he had done all he could for the community, and it was now time to think of himself, to move on.

The letter from London which found its way to the village and eventually into Lambros's hands was to turn the young man's plans for the future upside down and permanently transform his life. The sender was the president of the newly formed Orthodox church of Agios Andreas in the English capital and its contents were as unexpected as snowfall on a summer's day. Lambros held the envelope with great curiosity, examining its foreign stamp and trying to fathom who could have sent it, before he at last tore it open and started to read.

*We now have quite a large number of Greek Cypriots
living in London, mainly in the north of the city, whose
children need to learn the language of their motherland,
otherwise they will grow up speaking only English. For
this reason we must establish a school and we believe you
are a suitable person to help us undertake this valuable
mission for our community.*

Lambros stood open-mouthed, trying to grasp what he
was reading. Apparently, the Greek Orthodox community
in London had decided to set up a school affiliated to the
Greek church, and to his amazement he had been put
forward as the most fitting person to head the initiative.
Reading on, he discovered that the man who had recom-
mended him so highly for the job was his uncle Nicos
Christou, a first cousin of Maroula's, who had convinced
the church committee that his young nephew would be the
ideal candidate to head the school project.

A successful restaurateur who had immigrated to
London after the war, Nicos Christou was a generous
benefactor to the church and had originated the idea for a
school. His large donations and respect from the community had secured him the ear of the archbishop and church
committee, so his suggestion that his teacher-nephew from
Cyprus should fill the appointment to the school was met
with approval. He promised to undertake all of the young
man's expenses and lodgings and his contribution to the

church would be unpaid. As a wealthy man, Nicos Christou would take care of his nephew financially. He had been running his popular Greek restaurant in the predominantly Cypriot area of Camden Town in north London for years and had recently concluded that as he wasn't getting any younger it was time to bring in someone else to help him.

'I've done my share of hard work, and so have you. In a few years we can take a back seat,' he told his wife, a good-natured woman who had helped to build their business and whose biggest regret was her failure to bear her beloved Nico any children. 'Keep it in the family,' he added, reflecting that his dear cousin's son who had a good education would be the perfect choice to help with the restaurant and start the school. 'The boy is a teacher and I hear he is very clever. How different can it be, running a school or a restaurant? It's all a matter of brains, isn't it, and here he can do both! When the time comes he can take over.'

23

London, 2008

The next time Stella paid her father a visit was on a Sunday morning. A week had passed since she was last there. This time she found him sitting indoors: the summer rain was good for Lambros's garden, he told her when she walked in, but not for him.

'If I was in Cyprus now we'd be walking on the beach, my girl,' he announced when he saw her.

'I've been thinking, Papa,' Stella said, propping her umbrella against the big pot of scented geraniums by the front door, 'maybe we should all go next month. If the weather carries on like this, staying in London for the summer is pointless.'

Lambros ushered Stella into the sitting room, where he had been busy studying the *Radio Times*.

'What else can I do with this weather but watch television?' he shrugged, pointing at the magazine and pulling a face.

'Come on, let's make a coffee and sit down; moaning

about the weather isn't going to do any good, is it?'

'You're right,' he agreed, giving a little chuckle. 'Come and tell me more about this plan of yours about escaping to Cyprus.'

Soon father and daughter were settled on the sofa. Stella kicked off her shoes and stretched her legs, making herself comfortable in the hope of more family history from Lambros. He had been so expansive during her last visits that she was eager for more.

'So, how have you been, Papa?' She wanted to prompt him without making it too obvious.

He hesitated. 'I've been thinking a lot about our conversation, what we talked about last time we met,' he said. 'It got me thinking about the old days.'

'Me too,' she said hopefully. 'Want to talk about it?'

'I was remembering about when I first came to England. You know, before I met your mother.'

Stella put down her cup, folded her arms and leaned back on a cushion, ready to hear more. This part of her father's life she was more familiar with; her mother had often talked about the days of the restaurant, the years of his teaching. Stella was hungry to hear about the old days before they came to London, her mysterious aunt Anastasia, Orhan, and the circle of friends and family who were at last becoming familiar to her.

'You know, Stella, when my uncle Nicos sent for me I was troubled . . . it wasn't an easy decision to make. On the one hand it was the opportunity of a lifetime. On the other, I had enjoyed running the village school more than I could say. But I also knew that if I stayed I would be destined to move from village to village and eventually the novelty would fade and I'd be fed up with it.'

'But going to England was a huge move, Papa. You were going to emigrate, how did the family take that?'

'Your *yiayia* was distraught, but I kept telling her it wasn't that different from living in the village all that way across the other side of the island. The year and a half I was posted there I didn't go home, not once. But she still cried and wailed, convinced that once I'd gone to England she would die and never see me again.'

'Not so surprising, though, is it?' Stella replied. 'I guess she thought that she was now losing both of her children.'

'You're not wrong there, my girl,' Lambros replied, leaning back on the sofa and closing his eyes. 'She was right, my poor old mum. I only made it back to Cyprus once after I left and that was when she was ill and dying and I rushed back to see her.' Lambros took a deep breath and looked at his daughter visibly saddened by the memory. 'As if it wasn't enough for her to be separated from her children, the knowledge that she also had a grandchild that she had never laid eyes on really tore her apart. She died totally heartbroken.'

Stella couldn't imagine not seeing her own children for more than a week. On the occasions when they had gone on holiday without her she had missed them terribly, although they kept in touch with her via their mobiles. These days, unlike the past, Stella thought, the idea that you would leave your family and country never to return was inconceivable, yet then, it happened all the time, breaking many mothers' hearts and her poor grandmother was one of them.

'When I went back to Nicosia to prepare for England,' Lambros continued to reminisce, 'I went looking for Orhan. I decided I wanted to see him before I left. But I didn't find him. I just didn't have enough time, you see, I had to leave quite quickly, but I should have looked harder. Once I arrived in London I realized how small Nicosia was and that it shouldn't have been so hard to find him . . . but I never did.'

'How about trying to find him now?' Stella said, reaching for her father's hand. 'He might still be there; better late than – you know – never, as they say. We can try together, what do you think?'

24

Istanbul

After Hatiche and Leila left to return to Cyprus, Anastasia wrapped herself again in a dark cloak of depression which she did her best to shrug off for the sake of her baby.

Before the winter gloom and cold set in she forced herself to venture to Pera, to visit Myrto and her mother and show off her boy.

'This is Andreas,' she said, handing him to the older woman, who reached for the child the minute she entered the shop. 'I called him after his grandfather, my father,' she explained, her voice trembling slightly.

'He is adorable, *Maşallah*,' the woman cooed, cradling him in her arms. '*Phtou, phtou*' – she made the customary spitting sound to fend off the evil eye – 'may God and the *Panayia*, our holy mother, protect him always.'

'What a little beauty,' Myrto added, waiting for her turn to hold him. She looked at Anastasia: 'He has your eyes, my friend, such a beautiful colour, but the rest of him? I can't tell . . . does he take after his papa?'

'It's too early to tell,' she replied quickly, avoiding the question.

Despite her constant anxiety that her identity would be discovered, Anastasia continued to visit her friends in Pera while the weather permitted. Although she found solace and comfort in their company she felt tension too; as much as she loved being among these Greeks, she was also content in her new life with her baby. She acknowledged that her love for Enver was now different from the heady passion she had felt when they first fell in love, but she still cared for him, and he had given her the most precious gift of all; he had given her their beloved boy and for that she would be eternally grateful to him. Despite her regrets for what she had done to her family she accepted that it had been all her own doing. Nobody had forced her into this life. She only wished she didn't have to be so secretive, splitting herself between the two cultures, but that too was her own doing and that too she had to learn to manage on her own.

As time went by and her reluctance to entirely relinquish her Greek identity became clear to her, she realized that in order to stay loyal to her origins, she must abide by two religions in secret and accept that she had no option but to learn to live a kind of double life. With her Greek friends in Pera she was a Christian; with Enver and his kind she was a converted Muslim. She managed well enough, but as her boy grew so did her anxiety; her dilemma was what to do about him. It was not something she could discuss freely with her husband; as far as he was concerned his son was a Muslim and that was the end of it. But Anastasia begged that her son must at least learn to speak her language.

'I need to be able to speak to my son in Greek. I want him to know something of where I came from,' she explained.

Enver understood; after all, he was a man who had been raised in England by a mother who spoke no other language than Turkish, and she too had brought him up to be familiar with their heritage.

'You'll talk behind my back,' he mock-complained. 'How would I know what you're saying?' But he was an educated man and, Anglo-Turk that he was, he couldn't object seriously to her wish. Anastasia discussed none of her other concerns with him; her religious inclinations had to be kept to herself.

'It's time we moved from this little pigeonhole of an apartment,' Enver announced one day, soon after the boy had started to walk. 'I can afford it and we should live according to my status,' he added proudly. He was far too busy with work to look for a suitable property, he informed Anastasia, and so the task would fall on her shoulders. This turned out to be the perfect distraction and diversion from her melancholia: as time passed, her depression gradually lifted and she threw herself into setting up a new home and bringing up her son. Their new place was not far from their old apartment, still central and fashionable, but instead of living in two small rooms with a roof terrace she now had a leafy garden hidden behind an entire house with rooms enough to accommodate a large family.

Anastasia's inability to fall pregnant again caused her no end of heartache, and for Enver it caused no end of disappointment. She felt she was made for motherhood. Never had she felt happier or more complete than when she was with her child. Enver felt he should be the head of a big family and longed to have at least three sons, even if his friends kept pointing out there were never any guarantees.

'Look at me,' one of them said, a fellow doctor, 'I have four daughters and still waiting for a son, at least you *have* a son!'

'Yes, I know,' Enver replied, 'but as my old mother used to say, one child is like *no* child.'

'From what I understand, aren't you an only child yourself?' the friend asked.

'Yes, and that's the reason why my mother lived in fear of losing me, you see. If you have only one child, if something happens to that *one*, then you have *no* child!'

'It's a strange theory,' the other doctor replied. 'I say be thankful and praise Allah for what you *do* have.'

Anastasia knew that her husband was disappointed in

her for not being able to give him any more sons, or any more children at all – but who in those days would have even entertained the idea that it could be Enver's fault? She longed to be with child again and often found herself wondering how it was possible that she conceived the very first time she made love with Enver, yet, now try as she would, she was as barren as the desert. She tended to conclude that her passion for him was the reason for her earlier fertility and that perhaps now that Eros had departed, something in her had perished too. Another thought that preoccupied Anastasia was that if Enver was Orhan, he would be grateful for what God had granted him and not wish for more. In fact, she often caught herself considering what Orhan would say or do when she deemed that Enver was being unreasonable. She longed for her old friend's wisdom and advice, she yearned for his friendship and unconditional love. Once in a while she would write him a letter which she sent to Leila, asking her to pass it on.

He too wrote back to her through his sister, but his letters were always short and courteous, not representative of the Orhan that Anastasia had known and loved. She explained this to herself as due to his position as the pious, respectable imam that he now was, little knowing the real reason – that his heart still ached for her and he dared express no more in case he should reveal too much. She missed him greatly with the sisterly affection she had always harboured for him, wishing with all her might that Orhan was still in her life, watching her boy grow and passing on his wisdom. Since this was out of the question, then she would see to it that her son grew up knowing about her beloved friend who had been such an influence during her own young life.

Hassan Andreas was growing up to be healthy and strong and very much his mother's pride and joy, answering to both names, depending on who was addressing him. With the Greeks he was very much Andreas; with the Turks, Hassan.

However, while Anastasia was content with running her home and bringing up her child, the sorrow of abandoning her family and her faith was never far from her thoughts. At times the sadness flooded her being so completely that she thought she would drown if she didn't shake it off. Then she would take herself off to Pera to the Greek Orthodox church and light a candle and afterwards make her way to the shop to visit Myrto and her mother. There she could breathe again and recover her equilibrium before returning to her Turkish life. She resigned herself to the fact that she was condemned to a life of confusion and conflict.

While her son was small she would take him along to Pera. The boy spoke Greek as well as she did, she made sure of that. If any mistakes were made, they were put down to their Cypriot dialect, and he loved the fuss the

Greek women made of him. But as he grew older and more independent and spent his days at school, Anastasia would most often make these visits alone. There were many times when she felt the urge to confess, to tell Myrto and her mother about the secret she was carrying, about her inner conflict, but shame and fear prevented her. She was certain that she would be rejected, denounced; if her own parents had forsaken her, why would these strangers understand and forgive her? No, she could not afford to lower her guard. Their friendship was precious to her as it was all she had from her old life; she could not lose it.

25

Cyprus

Maroula never recovered from the loss of both of her children. All she had ever wanted was to see her daughter married to a good man and to help her to bring up her babies. For her son, all she had ever hoped and prayed for was that he would become the scholar he was destined to be and make them all proud. Instead they had both vanished to the dreaded *xenitia*, the distant foreign lands that would swallow them up for ever on alien soil.

'I will come back and visit you often, Mother,' Lambros tried to console her. 'Please don't cry.' But she sobbed and wailed, clutching on to his sleeve while they all waited at the port in front of the ship which was to take him away on his long journey to England.

As it turned out, Maroula wasn't wrong. Once Lambros arrived in London and settled into his new life and his work, the journey back home was delayed year after year and the one and only time he saw his mother again was to be the last.

*

The note was delivered to Maroula by Bambos himself. Leila had begged the old bus driver to take it to the Constandinou family by hand and of course, realizing the gravity of their circumstances, he was more than willing to oblige.

'It's addressed to you,' he told Maroula, handing her the envelope, 'but I think it's meant for all of you.'

She held it with trembling hands and after Bambos left she went straight to the kitchen. She felt a great need to sit down before she tore the envelope open and started to read.

'Please come quickly, please let's bury everything that separates us before we have to bury her . . .'

The note was short, just a few brief hurried words, but it said more than Maroula could bear to read. In no time she had packed a bag and hurried to the shop to inform Andreas that she was leaving for the village. She hadn't made the journey home for years and the tightness she felt in her throat while sitting on the bus made it hard for her to breathe.

Hatiche had been unwell with heart problems for the best part of two years, Leila told her when she arrived, and during the last few months her health had become noticeably worse, but as always, her mother refused to accept she had anything seriously wrong with her and put the back pains and fatigue she suffered down to her workload. The tailoring business was thriving, and she and Ahmet, with additional help from Leila, laboured all hours of the day and night to meet the demands of their customers. Hatiche's regret that she had so far been unable to find a suitable match for her daughter plagued her and she blamed it on herself for not providing her with a good enough dowry; now that their business was thriving, she was determined to work doubly hard to attract a husband for her girl.

'I knew you would come if I asked you to,' Leila said, tears rolling down her cheeks as she ran to meet Maroula when she saw her coming down the hill towards the house.

'How could I not?' the older woman replied, taking the girl in her arms.

'I used to beg her to let me help more at the shop,' Leila said as they made their way to the house, 'but she told me I was better off taking care of cooking and the housework, but what good did that do?' A little sob rose to her throat, cutting her sentence short. 'My uncle Ahmet was at her side when she had the stroke,' she continued, finding her voice again.

'How is she now?' Maroula asked, fearing the worst, as they entered the kitchen through the back door.

'You'll see . . . come,' Leila said, holding back her tears, and led the way towards the bedroom. 'She doesn't open her eyes or recognize any of us, not even Orhan, who came straight away. He spends most of his time by her side.'

Leila wiped her eyes with her handkerchief and pointed to the bedroom. 'She's alone now, my brother is at the mosque, praying for her.'

Maroula walked towards the bed where her beloved old friend lay motionless, her mane of hair, once so enviable for its mahogany lustre and richness, deprived now of its colour and framing her face like a pale halo. She looked as if in a deep peaceful sleep.

'How long has she been like this?' Maroula turned to Leila in a whisper.

'Since it happened. It's a week now, the doctor says she's in a coma . . .'

Maroula sat down next to the bed and reached for her friend's hand.

'I'm here, *askim mou*,' she said, softly speaking in Turkish and crossing herself. 'See, I've learned the words as you always wanted me to.' She brushed a lock of hair away from Hatiche's forehead and, leaning towards her, gently kissed it. 'But it's time to wake up now, *do you hear me*?' she said, more forcefully this time, as if her voice could snap her awake like the Sleeping Beauty.

She stroked her face tenderly with the back of her hand and went on talking. 'You have to wake up now, Hatiche *mou*, and then we will let all that has happened between us go with the wind.'

She touched the sleeping woman's shoulder, giving it a gentle shake, willing her to move. 'It's all water under the

273

bridge now, it wasn't your fault that Anastasia did what she did, I was wrong to blame you. I know that now. You couldn't have stopped her. It's all water that has run from the river into the big wide sea . . .' Maroula's voice faltered. She wiped her eyes with the back of her hand and continued, her words trickling out softly.

'You have always been my best friend, Hatiche *mou*,' she said, as if she was now a girl talking to her friend after they had had a little squabble. It was as if she had turned the clock back to their youth. She sat by Hatiche's side, holding her hand for timeless minutes or hours, speaking tender loving words; she couldn't tear herself away. Leila and Orhan came and went, bringing her coffee and water and slices of orange. Maroula refused to leave the bedside. 'We need to get some colour, some henna on that hair of yours,' she suddenly heard herself say and gave a little chuckle, remembering their youth and the days of Ayşe *Hanoum* and her beauty recipes, 'not to mention your legs. You must be as hairy as a monkey by now! I have a good mind to go and make some *halaoua*, and not just for your legs, look at the state of your face.' She gave another chuckle. 'You're growing a moustache as healthy as Ahmet's!'

While she spoke, Maroula fancied she felt the faintest squeeze of her hand. She dare not move in case she broke the spell. With her eyes fixed on Hatiche's face, she continued. 'What do you think your mother would say, eh?' This time the squeeze, which she was convinced she felt, was stronger than before, and holding her breath Maroula tightened her grip. Scanning Hatiche's face, she was certain that she saw a ghost of a smile on her lips.

'Oh! Mother of God!' she breathed as tears filled her eyes. 'I think she heard me.' And without looking away, she called for Leila to join them.

Whether or not Hatiche regained consciousness for a few short minutes to respond to Maroula's words, no one ever knew for certain, except for Maroula herself, who maintained that her friend had indeed been aware of her presence and that in communicating with her by squeezing her hand she had also forgiven her.

Hatiche died peacefully a few days later with her beloved childhood friend and her two children by her side. She was laid to rest straight into the earth with no coffin, wrapped as tradition required in seven metres of unbleached calico cotton and placed on her side, facing Mecca, in a grave beside her beloved Hassan. The funeral procession was attended by all the villagers, Christians and Muslims wishing to pay their respects by walking the mile-long distance from the mosque to the Turkish cemetery. In death, their differences faded away; Greek and Turk would always unite to mourn each other's dead.

Maroula stayed until after the funeral, which Orhan performed for his mother. Before leaving she took both children in her arms and kissed them tenderly.

'What has separated us until now should not matter any longer,' she said and reached for Orhan's hand. She looked deep into the young man's eyes but said nothing, deciding that she would leave it up to him to speak if he wished. Then she got on Bambos's bus and returned to Nicosia, promising Leila that she would come and visit her again. Meeting both of Hatiche's children, who Maroula had considered almost as her own until the family feud, gave her both joy and pain. She had lost her own daughter and was separated from her son but these two children that she had loved so fondly all through their early life were still here. For the first time in years, as she sat on the bus during the long journey back to Nicosia, she allowed herself to start remembering and revisiting all that had happened to divide the two families. How could she have allowed the dispute to fester, she asked herself, to be estranged from her best friend, her soulmate, her 'sister' who now had gone forever.

'I have always thought of you as a second mother,' Leila had told Maroula while they sat vigil by Hatiche's bedside.

'I know, Leila *mou*,' Maroula sighed. 'We were all one family.' The pain of regret pinched her heart.

'Anastasia was my best friend and I loved Lambros as much as my own brother,' Leila continued. 'We should never have allowed what happened to come between us.'

The mere mention of her daughter's name filled Maroula's heart with more regret.

'At the time I thought that Anastasia's actions were

unforgivable,' she replied, shaking her head, 'but now it's myself I cannot forgive.' As they sat hour after hour by Hatiche's side Leila spoke of their visit to Istanbul; she spoke of the beautiful grandson Maroula had so far away and of the life her daughter was now living.

'I know she misses you and I think Anastasia feels the same as you do. Perhaps it's time you both forgave each other.' Leila reached for the older woman's hand. 'It's never too late.'

Leila's words echoed in Maroula's ears all the way back to Nicosia. She had lost her most beloved friend by arriving too late to make amends. She must not make the same mistake again; she must go to find Anastasia.

As Bambos drove his bus away from the familiar landscape of the mountains and across the plain towards the city, Maroula made up her mind. She had to make the journey of reconciliation. She needed to make peace with her daughter; she longed to take her in her arms once again and there was no time to lose. Her only concern was how to break the news to the rest of the family.

She was less concerned about Andreas's reaction, knowing well enough that her husband was as torn as she was by the loss of their daughter. But she also knew that Penelope would have much to say about it.

'How can the girl be forgiven after what she did, turning her back on her family and religion?' she would often say, never allowing Maroula to forget the shame she had brought upon them. As far as her sister-in-law and the rest of the world were concerned, Anastasia had sinned and her actions were indefensible. Maroula knew that her daughter had done wrong; she too would pray at the little altar that her mother had given her when she got married, and ask the Holy Mother of God to forgive her daughter. But Penelope was not the girl's mother and she did not feel the maternal love Maroula had deep in her soul for her child.

The loss of her only daughter and the regret she felt was the cross Maroula had carried with her since the day Anastasia left without a word. Since the death of her old friend, she had made up her mind that she must act soon, before it was too late.

As Maroula had rightly predicted, the only person to raise vehement objections to her decision was Penelope.

'She chose the Turk over you! Over all of us,' she said, her lips tightly pursed. 'You gave her everything, and how does she repay her family? By betraying us and forsaking everything that is sacred.'

'Yes, Penelope, but she is my flesh and blood and I have spent long enough with this burden of blame; I must rid myself of it now because I cannot live with it any longer.'

'How do you know she wants to see you?' the other woman retorted. 'She left and never looked back.'

'That is a risk I am willing to take. She is a mother herself now and she might understand a mother's sorrow at the loss of her child.'

So Maroula wrote to Lambros, informing him of her decision and letting him know that it was time for her, if not her son, to forgive his sister. She sent a note to Leila, asking her to accompany her to Constantinople and to warn Anastasia of their arrival. Then she started to make arrangements for the long journey.

But much as Maroula wished to rid herself of her burden of grievance and be reconciled with her daughter, it was not to be.

The letter from Leila informing Anastasia of their arrival came too late and it lay unopened for days.

Early one hot and humid Istanbul July morning, after a heavy rainfall the day before, Anastasia woke at dawn and went out into her garden to greet the day and tend her plants. No matter how many years since she had arrived in Istanbul, she never became used to these summer downpours which brought annoyance to the people and traffic to a standstill, and caused chaos with leaking roofs, muddy potholes and slippery streets; nonetheless Anastasia welcomed it. Where she came from, it was drought that they feared, especially in Nicosia where July rain would have been a godsend. She loved the way her plants revived after rain and early morning was her favourite time to trim the spent flowers and patrol the pots and flowerbeds to see what needed to be done.

She made her coffee – she liked it strong and sweet –

and took it out into the garden to savour it alone before her son and husband rose from their sleep. She breathed in the cool morning air and gathered herself for her task ahead. The rusty nail on a plank of wood was hidden behind a tumbling rose and the scratch on her arm seemed so minor that she did not even bother to interrupt her gardening to wash the blood away.

By the time Hassan came home from school she was showing signs of a cold.

'These summer colds are the worst,' she said to him as he dropped his satchel on a chair and ran to see what ailed her.

'You never take care of yourself, that's your problem,' he scolded her. 'The rain was heavy yesterday. Maybe you caught a chill after you went shopping in the rain.'

'Maybe,' she said, smiling at her over-protective son. He saw a shiver go through her body. 'I'll be fine by morning.'

'Papa can give you something to help with it when he comes home,' he replied and made his way to the kitchen to get her a glass of water.

'Don't fuss, I'll be fine,' Anastasia replied, 'now go and do your homework.'

By the time Enver arrived home, Anastasia was running quite a high temperature; she prepared and served dinner for the three of them but had no appetite herself. The next morning her condition worsened, although she was still adamant that it was nothing but a cold, consenting at least to staying in bed. In the afternoon, when Hassan returned from school, he found his mother in a terrible state and at a loss as to what to do he telephoned his father at the hospital, who immediately sent an ambulance. The symptoms of sepsis were accelerating.

In hospital, Hassan sat at his mother's bedside for two days, talking to her and willing her to get better. She held on to her beloved boy's hand and tried to respond to him.

'I love you more than life itself,' she whispered at one point, her voice barely audible. 'I do regret some things in my life but having you, my boy, made up for everything . . .'

She struggled to breathe. 'I want you to do one thing for me, my son.' She turned to look into his eyes, her own pleading. 'When you are older I want you to promise me that you will go to Cyprus and find Orhan and tell him how much I loved him.'

The boy nodded, fat tears starting to roll down his cheeks, unable to believe that he had watched his mother transformed from a healthy and well woman one day to a dying one the next.

26

London, 2008

One day, while shopping in her favourite Cypriot bakery for some pastries to take to Lambros, Stella had asked the Greek Cypriot owner, Loula, if she might know anyone who could help her to trace her father's old friend.

'They were best friends when they were young back in Cyprus,' Stella explained, 'and he talks about him a lot these days. I would so much like to bring them together, but I don't know where to start.'

'Let me ask my husband's uncle,' Loula offered. 'His father lives in Nicosia. He's been there since '74, he might know something or someone, you never know. It's such a small place and these old people always seem to know one another.'

Stella knew that Loula, who was about the same age as herself, was married to a Turk – they often spoke about her family when Stella shopped there – and she mused on the irony of their conversation. Here she was, talking to a Greek woman married to a Turk as if it was entirely normal and unexceptional. Apparently families didn't break up or lifelong friendships perish because of a mixed marriage anymore.

The man who Stella went to meet was sitting in a coffee shop in the predominantly Turkish neighbourhood of Green Lanes in north London. She had been told that he had information about Orhan from the old days. He was sitting alone at a small table, a cup of Turkish coffee in front of him, smoking a cigarette. *Surely smoking is forbidden indoors* was her first thought, but on glancing around the cafe she realized that apparently this particular law went unrecognized in these premises.

Stella crossed the restaurant to his table. 'Good afternoon. Mr Ali Shafak?' she greeted the man, holding out her hand to shake his.

'*Ne!*' *yes*, the man replied in Greek, gesturing with his chin to the chair opposite him.

Stella pulled out the chair and joined him. 'Coffee or tea?' he asked, still in Greek.

'*Euharisto,*' *thank you*, Stella replied, following suit. 'Turkish coffee please, *sketo*, no sugar.'

'So, you are from Cyprus,' the man continued, raising his hand to attract the attention of the young man behind the counter.

'Yes . . . well, my parents are. I was born here in London, but I do consider myself a Cypriot,' she explained.

'I come from the Larnaka area,' he informed her, this time in heavily accented English, 'and not a day goes by I don't miss my village, even if I have been living here for nearly forty years now.'

'What made you leave?' she asked as the waiter arrived with her coffee and water.

'The war . . . after '74 everything changed. We all had to move, leave our homes, leave our friends. We moved to Nicosia first, then I came to London. Here is like old days in Cyprus. Greek and Turk live together again like before . . .' He let out a sigh and reached for his glass of water. 'In the old days, we were all Cypriots, not like now, torn apart . . . your parents perhaps tell you this, no?' He looked at Stella and then gestured to the waiter to bring him another coffee. 'In those days we always left our doors unlocked, no one came in, we would leave our tomatoes in the yard and our donkeys in the field.' He took a deep breath and exhaled slowly. 'My father had a donkey and some goats and always he left them outside, nobody touched each other's property. We respected one another. Now . . . after the war, all different.' Ali Shafak sat back in his chair and looked at Stella again. 'That's why I left, came here. Maybe here is what's left of old Cyprus, Turk and Greek live like old days. The way I see it we are all Cypriots.'

The segregation of the Turks and Greeks to the north and south of Nicosia respectively, which Ali bitterly lamented, had taken place in 1963 following political unease between the two communities, inflamed by the British regime whose colonial rule had come to an end three years earlier after a bitter struggle with the Greeks. However, after Turkey invaded Cyprus eleven years later the division became a militarized border and Turkish troops occupied the north of the island. From then on the Turkish and Greek populations became segregated across the entire island as well as the capital. For decades the Turkish north, guarded by Turkish forces, had been a no-go area for the Greeks in the south. No one was allowed to cross over, movement was prohibited, and friends and neighbours were separated with no hope of a reunion unless, as Ali Shafak explained now to Stella, they left the island and came to London.

'Do you go back there often?' she asked, remembering how much her parents longed to visit every summer and more.

'No, not often. No point if I couldn't visit my village,' he replied. 'I only go back to see my old father who lives in Nicosia. When the restrictions were eased I did go back to our village but only once; it's not the same now. I don't know the people there.'

'So how did you know Orhan Terzi?' Stella asked, hoping he could help her with the reason for their meeting while enjoying his tales of trust between the two communities, so reminiscent of the accounts she heard from her father.

'Imam Terzi conducted prayers and taught in my

father's mosque in Nicosia,' he started to explain. 'I met him when I went to visit my father. They were good friends and neighbours.' Apparently Orhan Terzi was a well-known imam and teacher in northern Nicosia, so well respected by his community that the road running past his mosque had been named after him, an honour indeed and indicative of his popularity.

'My father was very respectful of him. He is a good man who helped everyone.'

'Is your father still alive?' Stella asked and instantly regretted it in case she might cause distress.

'Oh yes, he is!' the man laughed. 'He is a tough one, my old man. He'll live to be a hundred I am sure and he's not far from it!'

'When did you last see Imam Terzi?' Stella enquired, concerned that *he* might not still be alive despite being nowhere near that age.

'It was about two years ago, when I last went to visit my father in Nicosia.'

'Did you speak to him? Was he well?' she asked, her voice betraying her anxiety.

'When I saw him at the mosque he was well enough. I heard he had been quite ill but had recovered. If something had happened I would certainly know. My father writes regularly with news of everyone,' he continued in his broken accent.

*

'Do you think we should go to look for him together?' Stella asked her brother as they sat in a cafe during their lunch break a few days later.

Both brother and sister worked in London's Soho area in nearby offices, and they often took the opportunity to meet for a quick lunch. Spiros was in advertising while Stella worked for one of the big accounting companies; her children always teased her about this, considering her job boring, unlike their cool uncle who worked in a fashionable industry. Stella didn't mind their jibes: she enjoyed her work, she liked numbers, and she was good at her job. *We can't all be creative*, she'd tell the kids. She could have been managing a department by now if she hadn't taken time off during those early years to take care of the children, but she didn't regret it. She found a job without too much difficulty once she decided it was time to go back. Yet even if she was able and efficient, she had to start on a lower salary than her qualifications and abilities deserved.

'You and I could go together,' Stella said and took a sip of her cappuccino, 'and if we find him, tell Dad afterwards.'

'Isn't he booked to go to Cyprus for a month with you?'

'Yes, but we could go a week or so ahead. We could at least *try* to find Orhan before he comes? He doesn't need to know anything now.'

'Yes, we could do that,' Spiros replied, taking a bite of his sandwich. '*If* we can find him . . .'

'Loula's relative gave me a good lead. He has told me where to go and look. But I really don't want to go on my own. I don't want to cross to "the other side" alone.'

Cyprus, 2008

August is far from an ideal month to explore Nicosia or anywhere else on the island, other than the high peaks of the Troodos Mountains. The heat is stifling on the plain and in the cities, and no one with any sense would step outside between early morning and early evening unless it was absolutely necessary. Cypriots choose to stay in the cool of their air-conditioned houses or offices, or better still in their bedrooms for the customary siesta, and people seen wandering the streets at noon can only be visitors.

That Wednesday morning, two days after they arrived in Cyprus, Spiros and Stella swallowed a quick cup of coffee at their seaside apartment in Larnaka and by eight o'clock they were on the road to Nicosia in search of Orhan Terzi. By the time they had arrived, met their cousin Yiorgos, who insisted on coming with them, parked the car and made their way towards the so-called green line, the border that separates the south of the city from the north, the rising temperature was already making them uncomfortably hot. Holding their British passports, they joined a group of tourists who were crossing into the occupied territory of north Nicosia and its Turkish community. Stella and Spiros had ventured north only once a few years previously and were surprised to see so many foreign visitors making the journey in the heat that they knew would await them in a few hours. For decades, the north of the island and capital city had been impenetrable to Greeks, a prohibited area imposed by Turkey; but nearly thirty years after the invasion by Turkey, a decision had been taken to ease the restrictions of movement. Provided that people reported to the Turkish authorities at a border checkpoint with their correct documents, they were allowed to cross over for a visit.

'I object to having to use a passport to be allowed to walk in my own city,' an uncle had snorted to Stella and Spiros when the two had expressed a wish to cross the border in 2003 after the restrictions were first eased. 'The international community considers it to be an occupied territory. Only Turkey recognizes it, and I refuse to give validity to an illegal state,' the uncle fumed. 'I will go when we are united as one country again, but not before!'

But Spiros and Stella were curious; they had never been to the north and as they happened to be visiting the family for Easter at that time, they decided to join the hundreds of people who were seizing the opportunity to cross the border after so many years. It was early afternoon on Easter Saturday, before people gathered in church on this holiest of religious days to hear the good tidings that Christ had risen, when the siblings joined the procession of Greek Cypriots to pass through the checkpoint and cross the green line. They mingled with a crowd of men and women of all ages who all wished to make the long-awaited journey to their old neighbourhoods and see their occupied homes. Young and old, sons and daughters walked together, escorting their elderly parents by the hand, to visit 'the other side' for this emotional return. As they approached the strange neglected stretch of no-man's-land, the buffer zone, they walked past once elegant neo-classical houses, now left derelict and crumbling. They continued past the famous Ledra Palace Hotel, in its heyday the most opulent and glamorous hotel throughout the Levant, now covered in bullet holes and used as the barracks for the peacekeeping UN soldiers. These were sights that neither sibling had ever encountered before when visiting the island.

'It was one of the most moving events I ever experi-enced,' Stella had told their relations on their return, still emotional after that day. 'There were so many people walking together, parents, grandparents, grandchildren, it was like going on a pilgrimage. One old woman who could hardly walk told me she wanted to see her home and her garden once again before she died . . . all I could do was cry.'

Stella and Spiros had never repeated their visit, although

over the years they met many people, friends from England and locals, who had walked across the green line to 'the other side' out of curiosity as they had done. Apart from the sadness she felt for all the displaced citizens who had lost their homes, Stella had found the city neglected and squalid in comparison to the sophisticated European south. That Easter Saturday when she and Spiros passed through the checkpoint, they had left a cosmopolitan southern Nicosia after lunch at an elegant cafe, and crossed into what Stella could only describe later on to her children as 'impoverished'.

Stella's curiosity had been satisfied that first time and until now she had had no reason to repeat the journey.

The wait for inspection of their passports was long and tedious and both brother and sister remembered their uncle's anger and frustration five years earlier. That first time when they had crossed over the green line they had been swept away by the novelty and emotion of the occasion. Then it had been a far less organized affair. Now that it had been accepted and formalized, the division seemed cold and calculating, and they keenly felt the injustice of being compelled to behave as if they were crossing into another country, when they were stepping over an imaginary line into one and the same city.

'It's all such a mess,' Stella whispered to Spiros in English as they stood in the queue to have their documents examined by the Turkish police and be permitted to proceed.

'Where will it all end?' he replied.

'It's been so long,' Yiorgos said with a sigh. 'Many of us hardly remember what it was like before. We only know what our parents tell us. Most of the Turkish Cypriots I know didn't want any of this either.'

'I know, our father can't stop talking about the old days,' added Spiros.

Stella watched a French couple ahead of them trying to communicate with the Turkish official in broken English and tried to imagine what their response would be once they passed into Turkish territory. Could they understand how it feels to live in a divided country? They were impartial observers, they were tourists curious to see something different from what they might see elsewhere in the west. Unless they had a personal interest or knew Cypriots, Turkish or Greek, who had explained their history to them, it was unlikely that they would have any strong emotional reaction. Probably, Stella mused, they were no more than casual spectators curious to visit a country with a colourful history and a disputed border that added a frisson of danger to their sightseeing.

'Let's move! Let's go!' Spiros suddenly called, leading the way out from the police cabins and bringing Stella out of her reverie. 'Get your map out, Sis, we've got work to do – no time to lose.' Aside from her absorption with the

French couple, Stella was now distracted by something else that caught her eye and made her come to a standstill. It was the street sign for the thoroughfare where they stood: a continuation of the same road that crossed the border, leading to the green line. On the Greek side its name was and always had been Ledra Street; here it was known as Lokmaci Street. She later learned that this policy had been imposed everywhere; after partition all streets were given Turkish names, villages and towns likewise.

'I hadn't realized they had changed all the names.' She looked at Spiros and Yiorgos, then remembered that all the street names that Ali Shafak had given her were in Turkish.

'Yes, I know. I was shocked too, at first,' Yiorgos replied, following the other visitors and stepping into a small piazza surrounded by souvenir shops and cafes. 'I don't like it, but you get used to it.'

The three made their way to the centre of the square, where a circular bench beckoned them for a moment's rest. Glancing around her, Stella realized she had indeed stepped into another country; this place reminded her of a Tunisian market square she had visited long ago, before she had children. Here the over-eager faces of vendors beckoning visitors to favour their shabby cafes, shops and stalls lent an atmosphere that contrasted sharply with the streets on the Greek side. Gone were the smart Max Mara and Gucci shop windows they had passed earlier, or the ubiquitous coffee bars Caffè Nero and Starbucks, where they stopped to fortify themselves before joining the queue at the green line. Here they met indifferent tourist touts and stalls selling mass-produced sunhats and sunglasses to catch the fancy of day trippers who were unlikely to return.

'Let me see your map and instructions,' Yiorgos said, reaching for the notes that Ali Shafak had given Stella. 'According to the map, Yenicami Mosque where Orhan preaches is north of the city.' He looked around him for clues to show them where they were and which direction they should take. 'I think we have to pass the Büyük Han, the Great Inn,' he continued, turning round to try to locate it. 'My father often talks about it. His mother used to take him there as a boy.'

The Han with its thick sandstone walls had seen many uses over the years, and before the partition had been frequented by both Turks and Greeks – now it was something of a tourist attraction with cafes and a souvenir shop.

'Yes, we do,' Stella agreed. 'It would be interesting to take a look, and I think we also pass by Agia Sophia' – she hesitated for a moment – 'but even if we don't, can we visit it, please? We have time, don't we? I've always wanted to see it!'

The first time Stella had visited north Nicosia, there had been no time to see anything of significance; she and Spiros had followed the crowd and meandered about for a short while before hurrying home to attend the evening Easter service. The cathedral of Agia Sophia, the oldest Gothic church on the island, had been converted into a mosque during the period of the Ottoman Empire; Stella had always wanted to visit it properly and see the interior. Often she had stood on her uncle's roof garden on the tenth floor of his apartment block just outside the old wall, her bird's eye view extending over the entire north and south of Nicosia, encircled by the enormous fortress built so many centuries ago by the Venetians to keep out the prowling Ottomans. The irony of its failure never ceased to strike Stella as she stood looking at the divided city. Agia Sophia loomed majestically, unobtainable and unapproachable, its two added minarets towering over its surroundings. Together with the Venetian wall, Agia Sophia, or Selimiye Mosque as it later became, was Nicosia's most prominent and oldest landmark, believed to have been built on the ruins of an earlier Byzantine church of the same name. Having read about this splendid example of Gothic craftsmanship, now that they were within a few streets of the building she was determined to pay it a visit.

'Maybe we can go there after we've found Orhan's mosque?' Yiorgos knew that although they had the whole day at their disposal, the heat would hinder their search as the day wore on. 'Let's visit on our way back,' he suggested.

Spiros studied the map. 'From what I see, Ali's father must live very close to the Yenicami Mosque, which means it wouldn't be too difficult to locate him if we ask around. But first we must find the mosque.'

Clutching the notes giving Ali Shafak's father's address, Stella, Spiros and their cousin made their way through the city. The commercial tourist quarter extended a little further with more cafes and souvenir shops, but as they ventured further from the checkpoint into the residential area they found a different scene. The houses were similar to the ones in the older part of southern Nicosia, but here decay and decline had taken hold. Whereas on the other side of the green line extensive renovations were being undertaken to restore the old villas and town houses, here they had been left to crumble. Residential neighbourhoods within the city walls in Nicosia had been mostly constructed around the turn of the twentieth century and traditionally the houses had their completion date displayed above their door in decorative wrought-ironwork. Stella found this custom charming and intriguing: who might have been the original owners of these family homes? She had enjoyed taking her children for a stroll on early summer evenings when they visited relatives in Nicosia, exploring the old residential areas and imagining the people who had lived there before the advent of cars, electricity or running water.

As they ventured further into the city, the houses that they passed looked as if nothing much had been done to them since the war: doors and windows in urgent need of repair, the narrow lanes littered with rubble and rubbish as children played there. Looking through a gate that led to a backyard, Stella saw chickens and a goat mingling with washing draped over the clothes line. Peering through open doors and windows, she saw poverty and deprivation. Many of the people living here, she had been told, were settlers from Turkey. Few were Turkish Cypriots, most of whom had chosen to move out of the city into the provinces and countryside.

'I never expected it to be as bad as this,' she murmured as they passed by a window with a broken pane where a man stood in his vest and underpants watching them walk by.

'Look!' Yiorgos suddenly shouted, stopping abruptly in front of Stella so that she bumped into him. 'Look,' he said again, pointing at a street sign, 'this points to Yenicami Mosque, so it must be down this way.'

They continued down several narrow lanes until they arrived in a neighbourhood where the streets were wider and the buildings in better repair, often surrounded by gardens. Following the directions shown by a signpost, they took a left turn and walked beside a high wall running the length of the entire street, which they realized was concealing a large garden.

'This is it!' Stella clapped her hands and ran ahead to the end of the street. 'Over here!' she shouted, turning left to find the very mosque they were searching for. They looked up as she pointed at the road sign on a telegraph pole above their heads: it read *Orhan Terzi sokak* – Orhan Terzi Street.

The mosque's walled garden was lush and green and flanked by two large sycamore trees. Four boys had climbed it to hide among its branches and observed the unexpected visitors waiting by the gate. Smiling, Stella waved and greeted them cheerfully; the boys responded with suppressed giggles, ignoring her. 'I like to see kids playing like this.' She turned to her brother and cousin. 'Climbing trees is surely more fun than sitting in front of an iPad.'

'I'm sure if they had an iPad they'd be sitting in front of it,' Yiorgos returned, mounting the steps to the gate.

'What do we do now?' Spiros said, looking at his cousin. 'Do you think he's in there?'

'Let's find out . . .'

'I think prayer time has been and gone. Are we allowed to go inside?' Stella added, concerned that as a woman she might not be welcome.

'Let's just go into the garden and see,' Yiorgos replied.

Entering the gate, they were met by a display of roses, geraniums, pinks and several jasmine bushes all competing with each other for the attention of bees and butterflies. In the centre of the garden stood an ancient stone basin with a tap above it for the mandatory ablutions before prayer.

Cautiously approaching the front porch of the mosque,

they saw that only two or three pairs of shoes were left outside.

'You two go in,' Stella announced. 'I shall stay and wait for you here in the shade.'

'It looks as if hardly anyone is here. Maybe we should try to find Ali Shafak's father's house,' Spiros suggested.

Stella reached for the note in her pocket and reread the instructions that Ali had given her. His father lived exactly diagonally across from the mosque, just as he had told her.

The two-storey house was well maintained and dated from 1905, according to the ironwork figure above its imposing door, on which was fixed a brass knocker at eye level in the shape of an elegant female hand like all the doors in the street. Stella lifted it and knocked twice. They stood waiting. It was almost two o'clock and the hottest part of the day was upon them – undoubtedly the worst time to be knocking on anyone's door, especially an elderly person. He could be in the middle of eating his meal or, worse still, having his siesta. They waited nervously, stealing glances at each other.

A voice from inside called out in Turkish.

'Friends of Ali,' Stella called back in Greek, hoping she had understood his question and he would understand her answer.

The front door was flung wide open by an old man who was smiling broadly.

'Mr Shafak?' she asked and extended her hand to him.

'*Hoşgeldin!*' he said in Turkish and immediately followed with '*Kalostous!*', the Greek Cypriot equivalent to his welcome greeting, indicating that the old man belonged to the rapidly diminishing generation of Cypriots who spoke both languages fluently.

'Are you all Ali's friends from England?' he asked cheerfully, again in Greek, and ushered them into the house, shutting the door behind them to banish the unforgiving heat of the day. The urgency with which he shut the door amused Stella, in contrast to England where doors were closed against the rain or the cold as opposed to the heat.

'Come, come inside,' the old man said, still smiling, 'too hot out there.' Stepping into the cool of the house they sighed with relief that they had found him at home and evidently glad to receive them.

'So, are you Greek from London?' he asked, looking at all three in turn. 'Ali has many Greek friends there.' As he spoke he beckoned them to follow him. 'My brother's grandson married a Greek girl from London, she is a very good girl,' he continued. *That would be Loula*, Stella thought. They followed him into a dark, deliciously cool kitchen where the old man had evidently been preparing his lunch. 'Please sit,' he said, showing them the chairs around the table. 'Some water? You must drink water, you must be thirsty. Then we eat together,' he said again, pointing at a bowl of salad, boiled potatoes, flatbread and olives in a jar. 'When too hot you don't want to eat so much . . . but we must drink water.' He fetched three glasses from a cupboard above the sink and poured water for them from a jug he took out of an old refrigerator before sitting down with them.

'So . . . friends of Ali!' the old man said again, beaming. 'You bring me news from my son?' Stella, the first to speak, began to explain. It was always that way between her and Spiros: he dealt with the practicalities, she did the talking. His excuse was that his work demanded a lot of talking so when not working he should do the minimum. Stella thought it was a lame excuse but she didn't really mind, she was good at communicating: her friends told her she brought out the best in people.

'Oh, my girl,' the old man said mournfully and sat back in his chair to look at Stella, after she had explained the reason for their trip and their quest to find Orhan. 'You have come two weeks too late.' His voice faltered.

Stella glanced at her brother and Yiorgos and held her breath, waiting for him to continue. 'I pray to Allah every day to return him back to us soon.' His eyes watered and his voice faded to silence.

'Why? What has happened?' Stella asked him, her own voice unsteady from the anticipation of bad news. It would be so unbearably sad if they really were too late. The thought flashed through her mind that she had been right not to have mentioned this visit to her father: they had come so close to finding Orhan, she could hardly imagine his disappointment.

Gradually the old man recovered his composure and he began to explain that Orhan had been unwell for several years now: 'He had the sugar, you see, too much sugar in his blood.' Orhan had apparently been suffering for years from diabetes, or 'sugar' as the locals called it. As the complications of the condition increased, he had been seeking medical treatment with Greek doctors, which entailed crossing to 'the other side' of Nicosia for appointments on a regular basis. Two weeks ago, Orhan had suddenly collapsed in the mosque while conducting prayers, Mr Shafak told them, his eyes sad.

'It was his heart, you see, it couldn't take the strain any longer.' Orhan's chronic diabetic condition, which he was not good at managing, had caused him to suffer a massive heart attack and he had been admitted to the general hospital in Nicosia, where he was now. 'I think a relative is here staying in his house across the street. He came to help him when he got sick.' The Greeks, the old man explained, have good doctors, and many Turks go to the south to be treated. 'If we want to see the Greek doctors they agree to see us, like in the old days,' he told them and the sadness in his voice reminded Stella of her earlier meeting with his son in London, or her many conversations with her own father. 'We used to all live together, not like now . . .' He picked up his glass of water and took several sips before continuing. 'Sometimes I would go with him to the hospital, for company, you see, I would wait outside when the nice lady doctor called him, she always looked after him well. May Allah bless her and her family. They are Christians, we are Muslims, but there is only but one God!'

They stayed with the old man for a while, accepting his hospitality and his offer of lunch with pleasure and listened to his stories. They ate a salad of ripe tomatoes and raw onions drenched in olive oil and lemon, shared his flatbread and olives, and drank cold water from the jug. After that they took their leave so that he could have his afternoon rest, though not before he told them where they could find Orhan. Then Stella, Spiros and Yiorgos ventured into the afternoon heat to make their way back home via Agia Sophia.

'I can do this alone,' Stella told Spiros when they returned to the apartment in Larnaka. 'I can go and see what state he is in and if he is stable, then we can go back to visit him together.'

'Only if you're sure,' her brother replied with apparent relief at being spared a possibly gruesome hospital visit. Neither of them knew what to expect.

The next morning she set off for Nicosia much earlier, so by the time she had located the hospital and parked the car

it was hardly past eight o'clock and the morning temperature still positively pleasant. She found a spot under a tree
to park, in the hope that by the time she had finished and
returned to it, it wouldn't be a pizza oven on wheels; but
she knew well enough that she was fooling herself and
that by then she'd be able to fry an egg on its bonnet.

Locating Orhan was easy, for there were few Turkish
Cypriots in the wards. Stella followed a nurse along
the air-conditioned corridors, feeling almost chilly but
knowing that in less than an hour she would be grateful
for it.

'He's in bed number four.' The nurse pointed at a bed
by the window. 'He is quite sedated and sleeps most of the
time. If you need any help, I'll be in the ward.'

Stella stepped into the room and made her way to the
window. There were four beds in the room, two side by
side against each wall facing one other. She stood by the
window and looked down at the old man lying motionless, wired up to machines. She hadn't considered what he
might look like now. A little like her father, perhaps, she
had imagined. Lambros had talked about him far more
than he had ever *described* him to her. She didn't have a
strong visual image of him; what she had was a strong
feeling, a loving feeling as conveyed by her father. He
looked much older than Lambros: probably because of his
white beard, she thought. Her clean-shaven dad always
looked dapper and younger than his years. She stood for

a while, watching him breathing, then she bent over him and softly whispered his name. After a pause she repeated it, then again, and touched the back of his hand, which lay by his side. She saw his lips move but his eyelids remained shut. A few minutes passed, she again touched his hand lightly with her fingers. Slowly he opened his eyes and looked up at her.

'Anastasia,' he whispered, his voice barely audible. 'You came.'

'It's Stella,' she said softly and reached for his hand. 'I came to see you. I'm Anastasia's niece, my name is Stella.'

'Ahh,' he breathed out and closed his eyes again, shutting her out; she sensed disappointment.

'I'm Lambros's daughter,' she said, her tears starting to gather.

'Lambros . . .' he murmured, eyes still shut, 'my old friend.' He slowly opened his eyelids and looked at her.

'Yes!' Stella said, gaining courage, 'Lambros, he wants to see you, I can bring him to see you.' She sat down by his side and took his hand in hers and waited.

'The *boy, he* came . . .' he whispered, his voice weaker than before. 'He came to see me. She sent him to me . . .'

27

Istanbul, 1960s

Anastasia's son was growing into a fine young man, but his mother's untimely death left a lasting imprint on him. The fear of losing anyone he loved would linger over him for the rest of his life. Mother and son had been so close, far closer than he had ever been with his father, and adjusting to life without her proved hard for both of them. Enver had always been obsessively committed to his medical practice and was absent a great deal, so Anastasia and Hassan had developed an exceptionally close bond with each other. Now, left alone with the thirteen-year-old Hassan, Enver was at a loss and unfamiliar with how to deal with the boy. Although he was a generous provider of the material things in life, he was oblivious to his son's emotional needs, so the boy spent his teenage years in a state of simmering and sometimes open anger towards his father. Anastasia had always been the one who cared for, comforted and encouraged him, as well as instilling in him the importance of his dual ethnic identity. She made sure the boy was aware that his mother's Greek background was as significant as his Turkish inheritance from his father; in fact at times his affinity to the former seemed stronger, to his father's irritation.

'We live in Turkey and we are Turks,' he would tell Hassan when he considered his son was being deliberately provocative in front of friends after Anastasia's death.

'While Alev was alive there wasn't much I could do,' he would explain to people apologetically, using the Turkish name which he had given to Anastasia when they first arrived in Istanbul. 'The two of them always spoke Greek to each other. But now he must take pride in being Turkish.'

However, this was no simple matter for the teenaged Hassan. He was beginning to feel much the same way as his mother had done when the full impact of her decision to change her religion and take on a Turkish identity struck her – conflicted and confused. Anastasia had imparted some of her Christian values to her son and had often taken him to the Orthodox church when she visited her Greek friends. Growing up with the acceptance of two faiths made his circumstances unlike any other family he knew, but this seemed quite normal to him when he was little. His mother made sure he understood their situation was sensitive and it was never openly discussed outside their home; besides, Hassan wasn't an unduly gregarious boy, often preferring the company of his family to boys his own age. He would regularly go to prayers at the mosque with his father – one activity he liked doing with him – but would also be taken by his mother to light a candle and kiss the icons at the Christian church.

During early childhood his acceptance of his dual cultures and religions was unquestioned but once he reached adolescence he began to be troubled. After Anastasia's death, when Hassan found himself alone during his father's long hours of absence, he continued to go to church. He would take himself most Sundays to Pera and into the Orthodox church to light a candle for his mother; then after the liturgy, continuing their habit while she was alive, he would pay a visit to her friends at the Greek community. There, with Myrto and her family, he would be Andreas not Hassan. He was one of them; he was their dear friend's son on whom they felt duty-bound to lavish love and affection. For his part he revelled in the women's warm attention, while always taking care not to divulge too much about himself, as his mother had warned. Myrto and her family lived in a spacious apartment above their shop and on Sundays, when there was no trade, they would invite him upstairs for refreshments. Myrto had married a personable young man from Greece and had two children of her own, a boy and a girl. The marriage was arranged by one of her aunts who knew the family, and her husband was now helping them to run the shop.

'Welcome, Andreas *mou*,' Myrto would greet him as she

took him in her arms. 'We miss and lament our Anastasia so much, I can't imagine what your own grief must be like, my boy.' Her eyes would brim with tears as she fussed over him while her mother or daughter would hasten to bring him some sweet delicacy with a glass of water. He enjoyed his visits to the Greek family, he felt a sense of belonging there, but he liked it even more on days when the shop was open; he loved it as much as Anastasia had done when she first discovered it. The fabrics and tapestries, the textiles and colourful yarns and above all the special aroma of the place, were all so evocative of visits spent there with his mother.

Hassan had always been a good student and Enver's plans for him were to follow in his footsteps and into medicine.

'Orthopaedic surgeon! That is what you must train for,' his father would advise when they were discussing the future. 'There's much money to be made in that profession – plenty of work, people break bones all the time.'

But Hassan had other plans. He was an excellent draughtsman and had an unerring eye for design. He was good with his hands, but he didn't intend to use them to mend broken limbs. He was far more interested in acquiring the skills of his grandfather's and mother's trade than in qualifying in his father's profession. Fashion design was his passion, the sartorial arts fascinated him; the sensuous fall of folds of fabric over the body, the sharp cut of tailored suits, the shimmer of silky yarns were where his mind dwelt after school. Sewing needles intrigued him more than syringes or surgical equipment. Every month he would visit the largest newspaper kiosk in Istanbul to buy an armful of whatever European magazines he could afford on his allowance. When he was small, while Anastasia made clothes for them both, he would sit by her side and watch her cut the fabric and pin the pieces together to transform them like a magician into a jacket or a blouse. She had never lost her own passion for dressmaking and preferred to make her own clothes, adapting the *Vogue* patterns as she had done when she worked with *Kyria* Thecla, although Enver could buy her whatever she wanted from the best shops.

'It's a matter of preference not necessity,' she would reply when he asked why she bothered to put herself to so much trouble. 'It's a pleasure not a bother, I love making clothes for myself – I know what suits me and besides, they fit me better,' she would try to convince him. Later, when Hassan was older, he would go shopping with his mother to the textiles bazaar to choose cloth for an outfit that she planned for herself. He liked nothing more than the smell of a fabric emporium with its bolts and rolls of materials stacked on the shelves; he loved the process of helping Anastasia to choose the fabric by its weight, colour, design and motif and then seeing how she adapted the pattern to her own shape and style.

These activities always took place without Enver. 'I don't think your father would quite understand the importance of what we're doing,' Anastasia would laugh, knowing that her husband would consider a boy taking interest in such matters as effeminate. On the odd occasion when he witnessed mother and son discussing the design of a garment he would protest.

'You're filling the boy's head with unnatural ideas,' he would complain moodily, 'this is women's work.'

'Didn't your family come from a long line of tailors?' she snapped back at him. 'Was *that* women's work? Your father was a tailor and for your information your uncle Hassan *Bey* was a master at his craft and a great inspiration to me.'

'That's *not* the same,' he'd protest, 'they made clothes for men! Not women's dresses!'

'Their work was no different from any seamstress I ever saw,' she would argue. 'Better get used to it, Enver – our son takes after your father, not you!'

But Enver persisted. After Anastasia's death and once the boy was ready to graduate from high school he continued to push him towards medicine. However, unfortunately for Enver, they were now well into the 1960s and Europe was ablaze with revolutionary new fashion, style and music with England as its Mecca. Hassan, poring over the pages of his magazines, was well informed; he knew that London was the centre of this carnival of youth. The

Beatles, The Rolling Stones, the wild music, the new boutiques of crazy clothes were all there in the British capital. Mary Quant, high priestess of fashion, was practising her craft there along with Biba, Ossie Clark and a host of others and he longed to become a disciple. Hassan had no doubts where his talents lay: London must be his destination, and nothing would dissuade him from following his ambition. But he also knew that the only way to achieve this was to convince his father to support him. His father, however, was of a different opinion; if he was going to spend money on his son's education, it had to be on something he approved of, worthwhile and respectable.

'No son of mine is going to become some kind of, what do they call them, some kind of degenerate *hippy*!' he shouted.

'I want to *study*, Father, not drop out!' Hassan would try to explain in desperation.

'Fashion! What kind of studies are these?' Enver would scoff and throw his hands up in the air. 'Next thing you'll be wanting to grow your hair long like a girl and wear flowery shirts!'

It was no use arguing: his father was rigidly set in his traditional ways and would not be persuaded. Hassan was in despair. Then, just as he was about to give up hope, Fatima arrived in their lives and changed everything. She could never have replaced his mother – no one could ever replace Anastasia for either father or son – but she brought brightness into their home and lifted their spirits in a way that only Anastasia had been able to do. Fatima filled the air with her feminine ways that Hassan had missed so much, and she caused his father to smile and walk with a lighter step.

It had been a few years since Enver's friends started to urge him towards finding a wife. From time to time they had tried to match him up with one or other unmarried female acquaintance: 'You are still young and vigorous, my friend, you need a woman by your side and maybe another child,' they told him. 'The years are passing, your son is growing up and you'll end up alone.'

Enver was not opposed to the prospect of a wife and kept a roving eye for a fitting match. Eventually he found this at work, in the form of Fatima. She was a young doctor, a paediatrician, who had just been appointed to the same hospital as Enver. She was petite, pretty, with bright sparkling eyes, a sharp mind and a good sense of style, which met with Hassan's approval. At first the young man resented the idea that she might hope to replace his mother and was irritated by this new woman's intrusion into their lives, until he realized that on the contrary, what she had introduced to the household was love, peace and tolerance.

Enver had asked Fatima to marry him soon after they met, and within a short time Hassan could see the softening influence she was having on his father. She was able to infuse in Enver a sense of acceptance and understanding towards his son that he had never seen in him since Anastasia died.

'Times have changed, my love,' the young man heard Fatima tell his father one balmy summer's evening as the pair sat in the garden drinking coffee after dinner. Hassan had gone upstairs to his room to work on a drawing and as he sat by the open window he could hear them talking.

'The boy has to follow his passion and his ambitions,' Fatima told Enver. 'If he doesn't want to be a doctor you can't push him into it and, besides, if his heart is not in it what kind of doctor would he be?'

'But what of this nonsense?' Enver countered, stretching his legs on the lounger and lighting a cigarette. 'What is this fashion trumpery that he wants to study? What kind of work is that for a grown man?'

'Oh . . . my darling,' Fatima replied with laughter in her voice and reached for a cigarette herself. 'These are modern times now, my love, and your son has talent, don't you see? If that is his calling you shouldn't stand in his way.'

It didn't take many weeks or many more such conversations for Enver's vehement opposition to begin to wane; eventually, grudgingly, he agreed to support his son in his preferred studies.

'I suppose if he's going to go anywhere it might as well be London.'

'Exactly!' Fatima told him. 'It's your birthplace, after all, and it would be good for the boy to get to know it.'

'In fact, I haven't been back for many years myself,' he replied, swept along by the young woman's enthusiasm and support for his son.

'You must have plenty of contacts for the boy to look up when he arrives, no?' she asked, already worrying on Hassan's behalf at the prospect of his new start in a foreign country.

'Of course I do! But better still, you and I will go with him. I will show you both the city where I was born.'

'I owe everything to you,' Hassan told Fatima, wrapping her in a tight embrace and landing a loud kiss on her cheek the day he heard that he had been accepted at Saint Martin's School of Art to study textiles and fashion design. 'If not for you, I might have had to run away . . . however much my father insisted, I would *never* have gone to medical school.'

In his wildest daydreams he had never foreseen that this next phase in his life could work out so well for him and for that he knew he had Fatima to thank. At last he would be escaping from Turkey, from his confusion and the constraints of his family existence. Now he could become his own man, whoever he chose to be, not the troubled being who had been moulded by his parents. He even chose a new name for himself. Once he arrived in England his name would be Hassandreas; he would be neither one nor the other, an amalgamation of the two.

'You owe it to your perseverance and talent,' Fatima told him, 'and besides, it will be wonderful for us all.' She too was thrilled, not only to have managed to help the boy but also to be making this journey of discovery with her new husband. She promptly started to busy herself with arrangements for their trip. They planned to spend a month in London, settling Hassan in lodgings and visiting the city. Once Enver came round to the project his enthusiasm grew too.

'It really was about time I returned,' he told them. 'It's been so many years, I may not recognize the London I grew up in.'

This would be Hassan's last summer in Turkey. He'd been reading about a *summer of love* in Europe and America and he couldn't wait to be part of it. Istanbul was hot and humid, and the most exciting news on the streets was regarding a championship of the Turkish football league – Hassan couldn't care less. Of far greater concern were the earthquakes that had been striking parts of the country lately but they too couldn't detract from his mood of optimism and thankfulness that soon he would at last be leaving. He was increasingly detached from the news at home; what was happening in the streets of the rest of the world was on his mind and he was buzzing with anticipation to be part of that world. His spirits were soaring with excitement, the future was now beckoning him, but before any of that began, before he set off on this new and exciting

path, there was one thing that he had to do first. There was
a promise he had to keep, a pledge he had made that once
he was old enough he would fulfil. The time had now
come, he informed his father and Fatima; before anything
else he must keep the promise he had made to his dying
mother. There was no time to lose: before he set off for
England he had to travel to Cyprus and find Orhan.

28

Cyprus, 1968

Hassan arrived at Nicosia's newly built international airport on a scorching day in mid-July with a letter from Leila in his pocket containing Orhan's address and how to find him. After Anastasia's death, Orhan would once in a while write to the boy via his sister, as he had done for his mother previously, but it was Leila who kept Hassan informed about everyone in Cyprus. After Anastasia's death Leila felt it was her duty to keep in touch with her young nephew and continue writing to both her cousin Enver and the boy. She had remained unmarried, to her great disappointment, and was still living in the village with her uncle Ahmet, helping him to run the family business. Hassan knew about the Greek family too from his mother, who made sure of it, and once in a while curiosity would get the better of him and he would brood about trying to find them but something always held him back. If they ostracized Anastasia, how would they view him, and besides he had no way of knowing where they were or how to find them.

'We should go and visit your aunt and your grandfather,' Enver would promise Hassan whenever a letter
arrived from Cyprus, but he was always too busy to keep
his promise and they never did. So now, after all this time,
Hassan was standing outside the airport looking for a taxi
to take him into the city centre, where he must find his way
around these unfamiliar streets that he had only ever
heard about from his mother's stories.

'Your flight was from Constantinople, eh?' the taxi
driver asked him after he settled on the back seat with his
small backpack next to him. 'Are you Turkish or Greek?'
he asked again in broken English, examining the young
man in the rear-view mirror.

'Both,' Hassan replied in Greek, causing the driver to
apply the brakes and turn to look at him. 'What do you
mean, both? Nobody is both,' he said. 'You Christian or
Muslim?'

'Both,' Hassan said again rather sharply, hoping to put
an end to more questions. His answer shocked not only the
probing taxi driver but also himself, as he realized that for
the first time in his life, with this single word, he had actually defined who he really was. He had been feeling as if
he was *both* for so long, yet he had never before consciously
expressed it verbally, because he had become used to
secrecy and besides, he understood it would have caused
distress to those who knew him. But here on this island he
was a stranger, no one knew him and what anyone thought

of him was utterly unimportant, which gave him the courage to be honest. *Honesty*, he now realized, was what he looked forward to most about leaving Turkey. In London he would be anonymous. He could leave all his conflicting feelings behind. In England he would be able to re-invent himself as he wished. He did not have to be one thing, or the other; not a Greek or a Turk, not a Christian or a Muslim. He could be just himself, just a member of the human race.

'Where shall I take you?' the taxi driver asked, speaking in Greek now, still stealing glances in the mirror above his head. 'Where shall I drop you off?' Hassan took the letter from his pocket and looked at his instructions from Leila.

'By Kyrenia gate, please.'

'Ah! You are going to "the other side" then, inside the wall?' the driver asked, burning with curiosity to find out who this young man was and what he was doing; Kyrenia gate being one of three main entrances into the walled city and the one closest to the Turkish north. 'They have taxis over there too, I used to work all over Nicosia before the separation,' he informed him. 'Or if you know where you are going you can go on foot.' Hassan made no reply. Leila had already explained in her letter how to make his way around the old city to find Orhan.

There had been little of interest to see in Nicosia's outskirts during the ride from the airport, other than a series of half-constructed modern houses on arid-looking plots of land destined for the same fate. The place was obviously expanding and undergoing extensive development and modernization. Cyprus so far was nothing like he had imagined – mountains and pine forest, streams and waterfalls as Anastasia had described to him over the years. The only similarity connecting it to his home city that he had just left was the physical sensation of the burning sun. The heat in the taxi had been oppressive and the hot air that blew in through the open window had no cooling effect whatever. Not until Hassan walked into the walled city did the landscapes become more familiar to him. Here the influence of hundreds of years of Ottoman rule was apparent, although there was none of the grandeur and opulence found in the centre of Istanbul; yet the confusion of architectural styles, Turkish, Greek and Venetian, along with minarets piercing the sky and church domes looming above the streets, made him feel more at home.

He made his way to a *kafenion* to collect his thoughts and make a plan. He sat inside under the huge ceiling fan to shelter from the unforgiving sun and ordered a sweet Turkish coffee and *baklava* – he decided he needed the sugar for energy – and then took Leila's letter from his pocket again.

'*Number 3 Kuruçeşme Sokak near the Yenicami Mosque where he preaches,*' Leila wrote. '*You pass Büyük Han and go straight ahead then take a left . . .*'

He read on: his aunt had taken good care to give him detailed instructions to Orhan's house. He took a sip of the thick syrupy coffee and sat back on his chair to check her notes again, feeling the energy returning to his limbs. *How hard can it be to find a house in such a small place?* he mused. *I've wandered the streets of Istanbul on my own since I was twelve, and besides if I get lost I'll just ask someone, it's not as if I don't speak the language . . .*

The mosque was easy enough to find, not only because of the directions he held in his hand but also because he had no option but to accept instructions from passers-by. The labyrinth of back streets he walked through were strongly reminiscent of Istanbul's poorer neighbourhoods, the women doing their washing and chores in the open air and children playing in the alleys. As he continued, he was soon to discover that many alleyways led into people's backyards, so he found himself in effect walking into their homes. It was obvious to all that he was a stranger and, their curiosity ignited, he was warmly greeted and welcomed. Once locals found out what he was looking for, they volunteered to direct him towards Yenicami Mosque. He eventually arrived as prayer was being called and he thankfully took refuge from the heat inside with the other faithful who had started to gather.

During prayers he caught sight of the middle-aged imam with a thick head of short cropped hair peeping through his white skullcap and wondered if this was

Orhan, rather than the old imam with a long white beard. But he decided to wait before approaching him, preferring to pay him a visit in his home where they could talk more privately. He hardly had to ask where he could find Orhan at home, for everyone knew him. He had been teaching at the mosque, Hassan was told, for several years alongside their old imam and was living across the street, just as Leila had told him.

After prayers ended, Hassan walked into the mosque's garden and sat under the sycamore tree to gather his thoughts. He wanted to compose himself and consider exactly how and what he would say to this man once he came face to face with him; this man who he had never set eyes on before, yet whom he thought he knew from his mother. Anastasia had made him promise to convey her love to him, but what kind of love was it that his mother had for him? Was it possible that she loved him more than his own father? When he thought now about the way Anastasia referred to Orhan, perhaps she did have even deeper feelings for Orhan than for Enver. Faced with the reality of meeting the man after hearing so much about him, Hassan's mind was alive with questions which he had never considered or asked himself before. Could it be that his mother and Orhan harboured a secret love for each other – or worse still, what if Orhan didn't care for his mother at all; what if she had lived with a fantasy all her life, and what if Orhan did not welcome his visit? He felt nervous, the anxiety played on his stomach. He took a deep breath and exhaled slowly; he had come all this way to honour his mother's dying wishes and no matter what his reception would be, he would go through with it. Finally, he got up and hesitantly left the garden; he walked across the street to house number three. He lifted the brass door knocker in the shape of an elegant female hand and knocked three times.

Enver had never been a man who showed his emotions; even when Anastasia was dying, and afterwards, he held on to his feelings in the manner he deemed a man should behave and would reproach his son if he thought he was not following suit. Hassan had therefore never seen a man cry. Sitting across from Orhan now, observing an unashamed display of emotion from a grown man openly showing his grief was something of a revelation. The unfamiliar sight of shedding tears, tears that flowed freely without embarrassment or restraint, touched the young man deeply.

'Did she suffer?' was the first question Orhan asked, then without waiting for an answer he quickly added, 'How could such a thing happen to her?'

'It was so fast,' Hassan replied, stifling a sob at the memory of his dying mother. Orhan knew about Anastasia's death as his sister had informed him and he had shed tears of grief then, but now sitting down with the boy, the sorrow came flooding back for both of them.

'Oh! My Anastasia,' Orhan whispered, his sadness etched all over his face, 'always so full of life . . .'

'I grew up knowing you,' Hassan told him. 'She talked about you often.'

'Not a day went by that I didn't think of her,' Orhan replied, wiping his eyes with a white cotton handkerchief.

'She made me promise to come and find you,' Hassan said, tears welling up in his own eyes now, and for once he didn't feel that he had to hide them. 'She told me I had to come and tell you she loved you.'

'I know she did . . .' Orhan replied, his eyes welling up again too. 'But she didn't love me the way I loved her. I didn't understand then, I was too young, but now I do.'

Hassan stayed with Orhan in his house for two days. They talked together; Orhan wanted to know everything about the boy. They ate together and prayed together and then when it was time for him to leave, they promised that they would always keep in touch. *Perhaps*, Hassan wondered after he left, *my mother should have married Orhan instead of my father? Would they not have been better suited?*

Cyprus, 2008

The sound of the land line ringing from the kitchen made Stella and Spiros start. No one ever called on it anymore unless it was an old relative in Nicosia who didn't have a mobile. The two siblings were sitting on the veranda of their apartment to cool down and review the events of the day. It had been an exceptionally hot and emotionally charged twenty-four hours and there was much to think about and discuss. Stella's trip to the hospital earlier that morning and the mounting excitement of locating Orhan at last had taken their toll on her, but the ice-cold ouzo they were now drinking and the evening breeze blowing from the sea were helping to ease the tension and focus their minds on the next step.

Their father was due to arrive in a few days and although Stella was eager to see him, she told Spiros, she was also apprehensive of how Lambros would receive the news that awaited him. It wasn't that she thought her father would not be pleased, no, she didn't doubt that for a moment, but this meeting that the two of them had conspired to arrange could be crucial and she couldn't be sure of the emotional impact it might have on two old men, one of whom was gravely ill. Years of wishful thinking and regret on their father's part might be about to come to an end, but all the same, Stella couldn't be fully certain of how he'd respond. And that was not her only reservation. She knew Lambros wanted to see Orhan but could the same be said of Orhan? When she visited him, he was in no position to express himself fully; she hadn't even been certain that he had understood who she was.

They were discussing all this and more when the ringing from the flat's telephone cut into their conversation.

'I think Yiorgos should give his mother a mobile,' Stella said, getting up to answer the phone. 'I think she's the only one who ever uses this line, unless it's Lambros ringing her.'

'She's probably calling to ask if Dad has arrived,' Spiros replied.

As it turned out the phone call was not from their old aunt in Nicosia asking for Lambros but from Lambros himself in London, informing them that he would not be joining them as planned but had to delay his trip for another week, so he could attend the funeral of an old friend.

'Oh well, that's it!' Stella said, returning to the terrace and throwing her arms in the air in despair, 'I really don't know if he'll make it in time now.'

'Don't be such a messenger of doom,' her brother scolded her. 'You always think the worst – you never know, the poor man might get better.'

'You can say that, but you didn't see him today. Honestly, Spiros, he was in a bad state, I thought he was at death's door. I fear Dad will be going to another funeral once he gets here, not the grand reunion we were planning for him.'

'We'll go together to the hospital and see how he is soon,' Spiros insisted, trying to soothe his sister's concerns.

But a few days later when they attempted to visit Orhan again he was nowhere to be found. The patient was apparently undergoing surgery or rushed into emergency, they were told – no one could explain fully. *Come back in a few days*, the nurse told them with irritation, *and try calling before you do*, was her stern advice.

'You see? I told you!' Stella said as they left the hospital. 'He'll die, and they'll never meet, and everything will have been in vain!'

'For heaven's sake, Stella, stop it!' Spiros told her. 'You don't know that. He's having surgery, he hasn't been taken to the morgue.'

'Even if he recovers, he might not be well enough. Would he even know Dad when he sees him?'

'We shall just have to hope, keep calling the hospital and wait and see, won't we?' Spiros said and stalked off towards the car.

Stella found the waiting unbearable. She had set her mind on bringing the two old men together and had such high hopes for a glad ending; now each day that passed made her fear that disaster was imminent. She called the hospital every day, much to the annoyance of the nurses, until at last she was told that the patient was out of intensive care and could be visited again.

The distinguished-looking man sitting by Orhan's bed stood up to greet them as Stella and Spiros approached. *He must be that relative that Mr Shafak mentioned*, Stella thought, gliding quietly towards him.

'*Kalimera*,' she whispered, aware of the quizzical look on the man's face. 'We are here to visit Orhan Terzi,' she explained, approaching to stand next to him beside the bed.

'*Kalimera sas*,' he greeted them in return, speaking Greek, evidently perplexed by the apparently foreign elegant-looking couple who had come to visit the modest-living old imam.

'How is he?' Spiros asked also in Greek as all three stood at the bedside to watch the sleeping old man.

'He's getting better, but he's been in intensive care.'

'Yes, we know!' Stella replied, to convey that they were well informed. 'Last time I was here he was all wired up, he didn't look at all well.'

'How long ago was that?' the man enquired politely, taking another good look at the two of them. 'I didn't see you, I've been here a while.'

'About a week ago,' was Stella's reply, stealing a probing glance at the man, 'but my brother didn't come, I was on my own.'

'I must have gone out and missed you,' he said, clearly wondering who these visitors might be who seemed so familiar with Orhan. 'I've been here every day. Well . . . every day since I arrived in Cyprus, that is.'

'Oh! You don't live here! Aren't you Cypriot?' a

surprised Spiros asked – his turn now to scrutinize the stranger.

'Well, yes and no,' he replied and his face broke into a smile, a smile so familiar to Stella that it triggered something in her memory, though bringing no conscious recall.

'It's complicated,' he continued, smiling, seeing the confusion spread on both Stella's and Spiros's faces.

'Where did you arrive from?' she asked, curiosity getting the better of her: she had assumed he was a Turkish Cypriot.

'London,' he replied, 'I live in London.'

'Really?' Spiros raised his eyebrows, unable to hide his surprise.

'What part of London?' Stella asked, in English this time, with the same sense of disbelief as her brother.

The little cafeteria in the hospital's grounds was empty; locals apparently either went home to brew their own coffee or brought a flask to drink while sitting with their sick relatives, to avoid leaving the bedside. For these three, however, since their discovery there was no option; what they had to say to each other could not be discussed around the bed of a sick man nor could it wait till later. The only place for them at that moment, even in the fiery thirty-eight degrees of the August day, was the little coffee shop under parched trees beside the hospital car park. They had so much to find out about one another, so much to exchange. It could not be delayed for a second longer.

The moment of realization came to Stella first as they stood gathered around the sleeping Orhan. As they spoke she started to piece together who the tall slim stranger standing close to her might be, the man whose face seemed so familiar and whose smile she suddenly recognized as so closely similar to that of her own father. Instantly she knew this could be no casual relative of the sick man, but a member of her own family, a blood relative of the closest kind, her first cousin. He must be her ill-fated aunt Anastasia's only son and her father's nephew, his estranged sister's child – who none of them had known much about, let alone that he lived in London; and the familiarity, they were soon to find out, didn't stop there.

As they sat talking in the little cafe, brother and sister gradually discovered that the elegant man a few years older than them, who was their first cousin, was also none other than Hassandreas, the celebrated fashion designer whose creations were preferred by the rich and famous globally, and desired by Stella and Erini alike but which they could hardly afford. They sat under the August sun drenched in perspiration, establishing their identities, moved and fascinated by their meeting, trying to join up the first few missing threads of the yarn that was their family history.

By the time they finished talking some small pieces had been put in place, but the bigger picture could not be completed without the two old men who were the main protagonists. This they knew was only the beginning of their journey of discovery, there was so much more to follow. As the next generation of the Constandinou and Terzi families, it was now for them to continue where their parents and grandparents had failed and revive the shared family history that had tied two generations before them so closely together.

When they returned to the room they found Orhan awake.

'Ah!' he sighed and looked at the three faces turned anxiously towards him. 'Hassan, my boy.' He moved his head to look at him, struggling to keep his voice steady. 'This young lady, Stella . . . came to see me a few days ago, but I was not able to speak then, not much at all.' He gave her a weary smile. 'I am happy you have all found each other.' He reached for Stella's hand. 'I wondered when you were going to come back.'

'You knew I'd been to see you,' she whispered, pushing down a sob that was threatening to rise in her throat. 'You heard me – you remembered my name!'

'She is so much like your mother,' Orhan said to Hassan and closed his eyes. The three cousins stood mute, looking at one another.

The old man opened his eyes again at last and looked towards the door. 'Is he coming?' He turned to Stella. 'You said you will bring him to me, where is he?'

'Oh yes! He's certainly coming,' she told him, wiping her eyes with the back of her hand, crying and laughing at the same time. 'Lambros is coming to see you very soon,' she managed to say, as the sob that she'd been trying to suppress rose up. 'I give you my promise,' she said again through her tears.

A Brief Chronology of Cypriot Political Events

1878

The United Kingdom received the island of Cyprus from the Ottoman Empire as a protectorate. The Cypriots at first welcomed British rule, hoping that they would gradually achieve prosperity and democracy following the collapse of the Ottoman Empire.

1914

Cyprus's status as a protectorate of the British Empire ended when the Ottoman Empire declared war against the Triple Entente powers, which included Great Britain.

1923

International recognition of the new Republic of Turkey, in which the new Turkish government formally recognized Britain's sovereignty over Cyprus. Greek Cypriots believed the circumstances were now right to demand union of the island with Greece (*enosis*), as many of the Aegean and Ionian islands had also done, but the British opposed it.

1925

Britain proclaimed Cyprus the Crown Colony of British Cyprus under an undemocratic constitution.

October 1931–October 1940 proved to be a very difficult period for the Cypriots. The colonial governor at the time imposed a number of suppressive measures, erasing the flimsy democratic infrastructure of the island. This was done to the extent that the legislative assembly was summarily dismissed, the elections of town mayors and village heads were also abolished, and the entire island was governed by decree from the governor. The aim of this was to prevent local public interest in politics. There were strong protests against the regime, but the suppressive measures were not lifted until the beginning of the Second World War, during which more than 30,000 Cypriots joined the British armed forces.

1948

King Paul of Greece declared that Cyprus desired union with Greece. After the war, a delegation from Cyprus submitted a demand for *enosis* to London but the demand was rejected.

1950

The Orthodox Church of Cyprus presented a referendum in which around 97 per cent of the Greek Cypriot population wanted the union. The United Nations accepted the Greek petition and *enosis* became an international issue.

During the 1950s demands for *enosis* from the Greek
Cypriots emerged with renewed force, led by Archbishop
Makarios. Attempts to win world support alerted Turkey and
alarmed the Turkish Cypriots.

The British withdrawal from Egypt led to Cyprus becoming
the new location for their Middle East Headquarters.

1955
When international pressure did not suffice to make Britain
respond as required to *enosis*, an effective campaign began,
organized by EOKA (*National Organization of Cypriot
Fighters*), a guerrilla group which desired political union with
Greece, and violence escalated against the colonial power.
Makarios was exiled, suspected of involvement in the EOKA
campaign.

From mid-1956 onwards there were constant discussions in
NATO, but all efforts to create an independent Cyprus which
would be a member of the Commonwealth of Nations were
futile.

1957
Turkish Cypriots responded to the *enosis* demand by calling
for partition (*taksim*), which became the slogan which was
used by the increasingly militant Turkish Cypriots to counter
the Greek cry of *enosis*. Fighting was renewed in Cyprus
by EOKA, and violence between the two communities
developed into a new feature of the situation. Eventually

Greece had to recognize that Turkey was now a vitally
interested party in the dispute.

1958
The British prime minister, Harold Macmillan, prepared
new proposals for Cyprus, but his plan, which was a form
of partition, was rejected by Archbishop Makarios. The
archbishop on his return from exile declared that he would
only accept a proposal which guaranteed independence,
excluding both *enosis* and partition.

16 August 1960
Cyprus gained its independence from the United Kingdom
after the long anti-British campaign by EOKA. The Zurich
Agreement, however, did not succeed in establishing
cooperation between the Greek and the Turkish Cypriot
populations on the island. Both sides continued the violence.
Turkey threatened to intervene.

November 1963
President Makarios advanced a series of constitutional
amendments which the Turkish Cypriots opposed. The
confrontation prompted widespread intercommunal fighting.
In December, Makarios ordered a ceasefire and again
addressed the issue to the United Nations, which resulted
in partitioning the capital Nicosia into north and south. The
Turkish population moved north of the city and the Greek
south. The rest of the island remained mixed until 1974.

July 1974

Turkey invaded Cyprus in a two-stage offensive. Turkish troops took control of 38 per cent of the island and 200,000 Greek Cypriots fled the northern areas which were under occupation. At the same time, 60,000 Turkish Cypriots were transferred to these northern occupied areas by the United Nations and authorities from the British Sovereign Base Areas after an agreed temporary population exchange by Turkish and Greek leaders. Since then, and to the present day, the southern part of the country has been under the control of the internationally recognized government of Cyprus, now part of the EU. The north of the island is under the control of the government of Northern Cyprus which is recognized only by Turkey.

Acknowledgements

Although this book is a work of fiction, with the plot line and characters created from my own imagination, my gratitude goes to all those Cypriots, Greeks and Turks who so long ago lived side by side on this sunny island. Stories told to me over the years by my father, who had lived through more peaceful times, inspired me to write this book.

My thanks also go to my agent and good friend Dorie Simmonds for her constant encouragement and support, my editor Alex Saunders for his good advice and keen eye, Anne Boston for her brilliant editing skills and to all my friends and family for putting up with me during this time.

For research purposes while writing the book I had to pay a visit to north Nicosia, thus crossing the 'green line' and onto the occupied Turkish side of the city. I would like to thank my friend Lefki Demetriou for offering to accompany me on this journey – it made it much easier than doing it alone.

The poem at the front of the book was written by a man

called Orhan Seyfi Ari, not to be confused with Orhan Terzi, one of the main characters in this book.

The latter is a figment of my imagination and the former was a very real dear friend of my father's.

Among the Lemon Trees

By Nadia Marks

Anna thought her marriage to Max would last forever. They had raised two happy children together, and she looked forward to growing old with the man she loved. But when a revelation from her husband just before their wedding anniversary shakes her entire world, she's left uncertain of what the future holds.

Needing time to herself, Anna takes up an offer from her widowed father to spend the summer on the small Aegean island of his birth, unaware that a chance discovery of letters in her aunt's house will unleash a host of family secrets. Kept hidden for sixty years, they reveal a tumultuous family history, beginning in Greece at the start of the twentieth century and ending in Naples at the close of the Second World War.

Confronted by their family's long-buried truths, both father and daughter are shaken by the discovery and Anna begins to realize that if she is to ever heal the present, she must first understand the past . . .

'My book of the year. An utterly gripping
story of love and family secrets'
Vanessa Feltz

Secrets Under the Sun

By Nadia Marks

The truth will surprise you . . .

On the island of Cyprus, in the small seaside town of Larnaka, three childhood friends have reunited for the funeral of Katerina, the much-loved old woman who had a profound effect on their lives.

Eleni, Marianna and Adonis grew up together, as close as siblings. Although from humble beginnings – a house-maid from the age of thirteen – Katerina's love, wisdom and guidance helped shape them all.

Her loss leaves the friends bereft, but the funeral is not just a time to mourn and remember. Adonis's mother decides that with Katerina's death comes the time to share the family's secrets and answer the riddles of their childhood. A story of deception, forbidden love and undying loyalty unravels. What she reveals will change everything . . .